Saving Dawson

The Betrayed (A Rocker Series), Book 1
includes
Saving Grace, A Novella Prequel

COLBIE KAY

Saving Grace
Saving Dawson Prequel
Copyright © 2015 Colbie Kay
Editing by Jennifer Siegel
eCover design by Sierra Farris
Paperback design by Monica Langley Holloway
Formatting and interior design by Jersey Girl & Co.

Saving Dawson
The Betrayed (A Rocker Series), Book 1
Colbie Kay © 2016
ALL RIGHTS RESERVED.
Edited by Casey Heiter
Cover design by Cover to Cover Designs
Interior Formatting by Jersey Girl & Co. Designs

ISBN: 978-1539970644

Without limiting the rights under copyright reserved above, no part of this publication may be reproduced, stored in or introduced into a retrieval system, or transmitted, in any form, or by any means (electronic, mechanical, photocopying, recording, or otherwise) without the prior written permission of the copyright owner, except as permitted under the U.S. Copyright Act of 1976.

This is a work of fiction. Names, characters, places, brands, media, and incidents are either the product of the author's imagination or are used fictitiously. The author acknowledges the trademarked status and trademark owners of various products, bands, and/ or restaurants referenced in this work of fiction, which have been used without permission. The publication/ use of these trademarks is not authorized, associated with, or sponsored by the trademark owners.

dedication

I dedicate this book to all of my readers for hanging in there with me. I know you all have been waiting for this book and I hope you enjoy it.

other books by colbie kay

SATAN'S SINNERS MC SERIES

City Lights
Quiet Country
Night Sky

THE BETRAYED (A ROCKER SERIES)

Saving Grace (prequel)

Saving Dawson

acknowledgements

First I want to thank Lance Jones for giving me another awesome cover. You are amazing!!

Dave Kelley the photography you do is simply beautiful and without you I wouldn't have had the perfect cover. Thank you for all you do and keep on doing it.

Kari at Cover to Cover Designs you rocked this cover. I fell in love with it as soon as I saw it. Thank you for all of your hard work you do an incredible job.

Casey Heiter you rocked another book out for me and I can't tell you enough how amazing you are for always being there when I need you.

My betas I love you ladies!! You always give me sound advice and you make me the writer I am.

Sonya Covert thank you for always being there. It's been a rough year and you have stuck by me every step of the way. I love you!

My family thank you for being patient with me through the writing of this book and allowing me to fulfill my dream. I love you all!!

My readers thank you for hanging in there while waiting for this book. I know you guys have been waiting what seems like forever, but I finally got it. I hope you love these characters as much as my Sinners.

All of the blogs out there thank you so much for everything you do for us authors. We wouldn't be able to do what we do without you.

Saving Grace

Saving Dawson Prequel

one

I am fourteen years old and sitting in the local hospital waiting room all alone. I will never see my parents again and I don't know what is going to happen to me.

Why would God do this to me?

Why would he take my parents from me and why would they leave me?

All they wanted was an evening out by themselves to be kid free and have some fun. They always had that one night a month, I guess like a date night, who knew this one would change everything.

The nurse told me that I will be waiting for CPS to come get me and she explained that it stands for child protective services. She further explained they have employees who do home placement for children under the age of eighteen when it is needed, whether it be temporary or permanent.

I'm scared about not knowing what's to come and how I ended up here in the last few hours.

How in the world did my life get turned upside down?

—

I'm winning 47-7 on the new football game I got for my ps3, when the doorbell rings. I pause the game, jump up from the couch, walk to the door, and look out the window. A tall, brown-haired, and very muscled police officer is standing there. I open the door looking up at the officer as he looks down on me. I don't know what to say so I just stand there staring at him.

"Are you Dawson Gates?"

"Yes sir." I answer him, but at the same time wondering what is going on and how he would know my name. I don't remember getting in trouble. My parents would kill me if I had the police coming to the house.

"Son, I need you to come with me. There was an accident and I need to get you to the hospital."

"What happened?"

"The doctors will let you know everything I promise, but we need to go now. Your mom was able to tell me your name and address." I don't bother grabbing anything as I shut the door behind me. He opens the back door of his police cruiser ushering me in, then he climbs in the front. If I wasn't so scared and confused I would make a joke about riding in the back of a police car for the first time. I think I'll just leave that for another day seeing as how I am terrified this has to do with my parents. He hits a couple of switches turning on his lights and sirens as we speed away.

When we pull up to the E.R. he doesn't even turn his car off as he quickly gets out, opens my door, and rushes me inside. We pass the front check-in going right into the part where they have the exam rooms. I look around as nurses and doctors run around yelling out words that make no sense to me. One of the nurses is quickly striding by us when the officer grabs her arm stopping her. When she turns towards us she looks down at his hand, to his face, and then to me with a mix of frustration and confusion on her face.

Both of them seem to be young, but other than that they are opposites: Where the officer is big, she is small, his short brown hair versus her long blonde hair, and he is kind of intimidating, where she looks caring and sweet. She is very pretty with her hair pulled back into a ponytail and pink scrubs on.

"Grady I'm busy. What do you need?" So the officer's name is Grady

Saving Grace

and they must know each other.

"Did the lady..." I see the nurse shake her head. "Sarah, this is the son of the Gates couple."

"Oh God, okay just a second." Why is she saying it like that? I wonder as she rushes away.

"Officer..." He looks down at me with pain and sadness in his eyes.

"Officer O'Neill, but you can call me Grady."

"Grady, will you tell me what's going on?"

"All I can tell you is that your parents were in an accident. We need to wait for Sarah to come back because she will know more." My body is shaking in fear as I try blinking back the tears that are threatening to fall. I need to be strong so I pray to God in my head that my parents will be okay. For some reason, I don't think they will be though. It's kind of like when you get a feeling that something bad is going to happen. I have that feeling!

Sarah comes back just a few minutes later and stands in front of me looking the same way as the officer was. "What's your name?"

"Dawson Gates."

"Well it's very nice to meet you Dawson Gates. I'm Sarah O'Neill. This officer here is my husband." She says as she sticks her hand out for me to shake.

"Nice to meet you too," I say while taking her hand. "Can you tell me what is going on?"

"Yeah honey there was an accident. We don't know what caused it, but it looks like your father veered off the road. I don't think he could gain control back so the car ended up rolling a few times and hitting a tree. Your father was already gone by the time the police got there. Your mother died on the way here. I am so sorry we have done everything we can for her."

"No. No. No." I say repeatedly as I shake my head back and forth, tears blurring my vision. She grabs me up in her arms hugging me tight against her chest.

"I'm so sorry, Dawson. We have cleaned them up the best we can and...I will take you in to see them one last time if you would like." I pull back as I nod my head.

"Yeah, I wanna see them." I cover my eyes and cheeks with my hands wiping away the tears that have fallen.

"Okay honey come on." She grabs my hand while looking over to Grady.

"I'll see you at home Grady." I see her mouth I love you to him.

"Yeah okay Sarah. I love you too." He says back to her before turning and telling me, "Hey kid I know it may not seem like it right now, but everything will be fine. Sarah can give you our numbers in case you need anything." He gives me a pat on the back before he walks out.

I let Sarah lead me into the room where they have both of my parents lying on separate beds.

"We weren't sure if anyone would even be coming to see them and normally we only have one person per room. But just in case someone did, we thought it would be easier if they were seen together." I nod at her as I look at my parents and release her hand as I walk closer in between the beds.

Both of them are lying so still, not breathing, and covered in white sheets. It looks like they're just sleeping except for the scrapes, cuts, and bruises on their arms and faces. The hospital staff didn't do a good job of cleaning the blood out of their hair because I can still see it caked on both of their heads. The tears have come back now, but this time I don't bother holding them back. I let them flow freely down my face as I drop to my knees and beg my parents to wake up. I feel hands on my shoulders trying to comfort me.

"Sarah, why are they not waking up? They can't be gone. I need them to wake up. I need them!"

She walks from behind me, drops to her knees, and tells me. "Oh honey I'm so sorry they are gone. They're not waking up."

"I can't say goodbye to them."

Saving Grace

"Okay let's go sit out there CPS will be here in a little bit. Do you have any other family?" I shake my head no before she stands back up, takes my hand once again, helps me up, and leads me out of the room. Right before I walk out, I turn looking at my parents one last time.

I don't know how long it's been since I sat in this chair and started waiting, but finally a woman walks up to me.

"Are you Dawson Gates?" I look up at the older gray-haired woman with her glasses slipping down her pointy nose. She has on a dark pantsuit, her hair is in a bun on the top of her head, and her glasses are attached to a chain that wraps around her neck. She has a look of business to her so I'm assuming this is the CPS worker Sarah told me would be coming to get me.

"Yes Ma'am." She locks her pale blue eyes with my stormy gray ones as she takes the seat next to me.

"I'm Miss Carlson from CPS. They sent me over here to get you. I'm sorry about your parents."

I give her a tight nod and ask "Where are you taking me?"

"You will be going to a home for boys tonight and hopefully we can get you placed with a family soon. That way you won't have to stay there long."

"Can we stop at my house so I can grab some things?"

"I don't think we have time for that. I need to get you over there soon because they are expecting you." I don't like this woman already. I can't believe this! My parents just died, she's taking me somewhere I don't know, and now she won't even let me go to my house.

"I'm ready." We stand, turn, and start walking to the sliding doors that lead you out of the emergency room right when the doors open I hear. "Wait!" We both stop and turn to see that it's Sarah running towards us. I give a half smile at seeing her. She was so kind to me and I really liked her, unlike this old woman next to me.

"Wait Miss Carlson." Sarah says again.

"What can I do for you Mrs. O'Neill? I don't have much time I have to get this boy over to the home." She speaks like she's annoyed.

"That's why I stopped you. You're not taking him anywhere." Sarah states as she crosses her arms over her chest.

"I'm sorry Mrs. O'Neill, but I don't have time for this."

"After everything he has been through tonight, I'm not letting you take him to that home."

"You can't do that. It's against the protocol."

"It's not against protocol when I'm already a foster parent. You know this so go to your car, get your paperwork, let's get it done, then you can be on your way." Sarah grabs my arm pulling me away from the woman.

Miss Carlson let's out a loud huff before saying "I'll be right back."

Sarah looks over her shoulder "Yeah, I knew you would be." She looks down at me and smiles. "I hate that old hag." If it was under different circumstances I would have died laughing, instead I give her the best smile I can manage right now.

"Just take a seat over there my shift is almost over." I do as she tells me and wait for them to come back. When they do, we stay at the hospital until all the paperwork is done.

Miss Carlson says "We're going to need your husband's signature on these papers. Also we will be checking to see if his parents had a will."

"You can come by the house in a few days for Grady to sign them and everything can get settled then."

"I don't know why you keep taking these boys in."

"Why don't you let me worry about that and have a goodnight, Miss Carlson." Sarah grabs my arm pulling me with her outside.

As she is dragging me to her car I ask in a quiet voice, "Are you really taking me home with you?"

"Of course silly! I couldn't let her take you to that place after everything you have been through."

My head snaps up meeting her eyes and I inform her, "I don't understand why you are helping me, but thank you." It doesn't make sense to me why she would be so nice when she doesn't even know me. But really nothing about this night makes any sense.

We come to a black Suburban that she unlocks the doors to so we can get in. Sarah starts the car up, looks at me, and asks "Is there anywhere you would like to go?"

"Would you take me to my house?"

"Yeah no problem," she puts the car in drive. "Just give me directions." I do just that until we get to the only house I've ever known as home. When she pulls into the driveway she questions "Would you like me to come in with you?"

I feel like this is something I need to do on my own. "No I'll just be a minute."

"Okay I'll just wait right here." She responds with worry in her eyes. I open my door and hop out making my way up the driveway and opening the door.

Not bothering to look around right now I run up the stairs heading straight to my room. I grab my backpack that I have for school, start stuffing it full of clothes, and then place pictures of my parents and me on top before zipping it up. I go to my dresser and grab the guitar pick that my Dad gave me before heading into my parent's room.

When I open the door it's so eerily quiet I realize, I've never been in this room without one of my parents being in here with me. I don't want to be in here long so I go to their closet and grab my Dad's guitar. I don't need anything else so I take just a moment to look around the room thinking I have to leave the only home that I've ever known. I can't believe this has happened and my whole life is about to change.

I walk down the stairs going into the kitchen grabbing a plastic bag out of the cabinet and look around at the last place we were all together. Next I walk into the living room grab my ps3 with all my games and controllers putting it all in the bag before locking the house up.

I put all my stuff in the back and get back into the suburban. I close the door, and put my seatbelt on. As we are pulling out I ask, "Sarah can I ask you a question?"

"Yeah sure."

"Why are you doing this? You don't even know me, but you're taking me home with you."

"Because I have a feeling about you, Dawson. I think you're a good kid and that home she was going to take you to is awful. You don't belong there. We live about forty-five minutes away so you will have to change schools, but we'll worry about that after the funeral."

"Okay. What do I need to do for that?" I ask concerned. "I don't know how to deal with any of this." I say as I stare out the window.

"It's okay. We'll get you through it and the boys will help you get settled."

"I remember Miss Carlson saying something about other boys." I turn my attention to her.

"Yeah Grady and I tried to have kids of our own, but was never able to so we started taking in boys that needed homes."

"How many?"

"You will make four." She states proudly. "You will meet all of them when we get there. How old are you?"

Saving Grace

"Fourteen."

"That's good all you boys are around the same age then." The rest of the ride is silent as I turn back to look out the window. I start to remember the last memory I have of my parents from earlier today and I will hold on to it forever.

"Dawson." My mom yells at me from the kitchen. As I walk in there, I notice how dressed up she with makeup on and her hair done. I know what day it is because any normal day my mom is in jeans and t-shirts with her hair up is some weird bun on the top of her head.

"Yes mom?"

"It's your dad and my day so be good while we're gone. Do not leave the house and keep the phone close to you. Here are all the numbers if you need anything." She says the last part as she points to the refrigerator.

"I know mom we go over this every month. I'll just play my game and my bedtime is ten." I roll my eyes at her and smile as she grabs my face kissing both my cheeks and making both of us laugh.

"You're such a good kid Dawson. I don't know how we got so lucky. I love you. We should be back way before ten."

"I love you too Mom." I stand there hugging her when my dad walks into the kitchen. He comes over ruffling my hair and smiling causing us all to laugh some more.

"Be good while we're gone."

"I will Dad." I smile at him while trying to fix my hair.

"I know you will. You're a good kid, Dawson. I love you."

"Mom said that already, but I love you too, Dad."

"Hey you better get all the practice you can in on that new football game you got. We have our tournament tomorrow and I'm not going easy on you."

"You know I'm gonna kick your butt, Dad." He chuckles turning to my mom.

"You look beautiful babe," he kisses her cheek. "Are you ready to

go?"

"Yeah I just gotta grab my purse." *We all walk back into the living room where my mom grabs her purse. Everyone is smiling and happy as we say goodbye and I love yous one last time before they shut and lock the door behind them.*

"Dawson we're here." I hear Sarah say bringing me out of my thoughts.

two

We pull into the driveway of a two story house just like mine. It's dark outside so I can't see what color the house is, but I can tell there are dark shutters on the windows and a light on inside. The porch light is on illuminating white siding, so I assume the rest of the house is white as well. The front door is red with an oval shape window in it, and from what I can see it looks like a really nice house.

Sarah shuts the car off then turns to me.

"Okay Dawson are you ready?"

"I'm nervous." I respond with a shaky voice.

"That's perfectly normal all the boys were when we first brought them home, but you will fit right in. Everything will be just fine."

"You promise?"

"Yes I promise. Now come on let's get in there." We climb out of the suburban, walk up to the door, and Sarah opens it walking in with me right behind her. As soon as we walk in we're right in the living room and I see Grady sitting in a recliner, out of his uniform, and three boys sitting on a dark brown couch.

She shuts the door before saying, "Hey honey can I talk to you for a minute?" He turns his head looking at her and sees me standing beside her. He clicks off the flat screen TV while the other boys turn to look also. It makes me feel really uncomfortable that everyone is just staring at me.

"Umm...yeah let's go into the other room." Grady answers furrowing his eyebrows with a very confused look on his face. He gets up out of his chair and walks by her leaving the room. He doesn't look too happy. I hope this is okay, I don't know what will happen if it's not and I watch as she turns on her heels following behind him. I turn my attention back to the other kids to see they're all still looking at me. I drop my chin to my chest because this is really awkward. I don't know what to do so I just keep standing here. I can hear in hushed voices. "Sarah, what the hell are you doing?"

"Grady, I couldn't just let that hateful woman take him to that God awful place and you know it. Please let him stay, I already did the paperwork."

"Miss Carlson?"

"Yes!"

"Hey you," I look up with wide eyes. "Who are you?"

"My name's Dawson Gates."

"Are you without parents too?" He asks bringing the events of tonight back to the front of my mind and the tears well up again.

I nod while saying "They were killed in a car accident tonight."

"Shit man, I'm sorry." Another says.

"Colt! What did we tell you about using that kind of language?" I turn to see Sarah coming back into the room followed by Grady.

"Sorry." He drops his head with a smirk on his face. The other boys start laughing.

"Alright guys that's enough," Grady raises his voice to speak over all the laughter. "Boys this is Dawson Gates. He'll be staying with us from now on, if he wants to." Grady looks over at me "Do you wanna stay with us?"

Saving Grace

I give him a nod "Yeah, I would rather be here then at that place Miss Carlson was going to take me to." He gives me a tight smile.

"Okay then we met earlier, but these are our other boys. That one right there that got in trouble is Colton, but we call him Colt. He's the oldest being sixteen." Colt gives me a wave and I wave back. "The one right there with the black hair is Rico he's a year older than you, he's fifteen." Just like Colt he waves and I wave back. "The other one is Elijah, but we call him Eli. He's the same age as you being fourteen. Alright guys show Dawson to his room and get him settled."

They all jump up from the couch and Colt says, "The bedrooms are upstairs." I follow them out of the living room coming to a set of stairs, we all climb up and end up in a hallway. Colt instructs me as to where all the rooms are. "At the end of the hall over there is Sarah and Grady's room, here is our bathroom and the other three rooms are over here. Rico and I share a room so you can pick the empty room or you can share with Eli."

I look over at Eli while asking, "Do you mind if I share with you?"

"No not at all man, my room well I mean our room already has bunk beds. We got a flat screen TV, but the game systems are downstairs so that we can all play." Rico and Colt go into their room leaving me with my new roommate.

"I brought my ps3 if that's okay." I tell him

"Hold on I'll ask." We stand at the top of the staircase as Eli leans over the railing and screams. "Sarrrrraaaaahhhhh!"

"Eli you do not have to scream for us to hear you. Now what do you need?"

"Just making sure I have your attention." He smiles down at her and she huffs out a breath, shakes her head, and smiles.

"Dawson, my man, brought his ps3 with him. Is it okay if we hook it up in our room? He's sharing with me because I'm the sh…"

She points her finger up at him and glaring, shutting him up. "Do not finish that sentence. You can hook it up, but you will not be playing on it all night." "Thank you Mama S." He yells down to her. He turns to me laughing

"Let's go get you unpacked roomie." We go outside and get all of my stuff before returning to my new bedroom.

He opens the door and it's a big room the bunk beds are black metal with mattresses on both bunks and beds already made. There are two dressers, a closet, and a flat screen TV hanging above one of the dressers. He has posters all over the walls of different bands. "Do you like music?" I ask as I start pulling my clothes out and putting them away.

"Yeah man we all do. What about you I see the guitar case?" He asks while eyeing the case.

"Yeah it was my dad's. He taught me how to play a little bit."

"Hmm… That's good to know." We continue to talk about different kinds of music and bands we like along with what games are our favorites on the ps3. It turns out we have a lot in common which makes me feel more comfortable. I think it's going to be okay here. He tells me how Sarah and Grady are the best foster parents and how he ended up in foster care.

As soon as I get everything unpacked and we have the system hooked up, I hear Sarah yell, "Boys dinner's ready."

We all make our way downstairs and sit at the table in the dining room where boxes of pizza are piled on top.

"We thought you might be hungry Dawson usually we don't eat this late, but it was a hectic day. We also didn't know what kind you liked so we got a variety." Sarah says to me with

Saving Grace

a shy smile.

"Thank you I'm not picky though." I say back returning a half smile of my own. The smell of the pizza makes my stomach grumble letting me know just how hungry I am. I haven't eaten since my mom made me lunch and then everything happened making me forget all about food.

"Dawson, we need to go over the rules of living here." Grady says.

"Okay." I reply while grabbing a piece of pepperoni.

"Well we're pretty lenient, but your bedtime on week nights is ten and midnight on the weekends. You do your homework as soon as you get home from school and no getting on the game systems or anything until it's done. There is supposed to be no cussing, but you saw how well that's listened to. You will have daily chores and keep out of trouble." I look over at Colt and see the grin plastered on his face.

"Okay, those are pretty much the same rules as what my parents had."

Grady continues with his talk, "Good then you should have no problems. We understand you are all teenage boys so you will break some of the rules. We want you to be happy here."

"Did the boys help get you settled in?" Sarah asks.

"Yes. They showed me where all the rooms are and Eli helped me get my stuff unpacked."

"Good thank you, Eli."

"You're welcome Sarah it's gonna be fun having a roommate." Eli responds with a smile.

―

Over the next couple of weeks, everything happens so fast. Miss Carlson came over to get Grady's signature so all the paperwork was finalized and I was informed that my parents didn't have a will. I guess since they were so young they thought they had plenty of time for all that stuff. So now it is official I get to stay with the O'Neills. Thank God I never have to deal with Miss Carlson again she is a hateful woman.

The funeral for both of my parents was only three days after they died. Everyone was there giving me support along with all of my parents coworkers. It was sad that there wasn't any more relatives, but both of my parents were the only children in their families and my grandparents on both sides were already gone. I'm so glad they were there, I don't think I could of done it on my own. Sarah setup everything and also met with the lawyers about the house and all of my parents stuff.

Sarah enrolled me into my new school, which I won't be starting until Monday. I am adjusting to being at the new house, but I tend to hangout alone a lot. I miss my parents so much every day and I wish they were still here.

Everyone has been really great in trying to make me feel welcome. The guys always ask me to do stuff with them, but I'm just not ready yet. Sarah and Grady have asked several times if I want to talk about anything, but I'm not ready for that either. I just need some time, I guess it's the grieving process as Sarah likes to call it.

She says I was in denial at the hospital and then I had a bit of anger towards my parents for leaving me. Now she says I'm in the depressed stage. I don't remember how many other stages she said I will go through, but I know it sucks not having them anymore.

I start my new school today and hopefully it will be okay. I'm nervous because I don't know how I'm going to fit in. I've always went to school with the same kids, but now I'm the new guy. Will the other kids like me? At least I will have the guys with me.

Saving Grace

I just got done with my shower and getting dressed when I open the bathroom door and all the guys are standing there gawking at me.

"What?" I ask confused as to why they would all just be standing there staring at me. It's kind of creepy.

"Dude, you can fucking sing!" Colt states with shock in his voice. I didn't even realize I was singing out loud.

"Yeah, I guess." I drop my head in embarrassment.

"Man, you are good. Like really good!" Eli says with amusement.

"Thanks." I lift my head, but I can feel the heat rising in my cheeks. My parents were the only ones to ever hear me sing.

"You know what this means right?" Rico questions to the other guys.

When I look at all of them they're all wearing the same look. big eyes and blinding smiles.

"What?" I ask puzzled and furrowing my brows.

"Dude, it means our band is complete." Colt responds.

"Band? What band?" I ask getting even more confused.

"We'll show you after school. This is fucking awesome!" Eli answers fist pumping the air.

Letting it go for now, we all file out of the house and get into Colt's Camaro so he can take us to school.

three

    We walk up the sidewalk going into the double doors of the one story brick school. The hallway is noisy, packed with kids laughing with their groups of friends, and other kids walking to their classes. Sarah already got my schedule and supplies when she enrolled me so I don't have to worry about finding the office. I'm thankful for that because I don't want to be left alone in this craziness.

    My old school was the same way but I knew everyone and where to go, here I'm walking in blind pretty much except for Colt, Rico, and Eli. I stick to the back of the group as we walk down the hallway. I can feel people's eyes on me wondering who I am and where I came from. That's what I always thought when I saw a new kid at school for the first time, so I pay it no mind.

    A girl bounces up next to Colt and he puts his arm around her shoulders. "Hey guys," she cheerfully speaks with a bright smile.

    "Hey Kayla." Rico says nicely while Eli tries to mimic her voice, and has me hiding a laugh.

    "Kayla this is our new bro, Dawson." Colt informs her.

    "Hey Dawson! It's nice to meet you." She sticks out her hand for me to shake.

    I take and reply, "Nice to meet you too, Kayla."

    "Dawson, follow Eli he'll show you were your locker's at." Colt throws over his shoulder as he leads Kayla away.

"See you guys at lunch." Rico says as he walks off.

"Is that Colt's girlfriend?" I question.

"More like flavor of the week," Eli chuckles before continuing. "Come on man."

We start walking farther down the hall and as I'm looking all around me not paying any attention, I stumble. I catch myself on the lockers and look down. There on the floor is a girl with long blonde hair in pig tail braids picking up her books.

"I'm so sorry let me help you." I tell her as I bend down in front of her.

"Thank you." She responds with a small squeaky voice as she looks up at me.

"Hey man I gotta go, but your locker is right over here." He points in the direction it's at then goes on to tell me, "Your first class is English so take a right at the end of the hall and it will be on your right side." Before I get a chance to answer, he's already down the hall.

I turn my attention back to the girl in front of me she's a bit nerdy with thick black glasses, the braids, and has on a long-sleeved loose top and jeans. Who wears long sleeves and jeans in May? I don't even know this girl so I'm not asking, it's none of my business really. I continue to help her pick up the papers and books then we both stand only to bump heads.

"Ouch." We both say in unison while rubbing our heads and smiling.

"I'm Dawson Gates."

"Nice to meet you, Dawson. I'm Grace Sullivan." She uses that same squeaky little voice. We say our goodbyes as I hand her stuff over and make my way to my locker figuring out how to open it.

"Hey Dawson, I can show you where English is, it's my first one too."

Saving Grace

I look over giving her another smile and nod. "Yeah, okay thanks." She is kind of cute, even if she is a little nerdy. I grab the books I need, shoving the rest of my stuff in the locker, and close it before we head to our first class.

The first half of my classes have been good. I'm not behind at all since we were already going over the same subjects at my old school.

By lunch, I'm starving. I've had a couple classes with Eli and all four with Grace, which is nice I haven't been alone in any of them yet. I meet the guys in the cafeteria and we all sit at the same table.

"How's your classes going?" Rico asks.

"They're good so far. I'm not behind at all, we were going over all this stuff in my old school." I look over and see Grace standing there with her tray looking around. She looks so small in the big cafeteria with her oversized clothes on. "Hey guys do you mind if she comes and sits with us." They all turn their heads to see who I'm talking about.

"No." They all say smirking at me. Ignoring them I get up, walk over, and take her tray.

"What are you doing?" She asks with a surprised tone.

"You're coming to sit with me." I tell her confidently with a shrug of my shoulder.

"No that's okay."

"Come on Grace I saw you looking around just come sit with us. I haven't seen you talking to any other kids all day besides me. So do me the honor of sitting with me. Please!" I plead with her giving her my best puppy dog look.

"Okay." She finally gives in chuckling as I smile while leading her over to the table and introduce her to the guys. They all welcome her to the table telling her hello and their names.

While sitting at lunch I ask, "Grace, would you like to come over after school?" I see all the guys looking at each other with funny looks on their faces. "It's okay if we have friends over right?"

"Yeah it's totally fine." Colt answers.

"Why are you doing this Dawson?" She asks while bringing her gaze to mine.

"Doing what?"

"Being nice. Inviting me to do stuff. People aren't nice to me, Dawson. They don't ask me to sit at their table or carry my tray and they definitely don't invite me over to their house." She says as she drops her head maybe from embarrassment.

"Well Grace, I'm not other people. I like you and want to be your friend."

"That's it, that's all you want, to be my friend?" She questions cocking her brow at me like I have an alternative.

"Yeah that's all I want." I say chuckling.

"I'll have to ask and see if it's okay first so write down your address." I grab a pen and paper out of my bag, writing down the address, and handing it over.

"This is pretty close to my house so if it's okay I'll walk over."

"Okay." We all get up and head to our next class.

When the day is over and we're back at the house, they take me into the garage. Now I see what they were talking about a band. They have drums, guitars, speakers, a mic, and everything else they would need including a couch to sit on. All they were needing was the singer and that is where I complete the band. I agree to be the singer they needed so therefore the band, along with a brotherhood, are forming. Colt is on drums and the most serious about the band, Eli is on guitar, Rico is on bass, and I sing the cover songs because we don't have any of our own right now.

Grace did end up coming over and hanging out with all of us and that is how my friendship with her started.

four

I have learned over the last six months how to open up more to Sarah and Grady, they're starting to feel like second parents to me. The guys have become not only my bandmates, but also my brothers and I believe Grace has helped with that.

She always listens when I talk whether it be a memory or something my parents would always say to me. I've learned that it helps to talk about my parents instead of pretending they never existed. As good of a listener as she is, she never really has much to say about herself.

Somewhere along the way, she stopped being cute to me and became beautiful. I would like her to be my girlfriend, but Grace is my best friend. It scares me to think if we did change our relationship and it didn't work out I would lose her. I can't lose any more people that I care about, the pain from the loss is too much. I'm with her everyday whether it's to watch us practice, walking to the park, or being at school I don't want that to change ever.

I was always the outgoing kid with a lot of friends at my old school, and while I've made new friends, the accident did something to me. I am more withdrawn, I have no interest in hanging out with anyone outside of my brothers or Grace, and I don't let too many people get close to me.

In the last six months, I have yet to see Grace in anything other than the long-sleeved shirts and jeans no matter what time of year it is.

I think back to the first time I asked her why.

We walked to the park that's not too far from our houses. I sat on one swing while she sat on the other and I started kicking around the rocks with my feet feeling nervous, not even knowing why.

"Don't you get hot wearing those clothes all the time?" I asked her looking down at the ground.

"No." She responded in her little voice.

I lifted my head to look over at her, "Why do you wear them though?"

"Don't ask me that, Dawson."

"Gracie, I wanna know why you always wear them?"

She looks over at me, I swear I can see tears in her eyes even though she has glasses on. "It's time for me to go home. I'll see you tomorrow." Before I even got a chance to respond she had jumped off her swing and was running away.

I've asked her a few more times why, but she just changes the subject. I think it has something to do with her home life, but all I really know is that she is in foster care as well. I'm never allowed at her house so I can't say for sure if it's a good or bad environment. Grace comes over every day acting happy until it's time for her to leave then it's like she shuts down and goes into herself. I worry about her so much, but I don't want to upset her by asking questions.

We're all sitting in the garage when Colt pulls something out of his pocket that's white like a cigarette. "Guys we need to come up with a name," he says as he lights it up. "If people are going to take us serious we gotta have a name." He puts it in his mouth inhaling, exhaling, then starts choking. We all burst out laughing because it sounds like he is coughing up a lung and his face is bright red.

"What the hell is that?" Rico asks before stating, "And it

Saving Grace

smells like shit, Dude."

"It's weed, dude." Colt responds once he gets his breath back, but still coughing some. He holds it up teaching us, "This is what you call a joint."

He passes it to Rico who says, "I'm not smoking that shit."

"Rico, dude you're always so serious lighten the fuck up a little." Colt tells him as Rico gives in and takes it, inhales some then starts coughing also.

"If you get caught with that you're gonna be in so much trouble." I state to Colt knowing he doesn't give a shit. He likes to break the rules.

"Relax Dawson, Grady and Sarah won't be home for hours and there's spray in the house." He replies as Rico passes it to me. When I inhale I know now why they were coughing that shit burns the fuck out of your throat. The same thing happens to Eli and Grace as the joint makes it's rounds and by the time it's done we all have red blood shot eyes, feeling relaxed, and hungry. After we have gotten our snacks and the spray from inside the house, we sit back out in the garage and Colt wants to talk about names for the band again.

Eli pipes up through a mouthful of chips "Garage Monkeys." Making everyone except Colt burst out laughing. He takes this band shit serious like one day we will be big and famous.

"No fucking way dude." Colt responds.

"Okay fine what about The Raging Testies." Eli says making us laugh again, I don't know how he just said that shit with a straight face.

"Guys be serious." You can see Colt is getting frustrated.

I look over at Grace sitting on the couch always looking so small, but smiling at me. "What about Saving Grace?" I look back to the guys their smiles are gone.

"Dude I like it. You are the shit, Dawson." Colt states while the other guys nod their heads. "Okay so that's settled now, we need to really get some songs going. Are we going to the music festival next weekend?"

"Yeah if Sarah and Grady will let us." I tell him.

"Don't worry they will." He says so matter of fact with a smile.

The music festival is a big event they have once a year in Wichita where people set up stands. You can walk around to all of them and buy stuff like cds, jewelry, or shirts with band logos. There are usually two or three stages in different areas that have bands playing. My parents used to take me and it was always a lot of fun. I want to go with the guys, but the thought of me going without my mom and dad is unsettling.

Later that night after we are all back to normal from our high and after Sarah and Grady got home, we ask about going to the festival.

Grady is the first to answer, "Give us a minute to talk about it." That's their way of telling us to leave the room. We all get up out of the dining room chairs and head into the living room.

"You think they're gonna let us go?" I ask hopeful.

"Yeah they're just making us wait." Eli responds. After a few minutes they call us back into the dining room.

"Okay boys here's the deal, we know how much you all love music. You can go to the festival." Sarah informs before we all start smiling and yelling. She puts her hand up stopping us. "Before you get all worked up, Grady and I are both off this weekend so we'll be taking you."

"Dude, guys come on." Colt pleads with disappointment in his voice.

"Do you have to?" Rico asks defeated. Now it's their turn to smile.

"Yes, we have to, we're not letting the four of you boys

Saving Grace

go forty-five minutes away into Wichita by yourselves." Grady reprimands us.

"Can Grace come?" I ask not really caring if they take us or not.

"Yeah sure if her foster parents say it's okay." Sarah responds with a smile. I know she really likes Gracie, but worries about her too.

Today is the music festival in Wichita and we've heard a lot of crazy good bands. Some play rock, some bluegrass, and some jazz. I decide to walk around leaving everyone behind when I feel someone grab my shoulder. I just want to get away for a minute to do some thinking until I turn around seeing that it's Grace. "Where you going, Dawson?"

"Just walking around. You wanna come?"

"Yeah." She gives me a smile as I take her hand. "Dawson, why did you want to name the band after me?" She asks as we're looking around at the stuff people have for sale. I take her off where nobody can see us before I answer. This is it. This is the moment I have been waiting for. I'm tired of being scared of ruining our friendship.

"Because I like you, Gracie." When we started being good friends, I started to call her Gracie. She never corrected me so I guess she doesn't mind it.

"I like you too, you know that." She laughs and hits me on the arm in a playful manner.

"No I mean I like you more than a friend." I tell her looking into her eyes.

"Oh." Is her only response before I take her face in my hands and bringing her lips to mine. It's a soft tender kiss not like the ones I've seen Colt and Rico giving their girls.

Pulling away from her lips, I can see her eyes are closed,

her lips parted, and cheeks flushed.

"Will you be my girlfriend Gracie?" She slowly opens her eyes.

"I've liked you for a while now, so yes I will be your girlfriend." The smile lights up her face and I give her one in return grabbing her up and spinning her around.

We make our way back to the rest of my new family and I enjoy the rest of the day happier then I have been in a long time.

five

My relationship with Gracie has been amazing except for the fact she still won't talk about what her home life is like. I have this feeling she wasn't as lucky as I was. I thank god every day that Sarah and Grady are the ones that took me in so that I never had to go to that home for boys.

The band is doing great now that we have a name and know what genre of music we want to play, which is rock. Colt has been working on writing songs that are ours, but we still practice the covers until ours are ready. We made fliers to pass around school so now kids can come over on Saturday nights and we will play out of the garage. It's a start and Grace did so well at helping promote us, that we all nominated her to be our manager.

Tonight is the first night we are playing. Sarah set up a table with all kinds of snacks and we have a cooler full of pop. We have some lawn chairs set up and everything is ready. Kids start showing up around seven p.m. and we kick it off with covers of Hinder and end the night with some Journey. We stopped playing about ten that night, taking some breaks in between songs.

At first I was so nervous to sing in front of everyone, but when I stepped in front of that microphone and the guys started that first song it was like this is where I was meant to be. My nerves quickly disappeared when I opened my mouth and the words started flowing out. Excitement took over and then pure happiness and joy as our fellow students clapped for us. When it was all over, they told us how awesome we were and that they would be back every weekend.

It's the summer of Grace, Eli, and my junior year. Rico will be a senior and Colt graduated in May. As we all have gotten older the busier we have become. When each of us turned sixteen, Sarah and Grady got us cars not fancy ones by any means but they get us from A to B. The stipulation was we had to get jobs to pay for tags, insurance, and gas. I guess it's their way of giving us freedom, but at the same time making us have responsibilities so I got a job at the local pizza place making pizzas. Practice has become more difficult between work, Friday nights parties and Saturday night garage shows when we aren't working, and Sundays for family, it doesn't leave much time.

Colt moved out not long after graduation getting into a two bedroom apartment and has decided he doesn't want to go to college. The band is too important to him. He believes without a doubt that we will make it one day in the music industry. He has the rest of us so hyped up on the idea that I don't think any of us will be going to college.

Today is one of the few Sundays the four of us have off, but Grady and Sarah don't so we have been practicing for most of the morning. After the last song, it's hot as fuck in the garage so I ask, "You guys wanna go swimming?"

"Yeah dude this heat is killing me." Colt responds.

"Yeah let's go." Rico says.

"It's so fucking hot I got sweat dripping out of my ass crack." Eli states.

Rico and Colt get up right when I reply "Dude that's disgusting and my girls here she don't need to hear about your

Saving Grace

ass crack." I look over at Grace who has her head down laughing.

"Hey man I'm just stating facts, it's hot."

"We know Eli." We all tell him in unison. I walk over to Grace grabbing her hand and taking her in the house and up to Eli and my room.

"Babe just grab a pair of my boxers and a shirt." I tell her as I grab my swimming trunks out of my drawer about to head out of the bedroom.

"I'm not going swimming." She says right when I'm about to open the door stop immediately and turn to look at her. She has her chin to her chest and fidgeting with her fingers.

"Why not?" I ask as I walk over to her taking her by the hand and leading her over to sit on the bed. We have been over this before, every summer actually and I've always let it go but this time I'm not. She has been my girlfriend for a year now, it's time I knew what was really going on.

"I just can't."

"Don't lie to me Gracie. We do everything together unless it involves you showing any part of your body. You are my best friend and my girlfriend. Trust me and tell me why you won't go swimming."

"I can't show my body Dawson." She looks up at me her eyes shining with tears behind her big glasses.

"Are you shy? You know I think you are beautiful." She shakes her head.

"Gracie?" I say her name harsher then I meant it to.

"I'm covered in bruises Dawson. I have scars." She drops her head again, but I lift my arm gripping her chin lightly turning her to face me. I won't let her cower down and hide from me.

"From what?" I all but shout. I let her chin go so I can stand and walk over locking my bedroom door. "Show me."

"Dawson please." She swipes the tears away that have escaped her eyes.

"Gracie you need to show me now." I demand as she stands up nodding. She pulls her shirt up over her head letting it fall to the floor then lowers her pants down to her ankles. I have to brace myself against the door because of what I see. She is covered almost all of her pale skin is either yellow from fading bruises or black and purple from new ones.

"Gracie how did you get all those?" My voice has lowered and I swallow hard trying to remove the lump that has formed in my throat. I'm not even sure she heard me until her head comes up to look at me.

"My foster father."

"Oh Gracie." I say while walking over to her. I lay her gently on my bed and start kissing every bruised part of her skin while telling her "I won't let him hurt you again. You are beautiful Gracie, even more so now. You are strong and brave for making it through this. I'll get you away from him." I can hear her sobbing loudly as I give her my words of comfort and meaning every single word. I don't know how yet, but I will make it my mission to get her out of that house. "Roll over." I command as I sit up letting her roll onto her stomach. I see the scars marring her back and thighs, her pale skin just as colored as the front of her body. I trace them with my finger before putting my lips to each and every one kissing my way done her body. "Are these from a belt?" I ask as she nods her head. "How often does he hurt you?"

"Almost every day, he has a really bad drinking problem. I make him mad a lot. I don't mean to, Dawson. My foster mom lets me come to your house so I can get away, but when I have to go back he is usually waiting for me."

"Gracie it's not your fault. He shouldn't treat you like that for any reason." I hear the knock at the door.

"Dude let's go." It's Colt.

"Give me a minute." I yell back. I lean down whispering in her ear,

"Please go swimming with me."

"Okay." I can see her smile against my sheets.

"Good; if you would have told me no I would have just tickled you into agreeing." I sit back and start tickling her anyway until she is squirming underneath me.

"Dawson stop." She says between giggles.

"C'mon let's go." I say as I stand up then help her up too. I gather all the stuff we will need before heading out.

—

When we get to the beach, we go our separate ways into the different restrooms to change. I get done before her so I stand at the door waiting for her. When she walks out she has on my shorts and shirt and she looks sexy in my clothes. I try to adjust myself without her noticing. For the first time I see her with her hair down; it covers her breasts in waves flowing down. She takes her glasses off and she literally looks like a whole new person. She is gorgeous and takes my breath away. I take her hand pulling her to me giving her a sweet soft kiss on the mouth.

"You are gorgeous." I whisper against her lips.

"Thank you," she whispers back a smile tugging at her lips. She pulls back from me with the biggest grin I've ever seen from her. "Catch me if you can." She states right before she takes off running. I turn chasing after her hot on her heels when she drops her stuff in the hot sand and runs right into the water. I drop my stuff next to hers running in after her. I start splashing her with water using my hands and she starts doing it back causing a splashing war.

The guys soon join in the war as water flies everywhere and you can't hear anything besides all the laughing. I've never seen her have so much fun and it fills my heart with more love for her. I always want her this happy and having this much fun. I swim over to her and grip her hip bringing her up against me for a kiss. "I love seeing you like this having fun and laughing not a care in the world."

"I'm so glad I came. This is so much fun. Thank you for making me come."

"You're welcome." I kiss her one more time before picking her up out of the water and throwing her away from me. When she comes back up, she is smiling and laughing. We swim for a while longer before I decide to take a break. I walk over to our stuff to sit with the other guys while she stays in to keep swimming.

"Dawson what happened to her?" Eli asks while looking out at the water. I'm surprised by his serious tone, he is usually all jokes and saying funny shit.

"All I'm gonna say is she wasn't as lucky as us, but I'm gonna get her away from there."

"Talk to Sarah and Grady." Colts advises.

"Yeah man that's fucked up whatever happened." Rico says.

Later that night after dropping off Gracie, I sit down to talk with Sarah and Grady.

"Can I talk to you guys for a minute?" I ask feeling really nervous. My palms are sweating so I rub them against my jeans.

"Yeah sure let's go sit at the table." Grady says.

When we all sit down I start, "I just want you guys to know how much I appreciate you guys taking me in and you didn't even know me. You have given me a wonderful home and taken great care of me. Some people are not so lucky; I know that now. I don't tell you guys enough, but I thank God every day that it was you guys there that night. So thank you for everything you have done for me."

"Dawson." Sarah says as I bring my eyes to hers and see the tears she's trying to keep back. Right then, all the guys come and sit at the table with us.

"What are you guys doing?" I ask confused as to why they would join in on this.

"Hey we are bros dude! We aren't gonna let you go through this alone." Colt informs me and I feel grateful that they got my back on this.

"Do what exactly?" Grady asks crossing his arms over his chest and cocking an eyebrow.

So I begin, "I want Grace to come stay here." Sarah holds her hand up

stopping me.

"We can't let your girlfriend come live with us Dawson."

"I wouldn't be asking if there wasn't a reason."

"Well what is the reason?" Grady asks.

"Her foster father beats her. She is covered in bruises and scars from his belt. She said it happens almost every day. Her foster mom let's her come over here just to get away, but most nights he waits for her to get home and then he unleashes his anger on her."

I look between them and Sarah is swiping tears from her cheeks and Grady looks pissed. "Is that why she always wears the clothes?" Sarah asks.

"Yeah. I had to talk her into going swimming and she showed me." I reply.

"Guys it was bad." Eli says hanging his head.

"We all think she should come here." Rico says with confidence.

"I know I don't live here anymore, but I agree. You guys took us all in when we needed it and that girl needs it." Colt says.

Grady stands from the table "Let me make some calls. I want you guys to know how proud I am of you for coming to us with this. For sticking together and I will do what I can Dawson. I promise." I nod my head at him knowing he is telling the truth.

"I never had a daughter before." Sarah says as she swipes some tears that have escaped.

"You could have dressed me up anytime you wanted Mama S." Eli tells her making us all laugh.

Within a few days, Gracie was living with us and both foster parents were in jail. Sarah made sure to take pictures of all her bruises and scars because she will have to testify in court when the time comes.

Of course Sarah and Grady sat her down giving her the rules talk and adding in some new ones for us because we are dating. They said they wouldn't stop us from dating, but we are not allowed to have sex under their roof. Even though we have never talked about going that far, I don't think Grace is ready for that.

The trial came quickly which I think Grady pulled some strings on that one wanting her to be able to get it done and over with so she could put it behind her and move on. So within a few months. we were sitting in the courtroom with Grace on the stand recounting every beating that took place. I don't know how I sat through all of it without getting sick. For years she was beaten to a bloody pulp for nothing by that asshole and no one knew. No one helped her. We all knew something was wrong but did nothing. I felt like the worst person on the face of the fucking earth for not pushing her hard enough to tell me sooner.

After all the bruising was gone, Sarah took her shopping and got her all new clothes and none were long sleeved or jeans. Now that the bruises are gone and not replaced with new ones, I can see her confidence growing.

six

Senior prom is quickly approaching so Grady took Eli and I to get our tuxes while Sarah took Grace dress shopping. Sarah loves having Grace here and it gives her somebody to shop with and do girl shit with.

When Grace first came to stay with us. she was real quiet and closed off, she walked on egg shells and was very jumpy. She was always scared she was doing something wrong and was always apologizing for things she didn't need to. We all had to be patient and keep telling her she was safe here and over time she started opening up and feeling more comfortable.

She has grown very close to Sarah and she often calls her mom, but I don't think she even realizes it. Sarah doesn't correct her. I think it makes Sarah real happy having someone call her Mom. The guys never do unless it's Eli calling her Mama S, but that's not the same as being called mom. Even though she is like a mother to all of us, I just can't do it. I think maybe it's that I would feel like I was replacing my mom.

Grace's confidence has grown so much now with wearing new clothes and she doesn't wear the braids anymore since Sarah started teaching her how to do her hair. With her new found confidence and a good home life, she has become more outgoing at school and has made a lot of new friends. I couldn't be more proud of her and my love for her has grown so much in the two years since that music festival. Kissing her that day and making her my girlfriend was the best decision I ever made.

Our relationship is perfect. We never fight or argue and I often find myself thinking about after graduation, if it will still be like this when we live together. Gracie is the only girl for me so as I see it the next step is graduation then living together in our own place. So far we have followed all the rules Sarah and Grady set for us, but that doesn't mean we don't sneak make out sessions here and there when they aren't home. I'm usually the one who has to put a stop to it and I've walked away with blue balls on more than one occasion. I can't wait for the first time I get to make love to my girl.

Eli is taking a girl named Stephanie to prom and she is one of Grace's new friends. Stephanie came over to get ready with Grace and Sarah couldn't pass up the chance to help them. So Eli and I are both in our tuxes at the hallway by the staircase with Grady waiting for the girls to come down. Sarah comes down first with tears in her eyes. Grady immediately takes her into his arms as she looks at me. "Dawson, she looks beautiful."

"She always looks beautiful, Sarah." I reply with a smile on my face and she returns it swiping away the stray tears.

Stephanie is next to come down, she has on a long gold fitting dress and she looks pretty. Eli goes to the bottom of the stairs taking her hand and helping her the rest of the way down. He gives her a kiss before whispering something into her ear that makes her face light up.

Then I see my girl. I start at her baby pink heels working my way up to her baby pink dress. It's short and form fitting around the top part and flaring out at the waist. Her hair is piled on her head with lots of curls and little flowers in it. Her makeup is done beautifully and she has contacts in. I have to breathe in deeply a couple of times because she just knocked all the air out of my lungs.

Saving Grace

I go stand where Eli just was helping her down and when she is off the bottom step I put my lips to her temple kissing her. I move my mouth to her ear telling her, "There are no words to describe how beautiful you look." I pull back cupping her cheek with my hand and see the tears building in her eyes. Mine are shining as well. She has come so far from that awkward girl I bumped into that first day.

Grady pushes me away from her so he can wrap her up in his arms. "You look beautiful Grace. You are the closest we ever had to having a daughter. I'm proud to call you ours."

"Grady stop you're going to ruin my makeup," Grace says as she laughs. "I'm so grateful for you guys, you are the closest to parents I've ever had." Grace's parents died when she was really young. She says she doesn't really even remember them. All her foster parents would ever tell her was that they died. They wouldn't tell her how or why. She wasn't allowed to ask about them or she would get beaten.

After all the pictures and hugs are done, we get in my car while Stephanie and Eli get in his. We head to the restaurant and have a romantic meal before heading to school for our prom.

The theme our class voted for was beach, sand, and fun. We walk into the dark cafeteria, there is a tiki bar off to the side and balloons and beach balls all over the floor. They have a inflatable pool filled with water and sand all around it, fake palm trees placed randomly all over the room. Over by the restrooms, they have a table set up with snack foods and drinks with little umbrellas in them and they have a photographer.

We walk into the gymnasium were most of the kids are dancing or hanging by the bleachers laughing. I pull Grace to me, "Would you like to dance?" I ask before kissing her on the cheek.

"Yeah." She says while smiling. I take her hand in mine leading her onto the dance floor. Classmates walk by us all the girls saying hi, telling her how great she looks, and that they love her dress. The guys saying what's up to me and giving me a pat on the back.

The song changes to a slow one as I pull her to me, we sway to the beat. I love having her this close to me. We dance, hang with friends, eat, drink, get pictures and have an amazing night.

Prom is coming to an end and kids are either staying for the lock in, going to the after party, or going home. Grace and I won't be doing any of those, tonight is the night we take our relationship to a whole new level.

Since you have to be eighteen to rent a hotel room, I had Colt do it for me. He brought me the key yesterday and now we are on our way to the Hilton. I wanted the best for Grace so I had him get a suite with money I had been saving.

When we get in the room I think both of us are a little nervous, at least I know I am, if my sweaty palms and shaking hands are any indication. The room is so nice with the beige walls and carpet, it has a huge window that takes up almost all of one wall. The lighting is low throughout the room and in the corner by the window is a table and chairs. I look to the big king-sized bed and there are a lot of useless pillows and Colt has thrown rose petals all over the beige comforter.

I try to make this as stress free as possible and not just jump into why we are here. So I sit at the end of the bed and turn on the flat screen TV that is hanging on the wall opposite of the bed. Grace comes over to sit next to me. "Dawson, I don't want to watch TV."

"Okay," I respond turning it back off and look at her, "What do you wanna do?"

Saving Grace

"I wanna do what we came here to do. Will you make love to me, Dawson?" Boy I guess she wants to just jump right in, maybe I'm the only on feeling nervous after all. My head swims with thoughts of this finally happening. I cup her cheek with my hand placing my other hand on the nape of her neck bringing her face to mine. Tenderly placing my lips against hers until she opens for me, deepening the kiss. We explore each other's bodies and soon I have a condom on as I press against her opening I ask "Are you sure about this?" She only nods and pulls me closer so I start entering her becoming one with her. We are a heap of sweat and tangled sheets as we take each other to the stars.

We finally graduated! Do you know how good it felt having that cap and gown on? Sitting through the boring ceremony I never thought would end, but when it did and we all stood up throwing our caps it was freedom. We are free! Free to be adults, free to move on to greater things, and free to start a new chapter in our lives.

After graduation, Sarah and Grady threw us a party of course with lots of pictures. Sarah cried because all of us will be out of the house now, I guess it's the empty nest shit she always talks about.

A week after graduation we were all moved out. Eli was moving in with Colt and Rico so they moved into a three bedroom apartment a level down from the other one. Grace and I moved into the two bedroom that they moved out of. It feels good to be this close to Colt and Rico again. I am still working at the local pizza place I've been working at since I turned sixteen. Grace works as a waitress at another restaurant she started at after moving in with us.

Our first night in our house I couldn't wait to get inside of her, prom was the one and only time we had sex. We respected Sarah and Grady too much to go against their rules, so we decided to wait. I gently laid her down on the bed taking her to heaven as I followed not long after. It was one of the best nights of my life, loving every part of her body while I told her just how much I love her.

seven

The first couple of months living together on our own was incredible. We couldn't keep our hands off of each other, lying in bed cuddling and talking after we made love, and spending every second of our free time with each other. Whether that consisted of hanging with the guys or going on a date, just having those moments made me the happiest guy on earth. Everything was perfect like I thought it would be until it all started changing.

The changes were subtle at first and then they started evolving and I don't know if it's the being on our own or the responsibility of it. The arguing started with who was going to clean what or who would pay what bill. They quickly escalated to how she thought I was trying to be a parent instead of a boyfriend. Grace says I try to control her and her life. I don't know why she feels like that because she won't ever talk about it. We fight, then she leaves and when she comes back she doesn't want to talk which leads into another argument. You would think since we lived together already things would be great, but that's not how it is. We don't have Sarah and Grady here holding our hands through everything. We have to take care of ourselves and it's not what I thought it would be. I'm starting to see a whole new side to Grace and I'm not sure I like it.

Within just a short six months we have grown so far apart. We used to be good at loving each other and making love to one another, now fighting is what we're good at. We no longer spend time together, on a daily basis Grace leaves to be with her friends and then I go spend time with the guys. Making love has basically stopped, but if it does happen she doesn't want to cuddle anymore nor does she want to talk afterwards. It's like we almost can't stand to be around one another and I find myself asking if it's even worth it anymore.

I find myself at the guys' apartment more than I am in my own. I've talked to them on countless occasions about what has been going on, her pulling away and all the fighting. They aren't really any help though because they just ask what's wrong with her and tell me that's why they're single. They say they see a new side to her also and they don't like it so they stay away from her.

She still helps with the band as far as the manager shit goes, but she doesn't come to watch us practice anymore. Sarah is also quite upset because Grace doesn't come to see her and never calls anymore.

Now that we have our own songs, Grace set us up with a small tour that lasts for a month. This will be the longest I've been away from her in three years. A part of me thinks it will be good for us and the other part thinks it will be the end of us. She seems a little too excited about us leaving and I remember when she first told me about it.

She came over to the couch and sat down beside me "Dawson I have some great news." I turned the TV off so I could give her my undivided attention.

"Yeah, what is it?" I see the smile light up her face, a smile I haven't seen in months.

"I've been making some phone calls and I got you guys a month long tour. You will be opening for the band Caged Animals. You will start in Kansas City, Missouri then go to Chicago, Illinois and keep

going until your last show which will be in Detroit, Michigan."

"Are you fucking serious? That's awesome! So when do we leave?"

"It'll just be you guys going. I'm staying here because I can't get off work."

"I don't wanna go without you."

"It'll be fine Dawson the month will fly by before you know it. You leave in two weeks."

"Let me call the guys."

I have to make it right with her before I leave. I don't feel right about leaving her here. I love Grace and I don't want to be without her. We may be having a hard time, but we can get past it. Right?

I decide to do some shopping and then I start making us a romantic meal of spaghetti with garlic bread and a salad. Well really it's one of the few things I know how to make. I don't think macaroni and cheese or ramen noodles would do for this. I set candles up on the coffee table because we don't have a dining room or even a table.

When she walks through the door, she stops suddenly when she sees what I have done. "Dawson, what is all this?" She asks with a perplexed look on her face.

"Well Gracie we've been having a tough time lately and I leave tomorrow for a month. I wanna make shit right with you before I leave. I love you Gracie and I'm going to miss you."

"I'm going to miss you too. I'm sorry for how it's been between us. I'm just stressed out with everything."

"I know we both are, but I couldn't leave with us hating each other. Let's eat." After dinner, I start the water in the shower. When I had us both stripped bare I helped her into the water with me. I washed her body and hair savoring every part of her. She did the same to me and when we got out after drying each other off, I picked her up bridal-style and carried her to our bed. I laid her down exploring her body with my mouth instead of my hands this time. When the condom is on and I enter her it has always felt like home, but not this time, this time it doesn't even feel like it's mine anymore.

What the fuck is going on with us? Will we actually be able to get past this? As soon as I pull out of her and we have both cleaned up, she rolls one way and I roll the other no cuddling or talking. I lay there thinking how I hoped it was going to be different this time as we both fall asleep miles away from each other.

We are getting ready to go on stage for the very first time since we had our rehearsal earlier to make sure all the instruments were tuned and the lights and sound were just right. I'm nervous as fuck, sweating bullets, and about to puke my guts out everywhere. Colt walks up with the other guys patting me on the back, "You ready to do this?"

"As ready as I'll ever be." I answer with a shaky voice.

"We got this man. We're gonna rock this shit." Eli responds as he fist pumps the air.

"Aren't you guys nervous?" I question. Why is it always me that's nervous about everything?

"Not at all. This is our moment; the one we've been waiting years for." Rico states with all the confidence in the world.

Then I hear our name being called. We take our places on the stage in the bar, the lights shining on our faces and I can see the place is packed people waiting for us to begin. Colt starts with a slow beat on his drums, then Eli comes in on the guitar and Rico on bass. The haunting melody calms me as I start the first lyrics of the song.

I see you standing over there.

Saving Grace

I walk up and you act like I'm not there
Girl you know you see me
Quit acting like you don't know me

The melody picks up and I start belting out the chorus, trying to keep my eyes on the audience connecting with them and having them feel every word that I sing. When the song ends, we go right into our next one and by the time we're done with our set we have a standing ovation. We leave the stage yelling and laughing so hyped up from the adrenaline of it all. We make our way out to the bar and the chicks are swarming around us. I have to push them off of me so I can get to our small bus to call Grace.

It's the same thing every night we perform; the audience loves us. Then I have to fight with women off with a stick. I'm homesick and I miss Grace. We've been on the road for two weeks now and I've called and text her multiple times every day, but she doesn't answer and she doesn't call or text back. It's driving me fucking crazy not knowing what she's doing. I'm antsy all the time and I can barely concentrate. Luckily for me the band we open for has to drop out of the last two weeks of the tour because one of the wives is having a baby.

That puts me at my front door of our apartment two weeks before schedule. I open the door, walk in, and look around at the trashed apartment. It's a fucking disaster. There is trash everywhere and empty food containers all over the place it looks like she hasn't picked up after herself the whole time I've been gone. The smell that lingers in the air has a stench of rotting food and it takes everything in me not to empty my stomach right here on the floor. I have to cover nose and mouth with my hand as I walk further into the apartment.

I look to my right at the kitchen and it's just as bad as the living room with trash everywhere and dishes piled up. This is the most disgusting shit I have ever seen. What the fuck is wrong with her? I walk down the hall stopping suddenly when I hear noises.

What the fuck?

I open our bedroom door and sure enough all I see is naked ass and not just Grace's. She's fucking some dude in our bed in our apartment! My anger bubbles to the surface I can't believe this is fucking happening. They don't notice me at first until I hit my fist against the door. They both turn and look at me with shock written all across their revolting faces. They both jump from the bed as I walk over to the guy punching him in the nose blood flying out.

Good I hope it's fucking broke!

"Get your fucking clothes and get out of my goddamn apartment," I tell him as he goes to put them on. "No I didn't say stand here and put them on get the fuck out of my goddamn place. Now!" I yell picking up his shit throwing it at his chest. I walk over grabbing a handful of his hair pulling him through the apartment. Grace following close behind. "Really Grace? Is this why you didn't wanna go on the tour? You said you couldn't get off work." I open the front door pushing him outside, naked ass and all.

"Dawson, wait please it didn't mean anything." I turn on her anger clear on my face.

"You couldn't even wait two more goddamn weeks for me to come home. And look at this fucking place! What the fuck is wrong with you? You couldn't even keep the apartment clean!" My face scrunching up in disgust as I add, "Who fucking lives like this?"

"Dawson I'm sorry."

Saving Grace

"No you can't apologize for this. It's done. We're done, get your shit and get out of my fucking place."

"It's mine too Dawson. Maybe this wouldn't have happened if you paid a little attention to me."

"You wanna stay here fine. I'll get my shit. I gave you all my goddamn attention. You wanted to be with your friends instead of me, you chose to fight with me all the time. Don't you fucking dare put this on me. You did this Grace. You not me! You want me to apologize for working and doing what I had to for the band? We are grown now Grace, we have responsibilities. I'm serious you and me we are fucking done. I don't want to hear from you again." I scream this shit to her as I go back in the bedroom grabbing all the clothes I can fit in my arms. I add, "You're a selfish bitch, Grace. Everything I ever did was to help you and take care of you."

"Dawson I'm sorry. We can fix this."

"Fix this Grace? There's no fixing this. You repay me for everything I ever did for you by fucking some dude in OUR goddamn bed. You couldn't even have the decency to break up with me first."

"Dawson!"

"Fuck you." I scream as I slam the door shut. I jump on the elevator, hit the button going a level down, and walk to the guys' apartment knocking on the door.

"What's up dude?" Colt says with a dumbfounded look on his face when he answers the door.

"You got extra room for me?"

He furrows his brows opening the door completely letting me in. "Yeah man, come on in." He yells out, "Shawna get your shit it's time for you to go."

A pretty brunette passes us in the living room on her way out and the smell of weed hits my nose. I take a seat on the couch, drop my shit next to me, and wait for them to pass me the joint. After I've taken a hit I tell the guys, "We gotta change the name of the band and we don't have a manager anymore."

"What the fuck happened?" Colt questions looking more and more puzzled by the second.

"Why?" Eli and Rico ask at the same time.

"Because I came home and she was in our bed fucking some other dude."

"Man." Eli states.

"Dude." Colt utters.

"Fuck." Rico voices.

"Yep, so can I move in?"

"Hell yeah," Colt says before adding, "Did you beat the shit out of the dude?"

"I punched him. I think I broke his nose and threw him out of the house naked."

"Right on! What the fuck is wrong with that girl? After everything you did to help her." Rico inquires while we all laugh at the first part.

"I don't know you guys the apartment was a fucking disaster. She hasn't cleaned the whole time we've been gone."

"I'm starting to wonder if she played us all; maybe she's mental dude." Eli says in a matter of fact way.

"That's fucking gross! So what should we name the band?" Colt asks. He's always about the band.

I think about it letting my high take over as I relax back into the couch. "The Betrayed."

"Fuck yeah." They all say at the same time with smiles. This is how we went from Saving Grace to The Betrayed. The name is fitting for all of us in one way or another.

I pull my phone out calling Sarah I want to let her know what happened. She finally answers on the fourth ring. "Hello

Saving Grace

Dawson." You can hear the exasperation in her voice.

"Hi Sarah. Why do you sound like that?"

"Because I just got off the phone with a very upset Grace. Why would you do that to her Dawson?"

"What did she say I did? I didn't do anything!"

"She said you went on that tour and didn't call or text her the whole time you were gone. She said you came home and broke up with her because you didn't want to be tied down anymore and you kicked her out of the apartment."

What the fuck?

"Sarah listen, I don't know what's going on with her, but that is not at all what happened. I'm starting to think she might be crazy, literally."

"Are you sure Dawson? Please tell me the truth."

"I've always told you the truth! I called and texted her every day. She wouldn't answer or return any of them. I came home and the apartment was destroyed. There was trash everywhere with dishes piled up. I was gagging from the smell. She didn't clean the whole time I was gone. Then I walked into our bedroom and she was in there with another guy and I don't need to tell you what they were doing."

"Oh no, I'm so sorry I accused you. What happened to her! I should've known something was going on when I haven't seen or talked to her since a couple of months after you two moved out. Then today she just called out of the blue. You're my son Dawson I will stand behind you and the decision you made. Are you okay though?"

"Yeah I'm good we were fighting a lot anyway and I kind of knew that when I left on tour it would be the end for us. I'm staying with the guys now."

"Okay good I'll let Grady know what happened."

"Thanks Sarah I love you."

"I love you too, Dawson."

After I get off the phone, we start talking about the band and where we go from here.

Grace kept coming to the apartment asking for me. Finally, we were all so tired of it that about a month later we all moved into a house in Wichita. We started playing at open mic nights in the bars and clubs. We didn't get a new manager, but we did start putting videos on the internet. They have taken off and given us a fan base.

Over the next 4 years we were happy doing it this way until one night we were playing in a club called Insanity. Jacey Rhodes was in the audience watching us, she changed everything for us. Jacey made what we had been working for all these years a reality and our dream came true.

Saving Dawson

The Betrayed (A Rocker Series)

one

DAWSON

As I sit in one of the four chairs opposite of Jacey Rhodes desk, I get angrier by the second. "Why the fuck do we have to get a manager? We've been on our own, doing everything ourselves, and we have been just fucking fine. Why do we need to bring someone else in?"

"Chill the fuck out, dude. This is the break we've been waiting for, and if we need to find a manager, we will. Stop being an asshole about it," Colton says to me from his seat next to Elijah. I may be acting like a petulant child right now, but I couldn't care less. I don't want a new fucking manager, not after Grace.

"Dawson, I realize you four have done this on your own, but you can't anymore. When you sign this contract with me, it's only forward from here and you won't have time for everything that will need to get done. All of the paperwork, promoting, social media, and booking your tours, do you really think you could handle all of that? Because the truth of it is you won't have time, not when you are in there recording your first album. You guys need someone to take care of you while you four focus on your music and making sure the crowds love you. I believe in you guys and I only want what's best for you," Jacey tells me from her side of the desk with a smirk on her face.

Still being defiant but knowing she's right, I cross my arms over my chest and narrow my eyes. "Fine, we'll get a manager."

"Great. I have some people in mind so I'll set you up with interviews that you can have here down in the studio." With a clap of her hands and exaggerated sighs from the guys, we move on to the rest of this meeting. "You will need to get in the studio as soon as possible and start recording. If all goes well, I see you on tour in about six months. Does that sound good? Also, here is my offer for a sign on bonus and I'll cover your tour bus when the time comes." Jacey slides a folded piece of paper across the desk.

Rico is the first to grab it. "Holy shit! Are you for real? That's a lot of fucking money, plus six months before touring? Hell yeah that sounds good!" The rest of us look at the number and I swallow hard. This can't be right!

Her laugh rings out in the now quiet office. "I don't joke about money. Ever. I will make my money back because you guys are something special. I know it and everyone else will too. When that contract gets signed, we become a family and I'll be here if you need anything. I'm not like the other labels out there, okay? Most of them are money hungry dicks that only look out for themselves, but that's not me."

We're all still speechless from her offer so we just nod. "Okay guys, be here Friday at eight in the morning to start your interviews. Remember, the person you choose will be on tour with you and you'll be working closely with the person. So...choose wisely." I'm not sure I like the smile playing on her lips, but giving one last nod, we get up out of our chairs then leave Jacey's office.

The four of us climb into Colton's Camaro that Grady and Sarah had bought him when he was sixteen. After the car is started and we're heading down the street, Rico is the first to speak. "What do you guys think?"

Saving Dawson

"I think we're gonna be fucking rockstars and have so much pussy laying at our feet, we won't know what to do." Waggling his eyebrows and a goofy grin, Elijah answers first with his ridiculous thoughts.

"I'm pissed about having to get a manager, but Jacey seems like the real deal." I give my two cents. I can't help but to bring up the manager bullshit again. It may have been four years since the Grace catastrophe, but I've held that shit in like it was yesterday.

"You gotta let that shit go, Dawson. We all know how fucked up it was and we all thought of Grace like a sister, so it wasn't just you that she hurt. She may have hurt you the worst, but it affected all of us. Now you need to focus on what is best for the band and let the past stay in the past. Move the fuck on, dude." Colton gives his input on the situation, keeping his eyes on the road, but glancing at me every so often in the rearview mirror. I look around the car at Rico and Elijah to see their heads down. They agree with him. I slink back into the seat even more, huffing out a breath. I know the band comes first to Colton, so it's not surprising that he would be the one to speak his opinion before the others.

"You're right, I'm sorry guys." I mutter my apology. They don't get it. She might have been like a sister to them, but she was supposed to be my forever. I thought she was the love of my life and she was supposed to always be there. Instead, being our manager, she put us on tour and I came home early to find her in our bed with another dude's dick inside of her.

"Well I think Jacey's legit so let's get that new manager. All in favor of signing with J.R. Recordings, raise your motherfucking hand!" Rico chimes in, breaking the growing tension and making us all laugh. Then one by one we all raise our hands. So it's settled, we are going to be motherfucking rockstars! We have worked our asses off the last eight years for this moment.

We yell, holler, and laugh as we pull into the driveway leading up to our house. Later that night, we order pizza, get liquor, roll up a couple joints, they call a few chicks, and we party, celebrating our accomplishment.

We pull up and park at J.R. Recordings Friday morning at eight, right on the dot. I stop in my tracks when I see Bear open the door for us. Bear is Jacey's scary as fuck husband that I may have pissed off the first time I met him. I flirted with his hot as hell wife, thinking she was just another one of our local female fans. She has this sort of exotic look to her with her tan skin, dark hair, and different colored eyes. I couldn't help myself until he threatened to rip out my throat if I ever spoke to her like that again. Yeah, not a good deal. Especially when he's one of the members of the local motorcycle club, Satan's Sinners. And those guys you do not want to fuck with. Now when I look at her, I picture that old hag Ms. Carlson. A shudder goes through me just thinking about that woman.

"Uh, hey Bear. Where's Jacey?"

"You got a problem with me being here, rockstar?" His huge arms cross over his huge chest, one brow cocks and a deeper frown forms on his already unhappy face.

"Look, I'm sorry, okay? We got off on the wrong foot. If I would have known who she was, I would never have spoken to her like that." I stare Bear down, not letting him intimidate me. On the inside though I'm shaking like a leaf and ready to shit my pants. The dude is like ten times my size and I have no doubt he could break me like a twig with his bare hands.

"Fine. My Ol' Lady said to play nice and I do what I have to do to make my woman happy. So as long as you know your

Saving Dawson

place, then we won't have problems. Some shit went down I'm not discussing with you and she'll be out for a couple of weeks. I'll be here, or one of my brothers will be. She told me everything that needs to get done so we will take care of it. Your interviews start in half an hour so get your asses downstairs." Giving a tight nod, I follow behind the rest of the guys as we walk into the building. I swear I heard a growl come out of his mouth as I walked by. The dude hates me! It wouldn't surprise me if he had already thought of ten different ways to kill me.

As we open the door at the bottom of the steps, I look around the studio. Shit, this is nice with all the new equipment, the black leather couches, and it looks like the place has been newly remodeled with the red and gray paint. There are separate rooms: one with the recording equipment, one with instruments set up and a microphone so we can record, and one with toys I'm assuming for Bear and Jacey's son.

"Alright guys, like Jacey said, we need to choose wisely and we need to take this seriously. We don't want some fucktwat manager that we can't work with," Colton tells us as he gets into his business mode.

We choose to sit on one of the black leather couches, placing a rolling chair across from us so the interviewers can have a seat. We wait for the first person to show up. To say I'm nervous is an understatement, and I don't know if it's more from just the possibility of finding someone or to actually find the right one. I rub my sweaty palms on my jean-covered thighs as we wait. My pulse is racing with the anticipation of who we'll be meeting. Trust is a rough thing to give, and we gave it to Jacey, so she better not let us down.

Footsteps sound on the stairs and then the door opens. In walks a short, old, fat bastard with gray hair on the sides of his head and none on top. The dark blue suit he has on looks about two sizes too small, and I'm afraid one of those buttons on his shirt is about to pop right off, hitting one of us in the eye. What in the actual fuck? Where the hell did Jacey find this guy? The sweat rolls down his forehead and makes his too big glasses slip down his nose. I tried not to laugh, I really fucking tried, but when I looked at my brothers, I fucking lost it. Their heads are down, arms folded across their chests, and all of their shoulders are shaking with silent laughter. I couldn't help it, I busted a gut at this poor bastard's expense.

He pulls out a handkerchief that was tucked into his suit jacket and dabs at his forehead. He holds his free hand out for us to shake, but none of us take the offered hand. "Hi gentleman. My name is Gary..." I get my laughter under control by the time he makes it to the chair that is positioned in front of us.

Trying to be polite, I stop him from going any further. "Yeah, hey Gary, you're not gonna work out for us, but thank you for coming." There's really no point in wasting anyone's time when it won't be him we choose.

"But you haven't even heard why I should be your manager!" A frustrated expression plays on his face, matching the tone of his voice.

"We don't need to hear it. We already know you aren't a good fit for us. So thank you for coming. Goodbye," I tell Gary as he huffs out a breath and shows himself to the door.

Next came an old bossy bitch. When she first walked in, we thought she might work until she started telling us to sit up straighter. Then suggested if we are doing interviews, we should dress more business-like instead of in our jeans and t-shirts. As far as we were concerned, the interview was over so we kicked her out.

An hour went by before the next applicant showed up.

Saving Dawson

Her footsteps were so quiet that we didn't even hear her come down until the door opened. The girl that stepped through the doorway almost made me flip shit because of how much she looked like Grace when I first met her. She introduced herself as Jamie and that's all I heard. She had the nerdy glasses, the long blonde braids, the long sleeves and long skirt covering every inch of her skin. Her voice was soft spoken and she kept her head down. I couldn't take it, I had to leave the room. I felt like I was being strangled, I couldn't fucking breathe. I was suffocating and the walls were closing in on me. I ran up the stairs like I was in a marathon, taking in quick short breaths of air, my forehead drenched in sweat and vision blurry. I damn near passed the fuck out before I made it all the way upstairs, and didn't return into the studio until I knew she was gone.

"Absolutely not! Do not even fucking suggest her!" I told all of the guys, the seriousness deep in my tone so they know I'm not fucking around with this.

"She wasn't that bad, just a little shy maybe," Rico chimed in, being the only stupid one to reply as the others kept their heads down. *He can't be serious right now!*

I stand toe to toe with him and point my finger in his face. "No! You want me to be okay with this bullshit, then not her. No fucking way!" Dropping my hand back down and taking a few steps back, I continue on while looking around at each of my brothers. "When I was upstairs, Bear said we had a couple more people to interview." I try to calm myself, I'm still reeling from the panic attack.

The next girl came in looking like the typical groupie, with the too small dress that barely covers anything. Huge fake tits that didn't match the straight-as-a-board backside. The way she was chewing on that piece of gum she had in her mouth, you'd of thought that was the only thing she had consumed in days. Her finger twisted around her bottle bleached hair and she had a voice that could break windows, the way she would screech in happiness at being here. *Oh my God! I'm in front of The Betrayed. Oh my God, you are so hot!* Gah, don't even get me started on the ditziness and the dumber-than-a-box-of-rocks answers she gave. For example, when we asked how well she could multitask her answer was *Well, I am talking to the four of you so I think I multitask pretty good.* Yeah, that was the end of her interview. Then to top it off, before she left she had to tell us how much she loved us and wanted to have our babies. Can you say 'bitch is crazy'? I'm still wondering where the fuck Jacey found these people and why she would even consider them.

We've been sitting here, waiting for an hour and a half for the next person to show up, and I'm pretty sure they're late. It's already afternoon, we're all starving and ready to go. Right when I'm about to ask if the guys are ready, you can hear the sound of heels hitting the steps. The door opens and my heart stops. She must have lost her balance because it isn't a graceful entrance by any means, it's more like she barreled her way through the door. Thank God she caught herself before face-planting the floor in front of all of us. I hear *Shiiit!* from my brothers, but I can't even attempt to pull my eyes away.

Fire engine dyed red hair sits on the top of her head in big curls. Her knee length navy blue and white polka dotted dress hugs her body perfectly. The fuck-me red heels she has on make her legs look like they go on for days. The swell of her breasts tell me she's a good C cup, and combined with the luscious curves of her hips and tiny little waist, she has the perfect hourglass figure. Both of her arms, from wrists to shoulders, are covered in beautiful tattoos, along with one that goes across her chest. She looks like a vamped up, pinup style Dorothy from The Wizard of Oz. "Fuck me! This girl cannot

Saving Dawson

become our manager," I whisper under my breath so no one can hear me.

She rushes into the room. "Motherfucking sonofabitch! Can it get any fucking worse?" The explicit words fall from her bright red full lips that contrast with her cream colored skin. Her emerald green eyes meet my stormy grays, and I swear her face turns the same shade as her fire engine red hair. "I'm sorry I'm late. My name's Emery Ashland. And I'm sorry for my colorful language back there." She takes the chair that sits across from us and plops down, panting heavily like she had to run here.

"I don't know and don't care why you are late, let's just get this over with. I'm Dawson Gates, lead singer." I shake her hand and feel my anger rising towards the pinup beauty in front of me. The guys introduce themselves and we start the interview.

"So Emery how well do you multitask?" Colton asks from his seat on the couch. When I glance over at him he is bent forward with his elbows resting on his knees with his hands hanging between his legs.

Crossing one leg over the other and entwining her fingers, placing them on her top thigh, my cock starts to twitch at the sight. Her dress has risen up, showing off more of her bare, pale skin. "Well, I have experience in office work so while being on the phone taking calls, I had to file records, keep appointments straight, check people in, and do billing." Shit, she sounds like she knows what she's doing. Not good for me.

"How do you feel about living on a bus for months with the four of us?" Rico is the next to ask, while sitting up straighter. *Is he trying to impress her? I don't fucking think so, brother.*

"As long as I get the bedroom, and because I know every tour bus has one, we should be fine. If you guys are going to be doing what most rockers do on tour, I don't wanna be in the room nor do I wanna hear that shit. Also, clean up after yourselves and we won't have a problem." Fuck me she has a smart, sassy mouth too. Definitely not good for me. The others laugh at what she said, but I narrow my eyes on her.

I've been around this woman five fucking minutes and she is already affecting me. I have to keep changing positions on the couch because my jeans are growing tighter by the second listening to her musical voice and just being in her presence. Thank God no one is paying attention to me, I'd never live this shit down.

"Are you single?" Elijah questions from his spot next to me, but he is slouched back, one arm stretched out on the back of the couch, the smile in place that all the ladies love.

"I don't think that's any of your business and it has nothing to do with my job as your manager." Now her eyes are narrowing, matching my own. *Oh did he strike a nerve, honey?* As stunning as Emery is, I don't know how she could be single.

"Have you heard our music?" Is my question. I fold my arms across my chest, glaring at the woman while waiting for her answer.

Knowing my anger is visible, she doesn't back down. Instead, she mimics my expression and answers with a damn good response. "Honestly, I had never heard of you guys until Jacey called me. Then I looked on YouTube, watched your videos, and I have to say, I think you guys are really good. You have a lot of raw talent and it's refreshing to hear. I think we would work well together if you guys pick me to be your manager." God help me, she is perfect. This is fucking terrible for me.

"You're hired!" my three brothers reply immediately. I think I just gave myself whiplash with how fast my head snapped in their direction. Fuck me! I can't work with this chick. I know exactly what's going to happen and I can't let it. I won't let it.

Emery's mouth drops open, then closes like she's a damn fish. *I'd like to fill that pretty mouth so she better just keep it closed. Quit fucking thinking about her like that,* I tell myself but it's really not working. She needs to get out of here and out of my fucking line of sight. "What? Really? You're not fucking with me?" she questions before I witness the most beautiful smile in God's creation. It reaches all the way to her eyes, letting me know that it's real and true. Her straight white teeth shine and I have yet to find one flaw about this woman.

"Yes really, and no we aren't fucking with you," Rico answers while they all laugh again, except for me. I'm not finding this shit funny in the least bit.

"Thank you so much! It was really nice meeting you guys, and I'll be in touch with Jacey for what happens now." We all stand and I tuck my hands in the front pockets of my jeans while she shakes hands with my brothers. When Emery is in front of me, she says, "It was nice meeting you Dawson, even if you seem to be a little angry with me." She dips her head down, but not before I caught those teeth sinking into her bottom lip. The dimples from her pierced cheeks make her look fucking adorable. Finally she heads for the door and I can breathe again. Emery Ashland stole my breath from the moment she stumbled through the door, not just from the sight of her, but her smell too. Vanilla. So fucking good, my favorite flavor.

"Shit, she's fucking beautiful." Colton's remark pisses me off further.

"Shut the fuck up, Colt. And what the hell was that *you're hired stunt*? Shouldn't we talk about it first?" I ask, glaring at the three of them with their shit-eating grins.

"Don't take it out on us that Mr. Woody couldn't peck his

way out to play with the bombshell," Elijah says with a knowing grin while eyeing my crotch.

"Stop looking at my dick, Eli! Fuck, I didn't think anyone was paying attention. You assholes all know this is gonna end badly." I run my hand over my hair that's pulled back in the man bun. I've noticed it's the *in* thing with chicks, they've been digging it lately. Doesn't really matter to me though, it's not like I'm taking any of them home.

"Nah, we didn't notice. I think we all just had the same reaction to her. Fuck, she was hot! It doesn't have to end badly if you don't let it." Colton's brow cocks with that evil smile still on his smug face.

"Off fucking limits! You hear me?" I respond to Colton's statement that just pissed me off even more. They are egging me on and they know it. They better not touch her or even think about touching her. I'll break their fucking fingers if they do.

"Yeah, we hear ya, and no, we didn't need to discuss it. Don't be a shithead, you know she was the best one for us," Rico tells me as I follow them up the stairs.

"So did you guys pick?" Bear questions as soon as the door to the downstairs is shut behind me. He's a big sonofabitch with his arms crossed over his wide chest again. I swear they're bigger than my head.

"Yeah, we hired Emery," Colton answers for us.

Now Bear's the one with a smirk. "Good choice, that must be why she looked so happy walking outta here. Jacey said if you guys were to pick then you needed to sign these contracts."

We spend the next thirty minutes in Jacey's office reading over everything and then signing on every dotted line until our hands were cramped up.

"Alright guys, welcome to J.R. Recordings. Here you go.

Saving Dawson

Congratulations." Bear hands us each an envelope with our names on them. No excitement in his rough voice. "Give it a couple weeks for my Ol' Lady to be ready to come back and then you guys can start recording. Now get the fuck outta here, I'm ready to go home." The grin twitches on his face and I think maybe he isn't so bad after all. Yeah, right, he'd snap me like a twig if his woman would let him.

We follow Bear outside, he locks up and we get in the Camaro. All of us open the envelopes to find checks wrote out to each of us for twenty-five thousand dollars. Holy fuck! A hundred grand between the four of us I never thought we would be here. The ride home was loud with all of the excitement.

Over the next two weeks we worked on getting bank accounts, putting our songs together, and changing our looks to fit the rock star persona. The latter was Elijah's idea for the ladies, like he needs help in that department.

two

EMERY

Bang. Bang. Bang.

The loud sound of someone knocking on the door pulls me from my sleep. I jump up off the couch and run on my tiptoes to Sicily's room, not making a sound. I open the bedroom door, the only bedroom door we have, to see her sitting up in bed rubbing the sleep from her eyes.

Holding a finger over my mouth showing her to be quiet, I sit on the floor, patting the space next to me. The banging continues as she comes and sits down beside me. Sicily has gotten used to this drill over the last few months and I hate it. I hate that we have to hide because I know who is at the door. After a few minutes the knocking stops and she crawls into my lap. "Momma, who dat?" her sweet little three-year-old voice asks.

"No one for you to worry about, baby," I answer while running my hand down her long wavy chestnut hair and placing a kiss on her forehead. After a few more minutes of taking in the comfort of my daughter, we get up to start our day. I get her ready first, just like I always do. She always comes first. No matter what. That's why she has the bedroom and I sleep on the couch.

I style my hair in big curls on the top of my head, pick out my navy blue and white polka dotted dress and my red heels. Outlining my eyes in bold black liner because it makes the green of my eyes pop, I take a look in the mirror. I think I look pretty good for my interview today and I pray to all the Gods in heaven above that I get this job.

For the last three years I worked as the receptionist to an attorney, until yesterday. I walked into work like any other day, but got quite the surprise when Mr. Benson told me to pack up my shit because he was closing business. Luck was on my side for once because Jacey Rhodes had called me a few days before about a job, asking if I could do an interview. Of course I wasn't going to turn it down. She assured me that if the guys are serious then I will be hired. Jacey also told me it was for the band The Betrayed, I had absolutely no idea who they were until I checked out YouTube. After I packed up my stuff and left the office, I spent all day yesterday, while Sicily was at daycare, watching videos of their music, studying them, and I have to say, they are good. Really good.

I walk out of the bathroom and down the hall, coming into the living room where Sicily is sitting, watching her favorite movie. "Come on, little one, we gotta go." I go over to turn the T.V. off, grab her bag for daycare along with my purse, and make sure to pick up Pinky the Pig to take with us. Opening the front door, seeing the eviction notice taped there, I tear it down and throw it into the front room before locking and shutting the door. This just goes to show it was, in fact, the landlord knocking earlier. The same landlord I have been avoiding for the last three months because I can't pay the rent.

Shit adds up, ya know? I thought I could do this all on my own, I was determined to be independent. I was doing okay for awhile until the bills started coming in, and being a single parent isn't easy. Having a child isn't cheap. Medical bills, daycare, clothes for her, shoes for her, rent, utilities, food and

Saving Dawson

everything else - that shit adds up quickly! I'm not a woman to ask for handouts, I'm not a woman who wants shit for free. So I refuse to borrow money from my parents and I refuse to go on government assistance. Sicily and I may not have a lot, but what we do have, I worked my ass off to get. My momma raised me to be strong, she raised me to rely on myself, to have pride and to be proud of the choices I have made.

I strap Sicily into her car seat in the back of my Dodge Spirit that is no doubt older than me. The once blue paint is almost non existent and there is more rust spots than actual color. It gets us from point a to b, and is paid for, so that's all that matters to me. Opening the driver's side door, I climb in, shut the door and start her up. The sputtering sound makes it vibrate, but she starts up without a hitch, and then we are on our way.

Pulling up to the daycare, I get Sicily out, grab her hand, and we walk inside. As soon as we are in, she runs off to play with her friends while Ms. Theresa comes over to me. "Hi Emery. I hate to tell you this, but if we don't have a payment this week, Sicily won't be able to come back." I see the sadness in her eyes, she knows I don't have it easy, but I understand that it's her job. Me not paying keeps her in a bind and she has been lenient with me.

"I understand." I give no excuses because I have none to give. I walk back outside and climb in my car, feeling defeated. I start the car up again and head to my interview.

About a couple miles from J.R. Recordings, the car swerves a little on it's own and there's a loud pop. My fucking tire just blew! Pulling over on the side of the road, I check it out and sure enough, the tire is gone. Not salvageable at all, with all the rubber lying on the street. I pull the latch for the trunk, put all the pieces in there, and realize I don't have a spare. I grab my phone out of my purse and dial my parents' number. What else can go fucking wrong? Of course my phone ran out of minutes and I don't have the extra money to buy more. I also don't have the money to get the tire fixed or have someone tow the car. God help me, it's gonna be a long walk. I realize in this moment that asking for help may not be such a bad thing.

I make it to the studio an hour and a half late for my interview, and I'm sure they aren't going to hire me now. This has been a shit day and that will be the cherry on top. Jacey's husband Bear lets me in with a kind smile. "Are they still here?"

"Yeah they're downstairs. Make it good, they've sent everyone else out pretty quick."

"After the day I've had, they'll probably send me packing too." I give him a wobbly smile.

"It always gets better, girl." Bear gives me a pat on the back then adds, "The door for downstairs is at the end of the hall."

With a nod, I walk that way, open the door and shut it behind me. I make it a few steps and lose my footing, finally catching myself at the end after opening the door and basically bulldozing my way into the room. Well isn't this embarrassing, but it gets even better because I can't control my mouth. "Motherfucking sonofabitch! Can it get any fucking worse?" I say to myself, but when I look up, I'm met with three smirks and an angry expression.

I have a tendency to say inappropriate things when I'm nervous, or in times like this when I have exceptionally bad days. *Not the best way to start an interview, Emery.*

Although they are in a rock band, maybe it won't bother them, I can hope. My face heats up, I'm sure that matches my hair color. "I'm sorry I'm late. My name's Emery Ashland. And I'm sorry for my colorful language back there." Taking the chair that sits across from the four guys I spent my time watching yesterday, I plop down, panting heavily, finally trying to catch my breath from the walk.

"I don't know and don't care why you are late, let's just get this over with. I'm Dawson Gates, lead singer." I try not to let his broodiness bother me as I take him in. Gray stormy eyes, with pain hiding in the depths, are practically devouring me with a hungry gaze. A clenching jaw covered by a dark brown beard gives him a hard manly look. Dawson's long brown hair is pulled back in one of those man buns that doesn't work for a lot of men, but on Dawson Gates it works and works well. His toned chest stretches his t-shirt, making it look too small, and a half sleeve tattoo that's nicely done runs down his left forearm. Loose fitting washed out jeans cover what I know has to be thick muscular thighs. Dawson is a sight to see.

He is gorgeous, probably the most stunning man I have ever seen. I bet he would look like one of those Adonis statues if he was naked and in a pose. Shit, what I wouldn't give to see that. His voice is rugged and raw from the anger he is holding back, but it does things to my body that has never happened to me before. *What the hell am I thinking? Get it together, Emery,* I tell myself before meeting the rest of these good looking guys.

"I'm Colton James, drummer. You can call me, Colt."

"I'm Elijah Summers, lead guitar. Call me whenever you'd like, hot stuff." I laugh and instantly know he is the funny one of the four.

"I'm Rico Donovan, bass. Ignore Eli." A half grin plays on his lips, but he holds a seriousness to him.

"So Emery, how well do you multitask?" Colton asks me. Now we get down to business.

"Well, I have experience in office work so while being on the phone taking calls, I had to file records, keep appointments straight, check people in, and do billing." *Good answer Emery.*

Keep it up and you will have this in the bag, I chant to myself, going off the impressed expressions staring back at me. Even from Dawson, lead singer, angry man.

"How do you feel about living on a bus for months with the four of us?" Rico is the next to ask.

"As long as I get the bedroom, and because I know every tour bus has one, we should be fine. If you guys are going to be doing what most rockers do on tour, I don't wanna be in the room nor do I wanna hear that shit. Also, clean up after yourselves and we won't have a problem." I answer honestly because number one, I'm not their mother. Two, because they are trying to be rockers and rockers like sex, drugs, and partying. It's not my thing and well, having a child makes it kind of hard to be young myself.

I feel the heated eyes on me, but I try to ignore them long enough to make it through this interview. In my peripheral vision I can see that Dawson keeps moving around on the couch. I'm affecting him. Yeah, well guess what buddy, you aren't the only one affected. He might be angry at me for some unknown reason, but there is more in his eyes, in his body language, even in his voice.

"Are you single?" Elijah questions with a sneaky grin.

"I don't think that's any of your business and it has nothing to do with my job as your manager." My eyes narrow. *Is he really trying to hit on me?*

"Have you heard our music?" Dawson questions with folded arms across his toned chest. His glare bores into me while waiting for my answer. I don't hesitate.

He will not intimidate me and I will not back down. So, as if challenging Dawson, I copy his expression. "Honestly, I had never heard of you guys until Jacey called me. Then I looked on YouTube, watched your videos, and I have to say, I think

Saving Dawson

you guys are really good. You have a lot of raw talent and it's refreshing to hear. I think we would work well together if you guys pick me to be your manager."

"You're hired!" all but Dawson shouts out.

"What? Really? You're not fucking with me?" I'm in shock, I wasn't expecting it so soon. Jacey was right! If it wasn't unprofessional, I would start dancing like a fool right now in front of all of them. I'm so happy! After all the bad today, these guys just made it all worth it.

"Yes really, and no, we aren't fucking with you," Rico replies while we all laugh, except for Dawson. So broody. I'll make him smile one day, even if it kills me trying.

"Thank you so much! It was really nice meeting you guys and I'll be in touch with Jacey for what happens now," I tell them as we all stand and I shake hands with three of them. When I'm in front of Dawson, I say, "It was nice meeting you Dawson, even if you seem to be a little angry with me." Momma always said kill em' with kindness, not weakness. I bite down on my bottom lip because he smells erotic, sexy, divine. Oh God, he is going to be trouble for me. I dip my head down and quickly walk out, making my escape from the man I'd like to rip the clothes clean off of.

I get upstairs to find Bear standing in front of the window, looking outside with his arms crossed over his chest. He must hear me because he turns around instantly. "You were down there awhile, how'd it go?"

With a smile on my face I answer, "I'll let them tell you. Can I borrow a phone?" He pulls his cell out of his vest pocket, gets it to the call screen, then hands it to me. I have no choice but to call my mom to come get me.

While waiting outside, I think about those four guys. All of them having kind eyes, but so broken behind the facade. They helped when I needed it most without even knowing it, maybe I can return the favor. Maybe, just maybe, I can help them get back whatever it is they have lost or are looking for. At twenty-one I have perfected the ability to read people. It wasn't always like that though, and at the tender age of seventeen I had to grow up fast.

I couldn't be that dumb, naive little girl anymore and that's when I started watching and studying people. Watching body language, different sounds in their voices or the way they breathe, watching their eyes. There's so much you can read in a person's eyes. They think they can hide pain, sorrow, even heartbreak, but they can't. It all shows. It's not a lie when they say you can see into someone's soul just by looking into the depths of the eyes.

What changed in me was for six months when I was seventeen, I was in love. The kind of love you read about in books. He was so handsome, sweet, and kind. We were inseparable for those months. Inseparable until the day he walked away without a word, without a goodbye, and without a backwards glance. He left me broken, and four weeks later, I found out he left me pregnant. I had to pick myself up, become strong, and I had to prepare to become a mother.

While other kids my age were out partying, the girls were getting their hair and nails done or going shopping whenever they wanted I wasn't able to do any of that. I was spending my money on my daughter, buying diapers, wipes, formula, and anything else she needed.

While the other kids my age were planning on leaving for college, I was trying to find my own place to live. While they were having fun taking trips or hanging out at the beach for the summer I was working my ass off to make it. They say when you turn eighteen you become an adult and it couldn't have

Saving Dawson

been truer when it came to my situation.

I didn't have medical insurance and couldn't afford the high medical bills from OBGYN's, so I found a clinic for people like me. That's where Jacey comes in to play. She was the doctor at the clinic and she took me on as a patient. Jacey helped me in every way she could until it was time for me to have Sicily. My baby was so stubborn she didn't want to get into position. She wanted to come into this world standing, feet first. I ended up having to have a cesarean section and that came with a hefty bill. I've stayed in contact with Jacey over the years, and I am grateful to her now that I got this job when I needed it the most.

My mom pulls up in front of J.R. Recordings, bringing me out of my deep thoughts. I open the door to her new maroon Toyota Camry, pull on my seat belt, and she starts driving away. "Where's your car?"

"The tire blew a couple miles from here," I answer with a shrug of my shoulder, voice even like it's no big deal. "Why didn't you call me? Did you walk all that way?" Her tone rises a couple of octaves and her head whips in my direction before she focuses back on the street.

"Yeah I walked, and I tried but my phone is out of minutes." I keep my eyes on the road so I don't have to see her pity or sympathy.

"Emery..." Her tone is one of worry mixed with sadness. I can't deal with that right now.

Putting my hand up, I cut my mom off. "I don't wanna hear it, okay?"

"Fine, but I think it's time you had help, honey. You have been so strong and you are an amazing mother to Sicily. Your father and I are so proud of you, but let us help you now."

The tears blur my vision. "I got the job." I try to change the subject to get away from all the mushy stuff. Today has been a rough one, I just need a little light in my life right now.

"Oh, honey that's so great! I knew you would."

After picking up Sicily from daycare, sitting at my parent's house while my dad fixed the tire and telling my mom all about my new job, I am exhausted. We finally made it home with enough time to give Sicily her bath. Thank God Mom fed us or she would be up past her bedtime.

I lie down with Sicily in her princess toddler bed and start reading her favorite bedtime story. "The End," I say as I give her a kiss on the forehead.

"Momma."

"Yeah, baby?" I question, looking down into her tired green eyes that match my own.

"Da pwincess has a daddy." I know where this is going and it breaks my fucking heart every time. My nose stings from the tears wanting to fall.

"Yeah she does."

"Why I don't?" And how do you answer that? Oh, I don't know, because he is a disco douche who left me?

"Because God gave you just to me so you can be my princess," I reply with the same answer as always. "Close your eyes now. Goodnight, sweet dreams, sleep tight, and don't let those bed bugs bite." I use my sing-song voice as Sicily tries to repeat my words while I tickle her, making her laugh. It distracts her away from the daddy subject.

"Wuv you, Momma."

"I love you too, Baby." I continue to lay there until she is asleep, holding Pinky the Pig. I make my way to the couch, falling down, and within minutes, I'm asleep myself.

three

DAWSON

Our two weeks is almost up before we have to go into the studio to record. We got the call from Jacey yesterday to meet her Monday morning and we'll start laying the lyrics on tracks. We've stayed busy over the last two weeks with changing our appearances, getting inked up, and deciding which of our songs were best for this first album. Which is good for me because I have tried real fucking hard to keep that pinup Dorothy outta my head. It's not working at all.

Because of everything that has been going on, we missed Sunday dinner with Grady and Sarah last week, so we promised not to miss again. That brings us to today walking into the home I moved into when I was fourteen years old after the accident that killed both of my parents. Colton, Rico, and Elijah already lived here by the time Sarah and Grady took me in. Eight years ago, I would never have thought we would be where we are today - getting signed with a label, putting out our first album, and getting a tour bus of our own.

That night changed my life forever. One minute I was saying goodbye to my parents because the were leaving for their date night they had every month, then in the next, I was sitting on the couch playing a video game when a police officer was at the door, rushing me to the hospital. I had to say goodbye forever to my parents that night, and one thing I learned from it all is never take anything for granted. Always let your loved ones know how much you love them because you may not have them tomorrow.

Elijah's shrill voice cuts through my thoughts, "Maaaamaaaa SSSSSSSS!" he hollers through the foyer, making our ears ring as he yells for Sarah.

"Eli, stop that! We are in the kitchen!" Sarah yells back with a hint of humor in her tone. The four of us guys laugh as we walk that way.

"Just trying to get your attention." Elijah uses the same line on her he's been using since we were fourteen.

Sarah and Grady turn at the same time and the mixing spoon falls from Sarah's hand, hitting the floor as her mouth hangs open, eyes the size of saucers. Grady's eyes are just as wide as he asks, "What the shit?" We expected this kind of reaction, especially because of Colton. The four of us double over laughing. I love coming here because this is my home.

"Grady!" Sarah scolds, making us laugh more.

"Sorry." He pulls her into his side with a smile and kisses the top of her head. Shaking his own head, he questions, "What the hell happened to them? Where did we go wrong?" The humor is clear in his eyes as we all huddle in for one big hug.

"You boys go wash up and go sit at the table. Dinner's almost ready." We do as we're told, chuckling all the way.

"Oh man, that was great. Did you see Sarah's face?" Colton asks as we sit at the table, then adds, "I thought she might pass out right there on the kitchen floor."

"Yeah, we saw it. Maybe you went a little far, Colt," I suggest through another set of laughter.

We can joke about it and we can surprise them, but we all know that no matter what we do, they will still love us. They may not be happy with choices we make or things we

Saving Dawson

have done, but that love never wavers. All four of us got lucky when it came to those two people who took us in and loved us everyday like we were their own kids. They never did adopt any of us, but we didn't need the papers or last name to know that Sarah and Grady were our parents. It took me awhile to finally accept it because I didn't want to feel like I was replacing my own. Sarah and Grady took it in stride though, never once pressuring us into anything, and they gave us all the time we needed to think of them as whatever we wanted.

They are kinda like our heroes, taking us all in, giving us homes when we needed it. Sarah and Grady couldn't have kids of their own so it started with Colton. Then Rico, next came Elijah, and I was the last to move in, except for Grace, but we won't talk about that. My point is that these two people opened their hearts to four boys that weren't theirs and they took care of us. They loved us and gave us the closest thing to a family we were going to get.

Sarah and Grady remind me a lot of my parents, with the love that they have for each other and us four boys. The night my parents died, Grady was the police officer standing at my door to take me to the hospital. When we got there, the nurse that helped me was Sarah. I was supposed to be shipped to some boys' home that night, I was supposed to end up in state custody, but Sarah didn't let that happen. She signed all the papers that ol' hag Ms. Carlson had and was allowed to take me home the same night because they were already foster parents.

Little did I know, my life would change once again. When I walked into the house for the first time and saw three other teenage boys sitting on the couch, I didn't know what to expect. Now, eight years later, they have become my brothers, we have a band, and signed a contract to be motherfucking rock stars. Colton always knew it would happen, the rest of us just hoped.

"We are so happy you boys could make it this time for dinner. We don't get to see you enough these days, so tell me everything that has happened. Tell me about this Jacey Rhodes," Sarah says as she sets the rest of the food on the table then falls onto the seat of her chair, Grady following behind her.

Rico takes over in telling her everything as we pile our plates with lasagna, garlic bread, and salad. "She came to watch us play one night a few weeks ago at Insanity. She wanted to sign us, but gave us time to think about it. Went we met in her office, she said all the right things except we had to get a new manager. Jacey is new to the music business and we are the first band she has signed, but she seems to know what she's talking about. The night we met Jacey, she said something about she used to be a doctor. Had her own clinic and everything." A look passes across Grady's face, but disappears just as quickly as it appeared. I caught it though.

Sarah looks over to me, with sympathy because of the new manager shit, before asking, "So what happened?"

Laughter erupts around the table from my brothers. "Ask Dawson on that one, we aren't allowed to talk about her," Colton spouts off while stuffing his big fucking mouth full of food.

"Dawson?" Sarah fixes her attention on me once again.

"These three assholes decided to hire a woman named Emery Ashland without us even talking about it." I try not to sound too whiny, but I don't think I pull it off.

"Don't let him fool you Mama S, Dawson is in love. He wants to suck her face off and stick his..."

"Eli!" Sarah cuts him off before he can finish that sentence. "Dawson, watch your language. Eli, do not even go there. Why did you guys hire her?"

"Truthfully, she was the best person for the job. She'll fit in with all of our craziness and she answered the interview questions with top notch answers. She aced it." Colton answers with a shrug of his shoulder, then adds, "Dawson didn't want her or anyone else because of Grace, but his reaction to her is what's really pissing him off. She's beautiful, Sarah."

Sarah gives a nod in understanding. "You three," Sarah points her finger at them, "need to be a little more understanding with the Grace situation. She hurt all of us, but Dawson the most. Not only did he lose his best friend, he lost his girlfriend." Sarah's eyes cut to me. "Grace wasn't the right one for you and you will realize that one day. When you meet "the one" it's going to be like an explosion inside of you and she'll consume you, as you do her. Dawson, you have to move on eventually, but you need to keep it professional with this girl. Are you guys going to go on tour?" Thank fuck for the subject change.

"Eventually we will, Jacey says in about six months. We go into the studio tomorrow though and start recording," Rico informs Sarah of where we are at with the music right now.

"Dawson, we have to tell you something. I don't want you to hear it from someone else," Grady says from his spot at the front of the table. I set my fork down and lean back in my chair. "Grace's foster parents are getting out of prison in six months."

"What? How? They were supposed to have a few more years!" I'm in shock. How could they be released after what they did to her?

"Good behavior." I feel the air closing in on me again. Even after everything Grace did to me, I don't want them to get out. They hurt her, they scarred her body. They're mean, ugly people that deserve to spend the rest of their fucking lives rotting in a prison cell. I push my chair back from the table, grabbing my plate as I go into the kitchen, away from everyone.

I clean my plate off and put it in the dishwasher when I feel a hand on my back. I spin around, wrapping my arms around Sarah tightly. I need her comfort.

"It'll be okay Dawson. It'll all be okay." She runs her hand up and down on my back, giving me words to ease my racing heart. "Your parents would be so proud of you. Just like Grady and I are, we are so proud of all you boys." My throat grows thick and I blink away the tears that are trying to escape.

Clearing my throat, I pull away. "Thanks, Sarah."

With a smile she says, "You wanna go out there and tell Grady why you changed your looks?" We both laugh and I mentally thank her for easing the growing tension.

We eventually make it into the living room where we sit around and explain to them why we changed our appearance. Elijah tells them, "We needed the look of rock stars, it'll help with the ladies." It makes us all laugh and roll our eyes at his ridiculousness.

"Like you boys need anymore help with that. I remember when I was still doing your laundry and finding girls' stuff all the time." Sarah puts her hand up while we are laughing. "And no, I don't want to know the things that were going on in this house when Grady and I were working."

I control my laughter to give my response. "I guess I needed a change, it's like leaving the past there and moving on to the future."

"It's a good start, Dawson," Grady answers from his recliner, with Sarah on his lap.

"I just think it's cool as shit."

"Colton!" Sarah scolds, like he is still a teenager. We all chuckle because you would think after all these years she would give up on the bad language, but she hasn't, and it's nice.

"I just wanted more ink," Rico tells them, because he did

Saving Dawson

the least to change.

My long hair is now gone, along with the beard. My half sleeve has turned into a full sleeve, and my back is in the process of becoming a full themed piece. I also got a few piercings; my labret and my nipples.

Elijah cut the sides of his hair short, but left it long on top so it goes into his eyes. He's working on both sleeves, so his arms will be covered in ink, and he got gauges put in his ears.

Colton is also working on his sleeves, as well as his chest and neck. He's now sporting a mohawk that he had dyed blonde so he can change the color whenever he wants. Plus, he got his ears pierced.

Rico didn't do anything crazy with his hair or get any piercings, he just started working on his ink.

We sit around visiting, playing board games with Sarah, and watching some shit on TV until late into the night. When it's time for us to leave, we hug the people that saved us and became like parents to us. Then we head home, and for all of us, it's a restless night. We're amped up and ready for what tomorrow's going to bring.

—

We walk into Jacey's office the next morning. There were a couple of guys from the motorcycle club out front, but they let us in without any problems. "Good morning guys, are you ready to get to work?" Jacey asks as soon as she spots us.

"Yes," we answer in unison, with smiles matching hers.

"I have one question."

"What's that, Dawson?" she asks, with a knowing smirk on her lips.

"Where the hell did you find those people for the interviews?"

Her laughter is loud and her head goes back. When she

calms down some, she has to wipe the tears from her eyes because of laughing so hard. "Don't be mad, but I had to make sure you guys were serious, so I gave you a variety to choose from."

"What the fuck are you talking about?" Colton questions with his arms crossed over his chest.

"Well, I knew that Emery would be best for you, but I didn't know if you guys would go based on what I said. I made it your decision without you knowing I helped to make it. The others came from the club, with the help of Bear. They just played the part I asked them to."

"I don't know if that was fucking brilliant or stupid," Rico tells her, shaking his head and laughing, but looking impressed at her antics.

"So you fucking tricked us into doing what you wanted." My eyes form into slits as I stare her down. One thing about Jacey is she seems to be tough and doesn't back down. In fact, she acts like my harshness doesn't even bother her.

"Oh relax, Dawson. You wouldn't be happy with anyone, so get the fuck over it. It's a done deal now, you guys made the right decision, and I've known Emery for awhile. She'll be good for you guys."

We spend the next hour learning about the equipment and how it all works. Jacey informed us that she will have to take some time off because she's pregnant, which is okay as long as we still get to work. She assured us that it will be fine and she'll teach Bear how to work all of it as well.

I stay with Jacey in the control room while the others go into the live room to record the beat for our first song. It only takes about thirty minutes for it to be perfected and then it's my turn. I walk into the room, grab the headphones, and then I start growling the words to *You Don't See*. We cut three times

Saving Dawson

before it's exactly how it's supposed to be. When I end the song, I walk back out, and we listen to it. It's crazy good!

We repeat the process with the second song and when I'm about halfway through the second chorus, Emery walks in the door. I lose all train of thought and mess up the fucking lyrics. God, she is so fucking beautiful!

Emery's hair is halfway down her back, with two big curls on each side of her head. Her makeup is done the exact same as the last time, and today she has on a black dress that has a strap which ties around her neck. The top half fits her like a corset, but the bottom flows out like a bell. Emery's legs are long and slender once again because of those red fuck-me heels. They must be her favorite pair because both times I've seen her, she has been wearing them. I would almost bet that red is her favorite color too. My dick jerks to life, wanting to come out to play with her.

Jacey pushes the button. "Come on, Dawson. Get it together." I give her a nod. We start over, my eyes on the red headed bombshell, and then she bends over, talking closely with Jacey. Her ample breasts peek out of the top of her dress, just trying to say hello to me. My dick starts to grow, pushing against the zipper of my jeans because wouldn't you know it, he wants to say hello back. I can't focus with her in the room.

I lose it again, fuck up again, and I can't remember the fucking song. Starting over for the third time, Colton walks over, getting too close to her for my comfort. Instead of singing the lyrics, I rip the headphones off my head and walk out of the room, slamming the door behind me. Everyone turns their heads, looking at me curiously.

"What the fuck is going on?" My face is red and heated, my nostrils flare, and the anger ripples off of me.

"We're just going over the scheduling, dude," Colton tells

me with a knowing smirk. *Yeah, that's right motherfucker, you know what I'm pissed about.*

"You need to get back in there, Dawson," Jacey says to me from her seat, not bothered one bit by my pissed off look or attitude.

"I'll get back in there when Dorothy leaves the room." I fold my arms across my tight chest, being defiant once again. Emery walks over to me, narrowing her eyes and hands on those curvy hips. Her attitude is sexy as fuck and her quick intake of breath lets me know that I affect her just as much as she affects me. *Yeah, well guess what honey, you aren't the only one.* I stay focused on her face instead of those tits I want in my mouth.

"And who exactly are you referring to as Dorothy? I'm pretty sure no one here is named Dorothy." Emery's emerald green eyes connect with my grays after she looks around the room for good measure.

"I'm referring to you, cupcake." Some of the anger receding with her in front of me and not next to Colton.

"I'm not your cupcake and the name's not Dorothy." The claws are coming out on this little kitten as she gets pissed.

"Oh, I know what your name is. But how about we go with sweetheart, darlin', honey? Will any of those work for you?" Egging her on, I throw the names out just to see how far I can push her.

"How about I have a name, try fucking using it." Emery brings her face closer to mine and I do the same, so our faces are mere inches apart. Her eyes fill with a mixture of hate and desire. I love her filthy, sassy mouth, it's a big fucking turn on. So I push on further.

"Alright baby, Dorothy it is. Now leave so I can finish working." The grin twitches on my lips, but I hold it back.

Saving Dawson

"I hope you can get as good as you give, playboy, because you have no idea who you are messing with." One hand leaves her hip, coming up and tapping me on the cheek twice. Emery backs up a couple of steps with a smile as she walks past me, not before bumping me in the shoulder. The door opens and right before she leaves the room, she says, "Now don't let me stop you from working, sweet cheeks." The door slams behind her, laughter fills the room, and I storm back into the live room.

We work well into late afternoon before we're done for the day. We laid the first three tracks so we are making good progress. My mind kept going back to that sassy little spitfire. Jacey said she wanted to have a word with me, so now I'm sitting in her office with her across from me. "Dawson, what the hell was that with Emery earlier?"

"Nothing." I look down at my feet and wait for this to be done.

"Listen Dawson, I know something had to have happened with an old manager because of the way you are acting. I don't know what it is and you can tell me when you're ready, but you have to work with Emery. She has to be here and she has to be in the studio. Can you try harder to get past the issue you're having? Goddamn, that shit was funny. I thought Bear and I were bad, you took the cake on that one." Jacey laughs some more, making me grin. "Don't give her such a hard time, she's going to be good for you guys."

Making eye contact, I tell her, "I'll try. I don't want to talk about shit, but I will try. She just gets to me, ya know?"

"Uh...yeah, that was obvious." Jacey laughs and continues, "Alright, I'll see you tomorrow. Let's have a better day, yeah?"

Giving her a tight nod, I get out of my chair and walk outside where the guys are waiting for me.

For the rest of the night, we talk about the day - the good

and bad of it, what we need to get done tomorrow, and I got another lecture on the way I treated Emery. Going to bed once again restless, but for a whole new reason, I toss and turn for hours before finally giving up. As I stare at the ceiling, my mind wanders to what Grady said about Grace's parent's getting out of prison. Even though I hate Grace for what she did to me, I wonder how this will affect her. I haven't seen or spoken to her in four years, and you would think I would've let the shit go by now, but I can't. I haven't let go of her either. I know I need to and I know that I would never be with her again, but she was the love of my life. I don't think I'll ever be fully free from her.

Some might say what we had was just puppy love, but it wasn't, not to me. She was my forever. At fourteen, she became my best friend, by fifteen, I was in love with her. By the time we turned eighteen, we were living together, everything was perfect and like a light switch flipping on and off, it wasn't anymore. If I would have had it my way, by twenty-one, we would've been married with a child on the way.

Grace was there when we started the band, she became our manager, and it was supposed to be the five of us becoming famous, living our dream, and leaving our shitty pasts behind us. I guess Grace grew tired of it, or of me, because when she finally did get us a tour, she didn't want to go. I came home early and there she was in our bed with someone else. I have questions, like why she did it, what happened to us, and when it all changed for her. I'll never ask those questions because I never want to see her again. I don't know what I would do if I came face to face with her again. In the blink of an eye, my present, my future, became a past that I can't let go of.

Shaking off the thoughts of Grace, I start thinking about Emery. I love her spitfire attitude, I love how she doesn't let my anger faze her, and how she doesn't back down when I

Saving Dawson

challenge her. Emery has a hot little body with curves in all the right places. I'd like to put my hands on those curves, use my tongue to shut that dirty little mouth of hers up, and stick my dick in her so deep that she has no choice but to surrender.

I can't though. Number one, it's a whole new ballgame. The band is signed now, we aren't just playing in a garage for our friends from school. Number two, I can't get mixed in with another manager of our band. If it ended badly like I know it would, it would be all my fault and my brothers would be pissed at me. Number three, I can't open up and let someone else in. Emery is the closest I've wanted to come to it though. That woman has the potential to destroy me in every way possible, worse than Grace ever did, and this time I wouldn't survive. I might not have known her for long, but the way she makes me feel, makes me falter, makes me want something I haven't wanted in a long ass time scares the shit out of me to be honest. I need to steer clear of the pinup Dorothy. I smile in my dark room at remembering how she reacted to the name. If she only knew why I called her that.

One night stands and casual sex have never been my thing, unlike the other guys. I flirt and say a lot of shit, but it's just innocent fun, like with Jacey when Bear got pissed at me. I've always been the relationship type of guy and I've tried to be with girls after Grace, but it never lasts. Either they want more than I have to offer or I get bored, no one has kept my interest for very long. If that happened with Emery, the band would lose a manager, the guys would be pissed so my best bet is just to stay as far away as possible. Now how the fuck do I keep her out of my head?

My thoughts turn to my parent's. They had a love most people dream of having but never find. It was the kind of love that would last a lifetime, and I always wanted what they had.

The way my dad would always find ways to touch my mom, or the way her face would light up when my dad walked into a room. I want that kind of love. They were always affectionate, always touching in some kind of way and not a day went by that they had to question their love for one another.

I thought I had that with Grace, but now I know different. I'm sure that I am one of those people that will never find "the one" and I'm okay with that now. I never want to go through, or feel again what Grace put me through. Even though Grace and I weren't exactly like my parents, it was close for awhile, probably the closest I'll ever come to it.

I look over to the bedside table at my alarm clock, four A.M. Fuck me, I have to be up in three hours, but I finally feel like I can drift off. It doesn't take long for me to fall into a deep sleep where my dreams are invaded by my little pinup Dorothy.

four

EMERY

Over the last two weeks, things have changed for me. Sicily and I moved into my parents' house for now, until I can get back on my feet. They have helped me a lot with bills, my car, moving, and even Sicily. So much has been lifted from my shoulders and I am grateful to have the parents I do. I didn't want to ask for help, and because of that, I let my pride get in the way. I realize now that I wasn't doing what was best for my daughter and that makes me feel like a horrible mother.

When the bills started piling up, or when I couldn't pay rent to keep a roof over our heads, or when the weeks started going by at Sicily's daycare that I couldn't pay, I should have sucked it up and asked for help. I didn't though, I kept letting everything grow higher and higher until I was sinking. I continued to let us drown until my mom threw that life preserver out there and saved us from the mess I created. Now all I can do is learn from my lesson, never let it happen again, and come back stronger than ever. This time, I'm going to swim, even if I have to deal with a sexy man that hates me while doing it. I won't be defeated again not by my own doing or someone else's. I will be that strong woman my mother raised me to be.

I walk into Runaway Tattoo and find Audrey at the front desk. "Hey Aud. Is Daphne here?"

"Yeah, she's in her office. Go on back." We share a smile

before I head that way.

One of the benefits of having a best friend that owns a tattoo shop, I never have to pay. Daphne opened up her own shop not too long ago, but before that we would hang out at my place. We had a lot of nights that consisted of girl talks, romantic movies, wine, and her tattooing me. Good times! Daphne has a story much like mine, but it's not my story to tell. We met at our neighborhood park when Sicily was a baby and have been friends ever since, even though Daphne is older than me. We just kinda clicked, ya know?

Let me tell you how small of a world this is. Jacey was my doctor when I was pregnant with Sicily and we stayed in touch. Jacey would check on me every so often, and I would take my daughter to see Jacey when she was sick because of the no insurance situation. When Jacey closed up her clinic, Daphne bought it and turned it into a tattoo shop. I guess some bad stuff happened at the clinic and that's why Jacey shut it down, but no information was ever divulged from Jacey or the newspapers. Whatever happened was kept under tight wraps. Pretty crazy how this world works in bringing people together.

I walk into her office, not bothering to knock, and plop down in a chair across from her desk, frustrated and turned on from my little confrontation with Mr. Sexy Pants, aka Dawson. His long hair and beard are now gone, just leaving a patch of facial hair on his chin. His libra is pierced and I wonder if he had it before and his beard just covered it. I thought he was sexy before, but now he went up a hundred notches on the hotness scale.

"Hey! Oh no, what happened?" Daphne's eyebrows raise at seeing the frustration mixed with anger on my face.

"Oh God, where do I start?" I huff out an exaggerated breath.

Saving Dawson

"At the beginning would be good." Daphne sits back in her chair looking worried.

"So... you know I started my new job today, right? Well, within ten minutes I got into a fight with my boss, he kicked me out, and I just don't know if I'm cut out for this shit." My cheeks fill with air before letting it out.

"Woah, back up. You got into a fight? Why?" My eyes narrow on her because I see those lips twitching, trying to hide her smile. *Bitch!*

"Because he is such a douche nozzle. He called me Dorothy, which I have no idea why, and then he called me cupcake! He listed numerous other names, and I told him I had a name and to fucking use it. Then he kicked me out so he could go back to work. Like it was my fault he couldn't work in the first place! I told him I hope he can get as good as he can give because he doesn't know who he is messing with. Then I proceeded to tap his cheek twice before I walked to the door, and then I called him sweet cheeks. I think I started a war that I'm not sure I wanna fight in. After that, I slammed the door and left." Daphne's laughter fills the room. I'm not finding this funny at all.

"Sweet cheeks! That's fucking great." She breathes deeply a few times, getting herself under control. "Well, he sounds like an asshole so he deserves it. Don't let him intimidate you. What's his name?"

"Dawson Gates. He's the lead singer of that band I was telling you about, The Betrayed." Her smile vanishes.

"You said he called you Dorothy?" I don't miss the knowing expression Daphne tries to cover up.

"Yeah, why?" I look at her curiously.

Her hand waves around in the air and the smile is back in place. "No reason. So anyway, are you going to continue to work for them?" she asks as she starts organizing her desk. Something is up with her.

Rolling my eyes, I answer, "I guess. I mean, I need this job to support Sicily. I just need to try and not let him get to me. Besides, the angry Dawson is seriously hot. Like H-O-T, sexy as hell, fire-in-your-pants kinda hot."

Daphne taps her pen on the edge of her desk while looking at me. *Why is she so anxious?* "Yeah, I understand that kinda hotness. The sex-on-a-stick, hot as sin and you just wanna tear their clothes off kinda hot. But let me tell you, those kind of men are trouble, serious trouble. And if you wanna keep that job, you better keep it professional. "

Now it's my turn to laugh. "Yeah, exactly! At least you get me and I love you for it. He hates me anyway, so I don't have to worry about anything happening."

"I'm sure he doesn't hate you. Maybe he's just dealing with some shit." My brows furrow. She is acting weird. "How is Sis dealing with the move to your parents' house?" Daphne uses the nickname that Sicily has been given by her son.

Maybe she's right, maybe he doesn't hate me. I know I saw the pain he tries to hide, like they all do, and I know I saw desire in his eyes. I just can't get a read on him like I can with everyone else. Maybe because he affects me unlike anyone ever has. Maybe it's not me personally, one can only hope.

"She's doing good. She loves her grandma and grandpa. It's been good for me, I don't have to take Sicily to daycare anymore. I don't have all the bills staying with them so maybe I can get myself out of debt. I could get back on track, especially if I can keep this job."

"Yeah, that sounds good just stay away from Dawson. Hey, let's tattoo you I clear for the rest of the day and maybe that'll get your mind off of it." I nod vigorously while getting up out of my chair and walking into the tattoo room across from her office.

After a long five hour session, I walk out of Runaway Tattoo with new watercolor lilies, blackbirds, and butterflies decorating my back.

Over the next few months, I have managed to steer clear of the band for the most part. If I see them, it's in passing and all of them are nice in greeting, except for Dawson. He still acknowledges me with the name of Dorothy and it still pisses me off, so I throw names back. It's childish, but fuck it, I don't care. If he's gonna act that way then so am I.

I love my job and I've come to realize that I'm pretty great at it. Jacey lets me work at home a lot if I don't need to be in the studio, which gives me more time with Sicily, not to mention the pay. I make more in a week working for The Betrayed than I did in two months working at the lawyer's office. I'm getting all of my bills paid off, I'm getting out of debt, and if a tour wasn't being set up right now, I could start looking into getting a new place to live.

That brings me to today where I can't avoid Dawson because we have a meeting. Jacey decided instead of having two offices, because I really don't use mine, to turn one into a meeting room. So here I sit with her at the eight foot table, waiting for the guys to walk in.

When they do, oh holy hell, Dawson looks good. Too fucking good! His perfectly full lips part as his tongue peeks out, licking across him bottom lip, I am practically squirming in my seat. Now that the beard is gone you can see his clenched, chiseled jaw. Yeah he's not happy to be here or maybe it's seeing me that's bothering him.

The dark gray Henley shirt stretches tight across what I

can only assume to be a well defined muscled chest that leads to a tapered waist. It looks like he has added ink to his half sleeve tattoo, maybe making it into a full sleeve. Dawson's jeans sit low on his hips, fitting him perfectly, The black riding boots he has on stomp the floor as he walks to his seat. The scent of his cologne wafts through the room, causing my breath to catch. I give him one more look over, staring at the tattoos and trying to make out what they are. Come to think of it, I would've known that artwork anywhere. Daphne tattooed him. *That bitch!* She knew who I was talking about as soon as I said his name.

"We asked you here today so we can discuss what Emery has been doing. We need to go over some dates with you, so I will let her take the lead," Jacey informs them, starting the meeting after everyone has been seated.

"Yeah, I'd kinda like to know what Dorothy's been doing so we know we aren't wasting our time on a shit manager." Of fucking course, Dawson has some snarky comment he just has to chime in with.

"Dawson!" He gets warnings from everyone around the table except for me. I don't need to warn him, by the time I'm done with this meeting, he will be looking stupid.

Sitting up in my chair and squaring my shoulders, I open the folder that's lying in front of me on the table. "Well, darlin', let me start with how I've been running all social media platforms for you. I started a Facebook page and a Twitter account for the band, and as of today, you have fifty thousand followers."

"Fifty thousand! How the hell is that even possible?" Rico asks, looking shocked as ever.

"Because I give updates, post your videos from YouTube, amongst other things. The number grows everyday, I have no doubt it'll be over a hundred thousand within the next couple of months with what I have planned. I need your permission for the Instagram account. I need to be able to take your pictures in the studio or when you are just messing around. The fans will think you're connecting with them, and they want to see what happens in your everyday life." I give them a confident smile while making eye contact with each of them. The smiles are returned and appreciation shines in their eyes.

I get nods from all of the guys so I move on to the next topic. "I have set up a P.O. Box for where the fan mail needs to go to. When you are on tour Jacey will handle the mail because I will be with you. The reason you want a P.O. Box is because some of those fans will get crazy and you do not want them knowing where you live. I'll go through all of the mail when we aren't on the bus so you won't have to worry about that. I will give you the important stuff and the rest can be trashed." Again with the nods.

"How did you guys like touring with Caged Animals?" I look around the room once again so I can read them.

"How did you know we toured with them?" Colton asks his own question, with a brow cocked and his fingers tapping against the table.

"Because I do my research." I researched everything I could to find out about these guys and their music. I stayed away from the personal shit because, well, that's not my business. Not right now, anyway.

"It was fucking awesome, probably the best two weeks of our lives," Elijah says with a smile and a far away look, like he's thinking back to it.

"Good. It just so happens that Caged Animals are going on tour in May. It's a summer tour in the southern states and the tour is called Rockin' in the South. I talked to their manager and if you guys can get the rest of the album done, then you're in."

"Are you fucking serious? A three month tour?" Colton is practically bouncing in his seat.

"Yes, I am very serious. I don't have the exact dates at this time, or the venues, but let's work on getting that album done."

"Let's get the album done? Don't you mean *we*? I don't see you in the studio with us and you sure as hell haven't spent every day busting your ass to lay down these tracks." Dawson has to pipe in, making sure to correct me.

"Dawson, stop. She means *us* because we're a family. I'm not going to be around because of this baby in my belly." Jacey's hand instinctively rubs her huge baby bump and continues. "So it will be you guys and Emery, and my husband of course. Work together and be nice, be happy for fucking once, and I will give Bear strict orders that if you don't then he can kick your ass. Understood?" Jacey looks right at Dawson, clearly getting frustrated with his questions. I fake a cough trying to cover my laugh because no way in hell he would stand a chance against Bear. He's a big sonofabitch and scary too, when he wants to be, which is most of the time.

"It's fine Jacey," I assure her before moving on. "So a couple of dates we need to go over, I set up a photoshoot in April because we need to get going on merchandise for promoting. The photographer will be doing the photoshoot for posters, your CD, t-shirts and tank tops, and for me to post on social media, along with the ones I take. Also in March, which yes, is next month, we will be doing your first music video. Does all of this sound good to you guys?"

"Hell yeah it sounds good," Rico, Colton, and Elijah answer with huge smiles.

"Why are we doing a music video before our album is out?" Dawson pipes in again while leaning back in his chair, arms

Saving Dawson

folded across that toned chest. *Is he ever happy? Does he ever smile?*

"Because we want it to be ready after the album releases. The video will be *You Don't See*. Jacey has given me the demo, and it's amazing guys, no doubt it'll hit number one. I'm working on radio stations now, getting them to play the song."

"It all sounds great Emery. You are doing a fan-fucking-tastic job being our manager."

"Thanks Colton." He gives me a grin and I smile in return. At least someone appreciates me.

"No problem. Someone needs to tell you, and not all of us are assholes." I dip my head to hide my smirk.

"Alright, so that's everything, just keep working hard and get that album done."

The meeting ends and we all go our separate ways. Maybe, just maybe, one day I'll get through that tough exterior Dawson protects himself in. I know he is hurting and I know he's in pain, but why does he hate me so much?

After dinner, bath time, and storytelling for Sicily, I lay with her in bed until her precious little eyes close and she falls asleep. Walking into the living room, my parents are sitting on the couch watching TV so I take a seat in the recliner.

My father's eyes meet mine and he stops flipping through the channels. "How'd the meeting go today?"

"It went pretty good. The band is happy with the work I've been doing." I leave out the part about Dawson because my dad wouldn't like how he treats me. It wouldn't surprise me if he tried to find out where the guys live so my dad could pay Dawson a little visit. What he fails to realize is that I'm grown now and I can fight my own battles, which I intend to do. "I need to make sure you guys are okay with watching Sicily when I have to leave with them on tour. You know it'll be for three months."

"Oh, honey, we'll be fine, but the real question is how are you going to handle being away from her?" my mother asks, concern laced in her voice, matching the expression on her beautiful face.

My parents are in their forties, so they aren't old and they look good for their age. My father doesn't have a gray hair on his head, but he has those little lines in the corner of his eyes. He's a tall man, over six foot, with the build of a linebacker. He's a very protective person when it comes to his family, especially my mother. He can be quite the alpha caveman type when it comes to her and she loves him so much. They're perfect together, and the love they have is the kind I always wanted, but I realize not everyone finds that person or gets to experience that type of love. I hope one day I could be lucky enough to find that with another person. I thought I had it once, but I was a young, dumb seventeen year old girl.

My mother has long chestnut colored hair, same as mine when it's not dyed and same as Sicily's. We have the same hourglass figure, attitude, and I look just like her when she was my age. My mother is the strongest, most beautiful person I know inside and out. She may be in her forties, but she doesn't look it because Mom is a stunning woman. She has instilled it in me from a young age to be strong, independent, and never to rely on a man. Her motto is if you can't do it for yourself, then you don't need to do it at all. We have one weakness though, and that's our children.

My eyes instantly water up just thinking about leaving my daughter for that long. I've never been away from her for longer than a night here and there so I don't know how I'll handle it. "I'm not sure," I tell them honestly, then add, "I'm hoping that maybe you guys would bring her to see me at one of the stops."

Saving Dawson

"Yeah, I think we can do that. I haven't taken your mother anywhere for awhile, she could use the getaway." My father smiles down at my mother then puts his arm around her shoulders and places a kiss on the top of her head.

"Well, it was a long day so I'm gonna go to bed. Goodnight, I love you." I stand up, stretch my arms above my head, and yawn.

"Goodnight. Love you too," they both say before I walk down the hall to my room.

I grab an old t-shirt and a clean pair of panties, then heat up the shower in my connecting bathroom. Once the water is hot, I wash away all of my makeup, wash my hair, shave, and let the water relax me. I start thinking about Dawson, remembering the way he looked today. I move my hand down between my legs and gasp at how good it feels when I run my middle finger over my clit.

I imagine what Dawson's tongue and fingers would feel like touching my pussy, and a moan slips out as my fingers start working faster. Hiking one leg up on the side of the tub, I start imagining what it would feel like to have him filling me. I push two fingers inside then bring them back out, over and over. My eyes close, head hits the wall as I finger fuck myself with one hand and use the other to rub against my clit.

My orgasm comes quickly, and I bite down on my bottom lip to keep from screaming out his name. Never in my life have I ever given myself such a powerful orgasm. With shaky legs, I get out of the shower, dry off, put my t-shirt and panties on, and get under the covers. Only halfway satisfied and comfortable, it doesn't take long for me to fall asleep. I say halfway because goddamnit, I wish I had the real Dawson, not just my fantasies. I'm such a stupid, stupid girl when it comes to that man.

five

DAWSON

I wipe the sleep from my eyes, stretch out my body, and decide it's time to get this fucking day started. My painfully hard dick reminds me of the dreams I've had for the last few months of the sexy little redhead I'd like pound my anger into. Show her just how frustrated she makes me, walking around in those little dresses like she's June Cleaver, a hot little housewife. *Fuuuck!*

Throwing myself out of bed, I grab a fresh set of clothes and walk to the bathroom, hoping none of the guys are up yet. Thank fuck they aren't, so I turn on the shower just like every morning, washing my body and hair, do a little manscaping, then grip my still hard dick. As much jerking it as I've done over the months since I met Emery, I'm surprised I don't have calluses.

With a hand gripped firmly around my dick, I tug and stroke in long, hard motions. I imagine those perfect red lips surrounding me. Emery's hot, wet, filthy mouth sucking me in so deep until I hit the back of her throat. My pace quickens, my eyes roll and close, my free hand hits the wall to keep my balance.

I imagine pulling my dick free from her mouth and thrusting into her tight, scalding pussy. Her cream colored skin would be flush to my tanned complexion. Skin against skin as our sweaty bodies would move together perfectly. Emery would be so fucking wet for me and as I pound into her, filthy words and my name would be ripped from those swollen lips. Her screams would fill the room as I pummeled and pounded into her as hard as I could. I'd fill her with my hot cum while she begged me to give her all I had.

I form a fist with my hand on the shower wall, I can almost feel her nails scratching into my back. My balls tighten and the tingling starts in my spine as one last picture of Emery's hard little nipples in my mouth, tasting her vanilla scent, brings the first jet of cum out of me. With shaky legs, I continue pumping my dick until I am bone dry, my cum coats the wall with the power of my release. When I've calmed my heavy breathing, cleaned my mess and washed myself again, and steadied my shaking legs, I step out of the shower.

My black boots make angry thuds on the hardwood floors as I walk through J.R. Recordings. I walk into the meeting room and take my seat across from Emery. One of Bear's guys are here today because Jacey in now on leave so she can have the baby. "What're we here for today, Sweetness?" I use the names on her because I know it pisses her off, and I can't help it, a pissed off Emery Ashland is a sexy one.

Her narrowed eyes meet mine and her voice is laced with venom. "Don't fucking start with me, darlin'."

A smirk forms on my lips. "Wouldn't dream of it, Almighty Queen." I salute her and it seems to have made her angrier.

Emery's hand comes down hard, slapping the table, and she leans over, trying to get closer to me. It was loud so I know her hand has to be stinging, but she acts like she isn't affected. "I've had enough of your shit, okay? It's been fucking months, you don't know me and I don't know you, so why don't you tell

Saving Dawson

me what your problem is with me?"

"I don't have a problem." My eyes turn cold, my voice is hard as I add, "Now start the goddamn meeting."

Her lips turn up in a half grin, half sneer. "Oh, what's the matter? Did I hit a button?" Emery stands, leaning over the table, going off on a rampage. "Oh, poor little Dawson acts like he can't work around me and doesn't want a manager to help his band better themselves. Poor little Dawson has to use stupid fucking names to get a rise out of me. Poor little Dawson should worry about his fucking job instead of how to piss me the fuck off. So cut the shit, it stops now, understood? You know what I think, Dawson? I think you are threatened." Emery's chest rises and falls heavily, panting breaths come, and my dick comes to life.

Now it's my turn to stand with hands balled into fists resting on top of the table, I lean in so our faces are just an inch apart and I laugh right in her face. "I'm the lead singer, Baby. What would I have to be threatened by you about?"

Emery's grin becomes a full smile now. "I'm not talking about being threatened with the band. I'm talking about being threatened here." She brings her hand up, touching my chest where my heart is. Her touch burns my skin, even through my old Beatles shirt. I'm about to knock her hand away when Bear's guy stands up, puts an arm between us.

"Christ, Bear said I would have to watch you two. Didn't know it was gonna be some kinda angry foreplay. Maybe you need to fuck and get it outta your systems, but for now, sit the fuck down, both of you, and get on with this fuckin' meeting." Cackles break through the quiet room as neither of us want to back down. Neither of us want to be the first to sit. "Sit. The. Fuck. Down!" he bellows, and now we know he really isn't fucking around.

115

We do as we are told, but I'm reeling from our little argument. I'm worked up to the hilt with a hard as cement dick. I turn my attention to Bear's guy. "And who the fuck are you?"

"You watch your tone with me, boy. The name's Hacker and believe me, the name fits. If you don't wanna find out for yourself then sit here, shut the fuck up, and get this over with." Cold, dead eyes stare at me and I swallow the lump in my throat. *Is he threatening to kill me?*

"Fine, let's get this done." I fold my arms across my chest and wait for Emery to start.

"Thank you!" Her eyes cut to me. "We have the video coming up in two weeks for *You Don't See*. I need you guys to tell me what the song is about and what you want the video to represent," Emery starts, ever the professional, acting like nothing even happened.

"It's about a couple once in love, she did him dirty, broke his heart, and she doesn't care about all of the pain and hurt she caused," Colton answers, giving a good analysis of the song I wrote.

"Okay, I take it this is from personal experience. So tell me, what did the girl look like? Which one of you did she hurt? Dawson, you are going to be the one mainly in the video you will act as the boyfriend."

"No! No fucking way! I'm not doing it." I get up outta my chair so fast that it flies back, hitting the wall. Practically running out of the room, I throw the door open. I need air, the panic attack is coming full force. My vision is hazy, but I make it to the bathroom and I stand at the sink. I turn the cold water on, splashing my face with it, hoping to calm myself but it's not working. My hands clutch the sides of the sink so tightly that my knuckles are white, my breathing is in heavy pants because

Saving Dawson

I can't get enough air into my lungs.

I feel a hand on my back, light and delicate, and I know that it's Emery. "Dawson, are you okay?" Her musical voice rings in my ears and has me spinning so fast. Before I realize what I'm doing, I grip her wrist and bring her in chest to chest with me. Surrounding her in my arms, I hold her to me as close as I can possibly get her. That one touch, those four words out of her mouth were enough to calm me. Why, I have no idea, but I'll take it. Sarah is the only other one that has ever been able to calm me. "I'm sorry," she tells me, sounding so sincere.

"For what? You don't have anything to be sorry for." I hold her to my chest tightly, with my chin resting on the top of her head, and one hand absently plays with her long hair. I know I shouldn't be this close to her, it's dangerous. I fight with her at every turn so she will want to stay away, but she didn't. She came running to make sure I was okay and I need the feel of her for just a moment.

Emery's hand comes up to lay flat against my heart, burning my skin once again. "I don't know, I think maybe I said too much."

I have pushed this girl's buttons in almost every way possible and she is worried about pushing me. "You didn't, it's just a past that I don't want to think about, let alone talk about." I tell her honestly while still stroking her hair.

"So it was you." She pushes against my hand, tilting her head up so those green eyes can meet my grays. "I'm sorry that you got hurt, Dawson."

"Me too. Just be glad you have never been there." The sadness in her glossy eyes tells me I might just be wrong.

"I know about that more than you think." Emery starts to pull away. "Come on, we need to get back out there."

When she's almost to the door, I call out, "Hey, babydoll?"

With a heavy sigh she turns to me. "Yeah?"

"Just remember, it might not be such a bad thing when I call you Dorothy." She gives me a nod and reaches for the door handle. "Hey."

"Yeah, sweet cheeks?" She turns again, this time with a beautiful real smile and I return it with probably the first real smile I've had in a long time.

"You are doing a real good job as our manager. I just wanted you to know that, Emery. All the fighting between us it's my fault." The smile falls and her mouth forms into a cute little "o" shape.

"Thank you." Emery dips her head and then leaves the bathroom. For a few more minutes I stay in there, looking back at the reflection of myself in the mirror. Will I ever get past the shit Grace did to me? I sure fucking hope so, and I think Emery might just be the one to get me there. She's resilient, tough skinned, she doesn't quit, and she may be just what I need. A new plan starts to form in my brain.

We have been working our asses off the last couple of months. Working day and night, we finally got our first album done, along with the photoshoot, and we got the video made.

After I left the bathroom that day, I went back in for the meeting where we decided on having a couple in the video instead of me doing it. We also chose to have the girl as a brunette so it wasn't hard to watch, it wouldn't bring me back to the past with Grace.

The photoshoot was a breeze and the pictures turned out fucking amazing. After editing, the band decided the best pictures were the ones with Emery in them, standing in the middle with us. She has been the best manager we could have ever asked for, even if I don't tell her. We needed to let people

Saving Dawson

know how important she is to us, so some of the merchandise will have just the band and others with be the five of us. I've quit giving her such a hard time after that day in the bathroom, but I still call her Dorothy, along with the other names. She takes it and dishes it right back, but now it's in more of a playful manner. I'm coming to terms with Emery being around and I can't deny that she is great at her job. Better than Grace ever was.

"Hey Dawson, we're gonna head out for the night are you coming?" Rico asks as he pokes his head into the recording room.

"Nah, I'm good I'm gonna go over the tracks one more time. I'll call you later for a ride."

As Rico shuts the door behind him, I push play on the system. I've listened to these songs a million times and I know they are perfect, but the tour is drawing near and my nerves are getting the best of me. Will people like them, will we make it, what happens if we fail? We have wanted this for so fucking long and now that we are here, what will happen if this was all one far fetched dream that we could never accomplish?

That's not the only reason I stayed behind tonight. Emery is upstairs in the meeting room, working late. It doesn't sit right with me, leaving her here alone. She mostly works from home, but when she is here, it's late nights getting whatever done that she's working on. Those are the nights I stay behind, giving some kind of excuse to my brothers. Emery doesn't know that I stay until she is safely in her beat up car, driving away.

After an hour, I shut down the system. Satisfied with the album, I turn the lights off and head upstairs. She should be walking outside to her car by now. Yeah, this doesn't make me sound like a stalker at all. I walk down the hallway, pull out my phone, and I'm about to hit send when I'm hit in the shoulder.

"AAHHH!" Emery's scream echoes through the room. My phone falls to the floor, I reach down to grab it then put it in my pocket.

"Oh shit!" I grab ahold of her shoulders to steady her balance. "I'm sorry, I wasn't paying attention. Are you okay?"

"No, I'm not okay! What the hell are you doing here, Dawson? You scared the shit out of me." Emery's hand goes to her chest, covering where her heart is.

"I stayed behind to listen to the album again. The tour is coming up and I guess I just want to make sure it's perfect." I realize just then that my hands have started to involuntarily rub up and down Emery's shoulders. I pull away quickly and stick my hands in the pockets of my jeans. My head drops to check out the hardwood floor. "What are you doing here?"

"I had some last minute paperwork to finish up. I forgot my car keys so I came back in to get them." I chance a look at her and Emery's head is down also.

"So... I guess we better lock up and get out of here." I'm stuck, rooted to the floor, I don't want to be the first to walk away.

"Yeah I guess so." She doesn't move either.

"Go get your keys and I'll call Rico for a ride."

"Right, my keys." She rushes to the meeting room, I pull my phone out and start going through my contacts. Out of the corner of my eye, I see her turn around. "Hey Dawson, I'm already here. I could give you a ride."

"Okay. Thanks." I get to be around her for just a little bit longer.

Emery took me home that night and it was a quiet ride, but from that night forward we would meet up in the lobby. She would give me a ride, it was always quiet in the car. I don't

Saving Dawson

think either of us knew what to say, but you could feel the sexual tension radiating between us. It grew stronger by the day. Only a few more weeks until tour, how's it going to be in the small space of a bus? I'm not so sure I'm gonna be able to stay away for much longer. I just hope I don't fuck everything up.

We head out on tour in a week so we wanted to have one last dinner with Sarah and Grady before we leave.

"I'm going to miss my boys so much," Sarah says as she starts getting emotional. She wanted to make tonight special so she went all out with steaks, baked potatoes, salad, and white cake for dessert.

"Mama S, don't get crazy on us and start crying. You know I'm sensitive and you will hurt my heart and make me cry. You act like we are going to another country and never coming back. You and Grady can come to one of the shows and give your parental support." Elijah tries to ease her mind while joking as always.

"Shut up, Eli," Sarah laughs while wiping a few of her tears away."It's just you boys have never been gone this long. Or so far away."

"Aww, Sarah," we all say while getting up, walking over, and surrounding her in a group hug.

After everyone is stuffed full of the delicious food, our mess is cleaned up, we move this party to the living room. I'm going to miss the Sunday dinners, this house, and seeing Sarah and Grady while we are gone. I turn on the stereo as we all talk, laugh, and just take this time to appreciate everything Sarah and Grady have done for us. If it wasn't for them, we wouldn't be where we are today. It's bittersweet thinking about my parents, I miss them every day, but if the accident wouldn't have happened then The Betrayed would have never come about. I would have went on to college, got a degree, and lived my life happily somewhere else. I would never have met Grace either. But as I sit here, looking around the room at the people I love, I can't imagine my life without them.

We take our turns dancing with Sarah to whatever song comes on the radio while Grady sits, laughing at all of us. When it's my turn, You Don't See starts playing. "Do you fucking hear that?" Elijah asks with excitement.

"Of course we hear it!" Colton and Rico say while I am still in shock. We're on the fucking radio!

"Eli, mouth!" Sarah tries to scold while laughing. "Congratulations boys. We are so proud of you."

"Congratulations sons," Grady tells us with a look of pride.

We take a moment to act like little kids, jumping around the living room because we are on the radio. Who wouldn't want to jump around at that?

I grab Sarah by the waist, spin around, and then dancing with her to the first song from The Betrayed that people will hear on the radio.

Later that night after we get home, we sit and talk about the tour, how we are on the radio, and what is to come in our future as we get high as hell from the weed Colton has.

Emery has done every single thing she said she would for us. She hasn't given up on us, no matter how hard I tried to break her and get her to give up her job as our manager. I'm starting to think she might just be worth the risk of getting destroyed. I don't know how the guys would feel if I went after her, I don't think they would be happy about it. Right now though, I don't care what they think. They don't know that she gives me rides home even though I have my own truck. They don't know how bad I want her. And I think I will keep it that way for a while longer.

As the days go on it gets harder and harder to be around Emery without telling her how I feel. I want her to break for me, I want her to give in to me, and I want her to submit and give me every goddamn thing she has to offer. I'm tired of my dreams, of the fantasies I need the real deal. I need her, I need to feel her, need to be inside of her and consume her. And when she finally falls I'll be there to catch her. I'll be there to break right along with Emery. I'm ready to give her all of me I just hope I don't fall and break alone.

six

EMERY

The time has come, we will be leaving tomorrow morning to start the Rockin' in the South tour. Our first stop is Lexington, Kentucky, two days from now at Rupp Arena. I hope they are ready for this, it's the beginning of their careers and thousands of people will be ready to see what they are working with. I have stayed in contact with Caged Animals' manager, but I don't know anything about the band. Guess I'll be seeing them at some point in the three months we will be gone.

Closing up my suitcase, I mentally go over everything, making sure that I haven't forgotten to pack anything. I think I have everything; clothes, bathroom shit, hair shit, and makeup. Walking into the bathroom, I look myself over one more time. I want to look good for when I go over to the guys' house to make sure they are ready. *Ugh, I don't know why. It's not like Dawson is even interested in me.*

I've given him rides home several times, that no one knows about. He doesn't speak, I don't speak. Neither of us try to make a move, but you can feel the change between us. There's no more anger, you could cut through the sexual tension, but I think both of us are a little afraid that if we were to take the next step, what would that mean for the band? Truth be told I started going into the office more just so I could have just a little bit of time with him. How desperate does that make me?

My hair is down in two braids with my black beanie covering the top of my head. My eyes are done more smoky today making the green pop. I chose jeans and a tight black t-shirt that says *love* with someone's face going through the letters all in silver. I have only worn dresses around the guys at work, and even though I'm not working today, Dawson's opinion matters to me. I know it shouldn't, but I want to look good for him. *Gah, I'm an idiot!*

Deciding I look fine, I walk into the living room where my mom and Sicily are playing. "Hey Mom, I have to run over and make sure the guys are packed and ready to go for tomorrow. Can you watch Sicily?"

"Yeah, no problem." They both laugh at whatever game they're playing and my heart aches because I'm going to miss out on three months of my baby's life.

I walk over to Sicily, bend down, and kiss her cheek. "I'll be back in a little bit, then it's you and me for the night."

"Okay, Momma. Wuv you." Her little arms wrap around my neck in a three-year-old tight hug.

"I love you too, little one." I hug her for just a little bit longer than normal before standing back up. Walking over to the table next to the door, I grab my keys and purse, then head out.

I park along the same curb I have been for the last few weeks and take note of all the cars parked in the driveway. I walk up to the door, and knock loudly so they can hear me over the music. *Are they really having a party when they should be getting ready to leave?*

The door opens to a very high looking Elijah. His eyes widen, "Um...Uh... Hey Em. What're you doin' here?" He stumbles over his words before trying to give me his sexy smile. *No way buddy. It won't work this time.*

My arms cross over my chest and I look at him sternly."Jacey said I needed to make sure you guys were ready to go and had all your stuff packed up." I try to go into the house, but he stops

Saving Dawson

me. "Elijah Joseph Summers, you let me in right now!"

"Em, don't be bossy." His bottom lip pokes out in a pout and I can't help but to chuckle. "Don't get all mama bear on us. We were just having a little fun with friends before we leave."

"I could give a shit less what you are doing. I have a job to do, so let me get to it." I slip past him this time and make my way into the smoky as hell living room. I see a lot of girls, along with Colton and Rico. "Where's Dawson?" I yell over the music so they can hear me. My gut squeezes tight at the thought of him in this house, doing who knows what with some little skank.

"What's up, Em?" Rico asks from his seat on the couch with a stupid grin and red puffy eyes. A girl wearing clothes that should be considered illegal sits on his lap. Em is the nickname the three of them have decided to start calling me. I guess it's better than Dawson's cupcake, sweetheart, and all the other ones. I'm starting to get used to babydoll and Dorothy though.

"Jacey sent me over here, so where's Dawson?" I cross my arms over my chest once again, letting them know I'm not fucking around.

Colton's head jerks back towards the hallway. "Go check the last door on the left. We'll clear everyone out." At least someone can still be in their right mind in this smoke filled house. I swear I'm getting a contact just from breathing.

"Thank you," I tell him as I start walking into the hallway, choking as I go. I hear laughter behind me, but I don't care enough to turn around. *No point in arguing with potheads.*

I knock on the door just as the music cuts off and hear Dawson's rugged voice. "Go the fuck away."

I open the door slightly anyway, checking around to make sure Dawson is alone. He is and it's a little unnerving at just how fast the worry and tension leave my body immediately.

Dawson's lying on his bed, staring at the ceiling with his hands on his stomach. Bare stomach, might I add! The sight causes me to gulp because oh hell, for the love of all that is holy, he is muscled and toned and tattooed and perfect.

With all of my gawking, I didn't realize that he had picked up something and thrown it at the door until it was making contact with my head. "Ow. Shit! It's me, Dawson." I place my palm against my forehead where the object hit me. I can feel the knot forming on my face. *Oh, this is just fucking great!*

"Dorothy!" Dawson exclaims as he quickly jumps off his bed, puts his shirt back on, and rushes over to me. "Fuck! I'm sorry. I thought you were one of the guys, come sit down. I'll go get some ice." He leads me over to the bed and sits me down before he runs out of the room.

Dawson returns a few minutes later with an ice pack. He gently removes my hand to examine the damage he caused, and places the ice pack in the middle of my forehead. He rubs his thumb across my fingers absentmindedly while holding the freezing pack against my head. "I'm so sorry. I didn't know it was you, I thought it was one of my brothers," he repeats. I know he is feeling bad about it, but it was my fault.

A shiver runs through my body, but it has nothing to do with the coldness and everything to do with him touching me. At least I can pass it off as being the ice pack. "It's okay really, it was my fault. I shouldn't have opened your door after you said to go away. If I wouldn't have been distracted maybe I could have caught the object. But with my luck, now I'll have a nice bump on my head."

A sexy grin plays on his lips. "Why were you distracted?"

"That's not important. What did you hit me with?" I roll my eyes, trying to keep my cool. No way am I telling him that his bare upper half caused me to forget everything around me.

Saving Dawson

"Not important...right," he chuckles before continuing, "It was a small basketball."

With a smile on my face, I tell him, "Great. So first you are mean, you call me names, and now you resort to violence by throwing balls at my face. Nice, Sugar." I try to lighten the mood and it must work, because for the first time I hear his laugh and it is beautiful. Simply beautiful, just like he is.

"Let me grab you some water and Tylenol, then you can tell me why you're here." He walks out of the room once again. I take the opportunity to lie back on his bed, still holding the ice pack against my head, I close my eyes. I imagine what it would be like laying here with Dawson, holding each other and just talking.

"Shit, Emery! Are you okay, babydoll? Don't fall asleep on me." Dawson's hands are on my cheeks and the shiver returns.

I start laughing and open my eyes, dropping the ice pack. "I'm fine." He helps me sit up then hands me the pills and water. "Jacey wanted me to come over to make sure you guys are ready to go. Do you guys have all of your stuff packed up? Also, I have to make a run to the store to get everything you guys want on the bus, food wise."

Dawson takes a closer look at the goose egg and winces. "I'll make sure we are all packed up tonight. Come on, I'm going to the store with you, I'll drive. I wouldn't feel right if I sent you outta here after what I did." He holds his hand out for me to take, so I do, and he leads me out to the living room where it is now just the guys.

"Jesus Dawson! You trying to kill the girl?" Colton questions, with a smile on his handsome face.

"What's going on here?" Elijah comments while zoning in on our hands still connected. Both of us look down at the same time and jerk away from each other like we were on fire.

"Shut the fuck up, Colt! It was an accident I thought it was one of you idiots. And nothing, Eli. I'm taking her to the store and you guys need to get your stuff packed up. What do you want to eat on the bus?"

"Cookies."

"Beer."

"Pringles, lots of Pringles."

"Alright, got it. I'll see you guys tomorrow morning," I tell them with a smile and a wave before heading back outside.

"Bye, Em." I hear the chorus before the door is shut and realize that I have no idea which vehicle is Dawson's, so I wait on the porch.

"Mine's the truck over there," he tells me when he comes out a few minutes later.

It was a quiet trip to the store, through the store, and on the way back to Dawson's house. I didn't bother going back inside when he pulled into the driveway. There were no goodbyes or *I'll see you later,* we just went our separate ways. I could, however, feel his eyes on my backside as I walked away. I couldn't bring myself to turn around though, because if I would have, I probably would've done something really stupid like run over, throw myself into his arms, and kiss him like in one of those cheesy romance movies. I can't let that happen so it's best that I just kept on moving, no matter how bad I want to go back over there.

"Momma, are you lissenin' to me?" Sicily hits me on the arm while looking at me.

"Sorry, baby. What did you say?" I give my best innocent look, which does no good because she has perfected her irritated look. It consists of huffing really loud, crossing her arms, and narrowing her eyes.

Saving Dawson

"I want you ta tell me 'bout da pwincess." A big yawn slips from her mouth.

"Okay, but I have to tell you something and it's really important." I stare into her eyes, giving her my best serious mom look. "You know momma works with that band, right?" She gives me a nod and places her hand against my cheek, tapping a couple of times. "Well, tomorrow I have to leave with them for awhile. You are going to stay with Grandma and PaPa until I get back." Another nod and yawn. "I'm going to miss you so, so much little one, and Grandma and PaPa said they will bring you to see me."

"I miss you too, Momma. Tell me 'bout da pwincess now?" Her little lip pouts out and her arms go around my neck for a hug. I kiss her forehead and she kisses my cheek. I know she's too young to understand what is really going on.

Chuckling, I tell her, "Yes, baby." Then I proceed to tell her about the princess, amongst many more stories. I read to her long after she falls asleep. She must be exhausted because of our day.

After I got home from Dawson's, I played every game she wanted to play. We watched her favorite movie more than once, and we had her favorite dinner, which is pizza and ice cream. I basically did anything and everything she wanted for the entire day because I wasn't going to see her for awhile.

I decide to carry her into my room and sleep with her in my bed for the night. I don't want one minute away from her until I have to leave. I lay here next to Sicily while my hand runs down her long hair, over and over. The tears start falling as I think about leaving. I don't want to leave her at all, but I know that I am doing what's best for us. This job is helping us and I need to stay focused on that instead of Mr. McHottie, aka Dawson. Finally after hours of crying, my eyes get heavy from the exertion and I fall asleep.

seven

DAWSON

Jacey and Bear, along with their kids and dog Karma, came to say their goodbyes. We were all curious as to why they would name the black and white pit bull Karma, so Elijah, being the brave one, asked Jacey. I swear she literally doubled over laughing so hard while Bear looked pissed. Jacey then explained that Bear didn't talk to her about the puppy before he brought her home, and she was pissed because she was going to have to take care of the dog and a baby. So, and this is where it gets good, she trained Karma to bite Bear's ass on command when she would get pissed at him. Jacey said it only happened that one time because she felt really bad afterwards. By the time she finished the story, we were all laughing so hard we were crying, except Bear of course. We all knew Elijah was about to ask for a demonstration until Bear stepped up and told him not to even think about it because if he did, he would rip Elijah's tongue out of his mouth and then Bear would pluck his eyeballs out and shove them down his throat. That shut us all up because have I mentioned how fucking scary Bear is? Well he is, and he would do just what he threatened. But that pissed Jacey off so she told him to leave us alone or she would make him regret it. After a growl from him and a slap to her ass, they left.

Sarah and Grady also came, and of course Sarah cried, but

they didn't stay long since both of them had to get ready for work. Now, we are just waiting for Emery to show up. We got here a little early so she still has a few minutes.

Yesterday was a good day for us, except for the whole ball-to-the-face incident. I felt horrible about it. I thought she was one of my brothers or worse, one of those little groupie bitches. It's not really my scene, with the parties and all that. Don't get me wrong, I'll drink and smoke a little Mary Jane, hang out with the guys, but when all the people start coming over, that's when I retreat to my room. I'm not like the other guys when it comes to women, I don't want the one night stands.

The trip to the store with Emery was quiet, but it wasn't like those awful uncomfortable silences, it just was. I felt like she belonged there with me, next to me, not just in my truck either, and I liked having her there. She looks gorgeous in those dresses she wears, but seeing her in jeans and a fitted tee, she looked cute as hell. That plan I have is about to take effect once we get on the road, no more angry Dawson. The old me is returning and I can feel it inside, I want to take care of Emery. I want her to see the real me, not the cover up she has seen all this time because I got hurt four years ago. It's time to let all that shit rest, and I also know that I'm so fucked when it comes to that woman.

"Hey Em. It's about time you got here." Elijah tries to joke, pulling me out of my thoughts at the sound of her name. Sure enough, there she is, walking to the trunk of that death trap she calls a car. Looking sexy as ever in another pair of jeans and a black, tight t-shirt like yesterday.

"Piss off," Emery replies, not joking. I guess somebody woke up on the wrong side of the bed. She gets closer and I notice she has no makeup on, which is really unlike her. Sunglasses cover her eyes, a bruise is in the middle of her forehead from getting

Saving Dawson

hit yesterday, and her face looks red and splotchy like Sarah's was. *Has she been crying? Why would she be crying?*

She bumps into my shoulder on her way by me. "You okay, Dorothy?"

"I said to piss the fuck off." You can hear the wobble in her voice, so no, she isn't okay. I realize then that I know nothing about her. Maybe she is leaving behind someone she cares about. A boyfriend perhaps. Just the thought has my fists clenching and my jaw grinding.

Emery walks right onto the bus with all of her luggage and the bags of groceries we got yesterday. I can hear the guys talking about her, worried and wondering if she is going to be okay. This isn't like her to be angry at them, me yes, but them no. I ignore everyone as I walk onto the bus behind her.

I place my hand on her lower back and she tenses immediately. "Let me take care of the groceries and you get settled into your room."

Shaking her head, she continues pulling stuff out of the bags without looking at me. "No, it's fine. Just leave me alone, okay?"

Grabbing onto her shoulder, I spin her around. "It's not fine and you aren't fine. Clearly something is bothering you so let me help you." I push the sunglasses to the top of her head and I was right, her eyes are red and puffy. She has been crying for awhile now by the looks of it. Bending my knees so I am face to face with her, I use my thumbs to wipe away a few falling tears. It does no good because new ones appear as I swipe the old ones away. "Why you crying, babydoll? You're so fucking beautiful, you know that?" I probably shouldn't be saying this shit to her, but I can't keep the words from spilling out. "This is the first time I've seen you without makeup. You are beautiful with it on, but without the mask, you are fucking stunning. Too beautiful to be crying."

She seeks the comfort by leaning into one of my palms, her glossy green eyes reach my soul as she stares at me. Emery uses both of her hands to grip the sides of my t-shirt. "Why? Why after all this time are you telling me this shit now?" Emery's grip tightens before she lets go of my shirt and tried to turn around, but I stop her. "You don't know me, Dawson. You have never even bothered to get to know me. You think what a few fucking words about how 'beautiful' you think I am is gonna do what?"

"You are right I don't know you and I don't know what crawled up your ass, but I do know that I don't have to know you to tell you how beautiful you are." I give her a half grin as I still wipe away the cascading tears.

She bites down on her bottom lip before pushing me away. "I can't. We can't do this. Please just leave me alone and put the groceries away. I'm going to the room, tell Thomas we're ready to go." Thomas is the bus driver that Jacey hired for us. He's an older guy, but seems to be cool from the little time I've spent with him.

"I'll leave you alone for now, babydoll cause it's clear to see that something is wrong. It won't be for long though so work your shit out then you won't be pushing me away again." I tell her as I step away from her, I know this is wrong. Emery gets to the door and I have to stop her, I have to know the answer to this one question. "Hey, Dorothy. Do you have a boyfriend?" Emery turns to look at me, her head tilted to the side, and I lean against the counter, waiting for her answer.

"No, there's no boyfriend." She walks into the bedroom and closes the door before I can ask any more questions. I walk back outside with a smile on my face.

Saving Dawson

We spent the rest of the day playing video games on the PlayStation, practicing, and watching TV. Emery hasn't came out of her room except to use the bathroom and I'm getting worried. It's getting late and she needs to eat something. All of the guys have already gone to their beds, which are small as hell with only a curtain for privacy.

I walk over to the small refrigerator and pull out one of the microwavable meals. After it gets done cooking, I go to her door and knock. "Who is it?"

"Sweet cheeks." I respond with the name she likes to use the most, hoping to get a laugh out of her. And it works!

I take that as it's okay for me to go in. "You haven't eaten so I thought I would make you something." I sit the meal on the bed beside her. "Can I sit?" She gives me a nod while eyeing the food. "If you don't like that, I can get you something else."

As I sit down, Emery grabs the food and picks up the fork I placed in it. "No, this will be fine. Thank you. What's your deal, Dawson?" She looks at me suspiciously.

"What do you mean?" I look around the small room. It's only big enough to have a twin size bed and dresser.

"The nice act," she elaborates, while taking a bite of food.

"It's not an act." I lay back on the bed while looking over at her and continue, "I wasn't always an asshole. I guess the old me is just starting to come back a little bit. You gonna tell me why you were crying?" I grab a section of her long hair, rolling it between my finger and thumb, feeling the softness.

"I guess it's just leaving my family. I've never been far from them." Emery looks down at her food before taking another bite. She's not pushing me away so this is progress I refrain from busting out the cheesy smile that's trying to form.

"Yeah, I get it. Neither have we, that's why Sarah was crying too."

Her head jerks back like I hit her again. "Who's Sarah, your girlfriend?" Emery begins to tense and pull away, but I shut that shit down real quick by placing one of my hands on her thigh and rolling towards her.

Chuckling, I tell Emery, "No, not at all. She's our foster mom."

Our eyes meet when she swallows her last bite of food, then questions, "Our?"

"Yeah, the four of us. Colt was the first one Sarah and Grady took in. Then Rico, Eli, and I was the last. I moved in when I was fourteen."

"What happened to your parents?" I can see the sadness and what seems to be understanding in her eyes. Thank fuck there's no pity. I don't think I could handle pity from her, I've had it too much in my life. I don't want it from Emery.

I roll onto my back, one hand on my stomach and the other still on her thigh. "They got killed in a car accident." The gasp leaves her mouth, then her hand is covering it. I pause, before asking, "How old are you?" I don't want to answer anymore questions about my past. I want to talk about her.

I take a chance and make eye contact with her. "I'm so sorry you had to deal with that," Emery tells me as her eyes get glassy once again, like she wants to cry for me. I don't want that.

I ask the question again. "How old are you?"

"Twenty-one, why?" She eyes me suspiciously.

"I was just thinking, I'm twenty-two and I didn't think you were much older than me. I don't remember you from school. Are you from Kansas?" I stare at the ceiling when I feel her hand start to run through my hair. It feels good, really good. Grace never did this.

"No, we moved from Arizona when I was seventeen. I took

some time off from school, but went back and graduated." I lay my head on her leg as she answers. Her touch becomes rougher, she's massaging my scalp now, and holy shit, it's about the best thing I've ever felt.

"Makes sense." Rolling over onto my stomach, I lean up on all fours and kiss her forehead where the bruise is at. "Well, it's getting late and now that I know you've eaten, I'm going to bed. Hand me the trash and I'll take it out there." I get up from the mattress, hold my hand out. Her eyes meet mine and she bites down on that lip like she's trying to keep from saying something.

After a moment of hesitation, Emery finally says, "It's okay, I'll get it. I slept earlier so I'll be up awhile. Goodnight, sweet cheeks." We both smile.

"Goodnight, babydoll." I leave the room, go lay in my bed, and for most of the night I think about the girl that is so close to me yet so far away.

Lexington, Kentucky, our first stop. Tonight is show number one. Savage will go on as opening act then The Betrayed, and closing out will be Caged Animals. We spent most of the day in the arena having sound check, making sure the lighting was working properly, and waiting for the road crew to get our equipment step up. We had a small break for lunch, but it's been non-stop and so much more different than the first time we toured.

Our first tour we left home in an outdated van that Grace had found us. There were no roadies and we had very few fans. We played in small bars for two weeks with Caged Animals, driving ourselves to every venue, setting up our own equipment, and not once did we play for thousands of people in sold out arenas like we are now.

Emery has been running around crazy all day as well, trying to get everything done and taken care of. She came over a few minutes ago to let us know we had ten minutes before we had to be on stage before she was off again. Back to business in one of her pinup dresses, hair in big curls on the top of her head, and makeup done beautifully.

Traxton Jamison, lead singer of Caged Animals walks up to me. "So good to see you guys again, we haven't talked in awhile. What's been going on?" He brings me in for a one arm hug. Out of the five members of Caged Animals, we got the closest to Traxton. He became like a brother to us when he took us under his wing and showed us the ropes. Over the last four years we've stayed in contact with him, but since he lives so far away this is the first we've seen of him since.

"Yeah, it's real good to see you again. Shit, we've been busy getting our album ready, we finally got signed. How have you guys been?" I smile, feeling alive and ready rock this shit.

Keeping his arm around my shoulder, we watch as Savage performs their last song. "That's fucking awesome, man. I can't believe it's been four years, but I'm happy it's you guys on this tour. We've had shit luck with some of the bands we've played with over the years. Shit's different now, no more little bars, ya know? It's the big time, the real deal, man. Alright, I gotta go find my bandmates. See you after the show. We're having an after party on our bus if you guys wanna join."

"Yeah, sounds good," I respond to his back as he walks away.

The guys walk up, we do a little huddle, pray to all the Gods in heaven that tonight goes well and that the crowd will love us. When we break apart, Emery's standing there, smiling. "Showtime, boys." She claps her hands together.

Fucking right, it's showtime! I give her a smile. "Let's rock this motherfucking arena!" I shout, getting the guys pumped up. Then we take our places on stage.

eight
EMERY

"Lexington, Kentucky! How you doin' tonight?" Dawson yells into the microphone. "I can't hear you! I said how the fuck are you doin' tonight?" He screams louder just as the crowd does. "You ready for us to rock this shit?" Screams and clapping sound out in the arena. Dawson knows how to work the crowd, that's for sure. "Good, because we are ready to motherfucking rock!" Colton starts in on the drums, followed by Elijah and Rico. When it's Dawson's time to start singing, his eyes close and his haunting voice sounds out. I thought they were good in videos, but it's nothing compared to live. Dawson is amazing, they all are.

Halfway through their set, Dawson leaves the stage to come get a drink of water. I hand the bottle to him. "You are doing amazing! You guys are putting on one hell of a show, sweet cheeks."

He takes a long swig from the bottle and starts to go back out, but turns first. "Thanks, Dorothy." Dawson gives me a sexy grin, winks, then he is back on stage. I laugh while shaking my head.

"So let me tell you all a little about us. I'm Dawson, Colt's back there on drums, lead guitar is Eli, and bass over there is Rico. We are The Betrayed and I hope you're enjoying the show." The crowd goes wild and it's almost deafening in the arena.

As they start the last song, the lights dim and the place quiets. The flames from lighters shine brightly, showing the thousands of fans. Dawson's voice goes to my soul and breaks my heart as he belts out the lyrics to their first single, *You Don't See*.

> When I had no one else, you were there.
> I turned to you, you turned to me.
> We went from friends to lovers like it was all meant to be.
> My best friend, my girl, my love.
> You don't see the pain you caused.
> You don't see the future taken away.
> You don't see my fucking heart breaking.
> You don't see me destroyed.
> You don't see me anymore.
> You don't see, ooh ooh ooh.
> Now it's all gone in the blink of an eye.
> You pushed, I pulled until we were miles apart.
> You threw it all away baby, but it's okay, I don't want it back.
> I fucking hate you now, you got what you wanted.
> You don't see the pain you caused.
> You don't see the future taken away.
> You don't see my fucking heart breaking.
> You don't see me destroyed.
> You don't see me anymore.
> You don't see, ooh ooh ooh.
> I'm moving on without you and I'm rocking this show alone now.
> You're not suffocating me anymore.
> Finally I can fucking breathe, but it took too damn long to get me here.
> I hope you're fucking happy now.

Saving Dawson

> You don't see the pain you caused.
> You don't see the future taken away.
> You don't see my fucking heart breaking.
> You don't see me destroyed.
> You don't see me anymore.
> You don't see, ooh ooh ooh.

Dawson growls out the last lyrics and the crowd explodes. "Thank you Kentucky, and remember we are The Betrayed!" All the guys run off the stage and Dawson reaches me first, picking me up, spinning me around and placing me back on my feet. "That was unreal, babydoll!"

"Here drink this." I hand him the water while laughing. "You guys did great. It was fucking perfect!" The rest of the guys give me hugs and we all laugh while soaking up the moment. The crowd loved them!

"Thanks, Em," they tell me before Colton says he needs to go shower. Everyone is amped up as we make our way to the bus, and one by one we each take turns in the shower. Of course I let them go first, so by the time I get in there I have about two minutes of hot water. After I get all my makeup off, body and hair washed, I'm rushing to get out. At least I shaved my legs before we left so the hair isn't that bad. I pull on a pair of little shorts and a tank, brush through my hair, and walk out to sit at the table.

Dawson comes to sit next to me, placing one hand on my bare thigh. "Hey, there's an after party at Caged Animals' bus. I'm sure it's just the bands and some groupies. Do you wanna go?" A shiver runs through me at his close proximity and the touch of his hand on my leg.

"No, I'm just gonna hang out here. You should go though." I try to keep my cool so I distract myself with a nonexistent piece of lint at the bottom of my tank. What I would like to do is mold myself to him and beg for more like a crazy person.

"Nah, that's not really my thing. I'll hang out here. Do you drink?" Oh for God sakes, now his hand is on my shoulder. Dawson pushes my hair off my arm and the feel of his fingers skating across my bare skin sends electricity through my body. I feel little tingles in my stomach and realize my thighs are clenching because an ache is forming that I would really like his mouth to take care of. *Shut up!* I scream at myself because those thoughts are not helping my predicament right now.

"You don't have to babysit me." I try making my voice sound strong, while still focusing on that nonexistent piece of lint.

"I'm not babysitting. If you remember correctly, I was in my room the other day when you came over." Dawson whispers in my ear, his breath hits my skin, and goosebumps coat my limbs while my nipples harden to an almost painful state.

I turn my head, looking at him for the first time since he sat down. Our faces are only an inch apart and that sexy grin makes me nervous. "Drink? Yeah, a drink. I could use one of those."

With a smile, Dawson gets up and heads off the bus. I breathe deeply, filling my lungs with oxygen. About ten minutes later he returns with that sexy ass grin. He holds up a bottle of tequila in one hand, two shot glasses in the other. "You guys going to the afterparty?" Rico asks from his bed.

"No, we're gonna hang out here." Dawson's gaze meets mine as he walks over and sits across from me at the table, setting everything down on top. After the other guys leave, he says, "Okay, now this is how it's gonna go. I'm going to fill both of these shot glasses. You ask me a question, I answer, then drink. Same for you, if we already know the answer then you have to drink both shots." He pulls a couple of limes out of his pocket and walks over to the small kitchen counter, grabbing a knife out of the drawer and salt from the cabinet. "Got it?" Dawson walks back over to the table, sits down with the now cut up limes and salt, and puts the items on the table.

Furrowing my brows, I tell him, "Yeah I got it, but I'll tell you now, I'm not much of a drinker."

"That's okay." Dawson gives me a sly grin. I'm not so sure this is going to work in my favor.

"Alright, I'll start. What's your favorite movie?" Watching Dawson down the shot and lick his lips is unbelievably hot.

"Pulp Fiction. If you could go anywhere in the world, where would you go?"

I down the shot and take the lime, sucking the juice, hoping it will ease the awful burn in my throat. "Italy," I say on a cough. Dawson fills the glasses back up. "What is your favorite genre of music?"

"I love 80's rock music." This time Dawson puts salt on his hand, licks it off before taking the shot. I don't know how much longer I can stand to sit here with the way he is licking and sucking and I know he is trying to get a rise out of me.

"I wouldn't have taken you for an 80's love ballads kinda guy," I tell him with a smile.

"It's what I grew up with. My dad would always say, 'Dawson, bands like Skid Row, Led Zeppelin, and Poison are the great ones son.'" He shakes his head with a half grin. "Anyway, what is your favorite color?"

"Red." I down the harsh liquid.

"I already knew that, so drink up." The devious smile on his face has me questioning if he really did know or he just wants to get me drunk.

Narrowing my eyes, I ask, "How did you know that?" The

second shot doesn't burn nearly as bad.

With a shrug of his shoulder he says, "It wasn't that hard to figure out and I pay attention. Your hair is dyed red, you wear red lipstick, and your favorite heels are red."

I look down at the table because I can't argue with that. Fidgeting with my fingers for a minute, I don't know what to say. He paid attention to the little things about me. Isn't that what every girl wants? My lips turn up in a grin, I know my question. "Why do you hate me... or did?" Truthfully, his actions since being on this bus have me questioning his intentions.

With a heavy breath he takes the shot. "I don't hate you. I never have. It was hard for me accepting the fact that the band had to get a new manager, and you affected me in a way that's never happened before, from the moment I laid eyes on you. It's been a long time since I let someone in and the last time I did, I got fucked over. I didn't want to get close to you, but over time it's getting harder to stay away from you. I'm starting to think it's inevitable." His eyes meet mine, Dawson's telling the truth.

"What does that even mean?" I question, my brows pull down because it's all so fucking confusing.

"Tsk tsk, babydoll, you're only allowed one question." Dawson says while chuckling and filling the shot glasses back up.

After a few more rounds, I've learned his favorite color is black, he didn't want to pursue music until he moved in with the guys, and that while he doesn't have the life he thought he would, he's happy with where he's at.

Dawson has learned that I have bad luck, I'm a sucker for romantic movies, and the reason I decided to take the job as their manager. Somewhere during the game, I started just taking shots without having to. "Okay Dorothy, it's my question. That day we were in the meeting, why did you say that you think I feel threatened?"

My drunken mouth starts babbling words before I can even stop myself. "Because I can read people. I know that every single one of you guys have been hurt in different ways. You maybe more than the others, the pain in your eyes shows it. You are the only one I couldn't read for awhile, but I knew that I affected you. The way you treated me and the names, it showed that whether good or bad, I affected you. You have your heart closed off and now I know it's because you've had your heart broken. You haven't let the past go yet, and you need to if you ever want to fully move on."

Dawson gives a nod at my drunken rambling, and the expression on his face is one of thought while he sits back in the booth seat. I take the opportunity to stare as he does the same. "You really are sexy, you know that? Oh God!" I throw my hand over my mouth, because apparently a drunk Emery has no filter.

Dawson's gray eyes remind me of the sky on a stormy day, right before the rain pours down on you. Over the last few months, little by little, you can see the tension has started to leave his shoulders, and his once hard jaw has eased some. He looks more relaxed sitting here with me and it's a strange feeling, being so comfortable around him. Our once hate relationship has evolved over time, no doubt, but I'm not so sure I'm ready to feel this way with him. Something within Dawson is changing, maybe with me, maybe with the band, who knows? He isn't one to push, so I'll let it be, let things take their course and only time will tell. Even if I'm not ready to feel comfortable around Dawson, I'm not so sure I am strong enough to push him away either. Especially after the ten shots of tequila running through my veins, affecting my judgment and my mouth.

A resolve washes over his handsome face and a smile plays on his lips as he stands from the table. "You think I'm sexy?" He holds his hand out to me. "Come on."

"Whadda ya' doin'?" Great, now I'm talking like my daughter. I look at his hand before slowly looking into his eyes. Oh my, they have darkened to almost a black color and I know what that means. I've read plenty of books to know that he is turned on. Dawson's eyes are filled with lust, desire, and want, all for me. The tequila hits me harder, and while I'm jumping for joy on the inside, I think I better just stay sitting where I'm at because I might actually face plant if I stand up.

Or I could embarrass myself further in my drunken state and act like one of those bimbos by tossing my hair over my shoulder, sticking out my boobs and ass, then walk to my room like something's stuck up there. As I flop onto my bed, I'll hope that he will follow me so I can give myself to Dawson like a sacrifice to the orgasm gods. *Yeah, I'll just stay where I'm at. I should not drink because not only does it make me babble, I have no filter, and now I have become stupid.*

Dawson laughs. "Come on, we're gonna play a new game." He grabs the half empty tequila bottle off the table and takes my hand, helping me up.

"Ohh, what kinda game? I like these drinking games." Once I'm on my feet, he pulls me closer so I'm chest to chest with him.

Dawson bends down, leaning his head close, mouth at my ear. "Then you're really going to like this one, babydoll."

I think my panties just got a little wet! I know I have fantasized about Dawson many times in the months since I met him, but not once did I think it might actually become reality. Until tonight!

"Just a little? Guess I need to rectify that because I want your thighs shining for me, Dorothy." Dawson grabs my ass with one hand, pulling me even closer so I can feel his erection against his jeans. Oh hell, it is huge!

Good God, I said that out loud. Wait, say what to the what? He wants me wet? What the hell is going on? Is this real or did I pass out at the table and I'm dreaming? Oh, but I'm sure that is really his hand rubbing my ass cheek and it feels pretty fucking great. As I'm trying to comprehend everything in my state, Dawson doesn't give me too much time before we are heading down the hall and into my room. He shuts the door behind me and spins so fast it makes me dizzy. As I'm pinned against the door, his muscular arms holding mine above my head, I ask, "Whadda ya doin'?"

"Something I've wanted to do since the day I met you." Dawson moves in and I brace myself for the first touch of his lips.

After what feels like a thousand years, it happens. His hot, wet lips mold to mine perfectly. My eyes close as the explosion happens within my body, this is something I have never felt before, not even with Sicily's father. I fight against his arms, and finally he lets me go without breaking from the kiss.

My arms wrap around Dawson's neck, I try getting closer but it's not enough. I willingly open my mouth for his invasion, the first touch of his tongue is light against mine, like he is unsure, but that doesn't last long. We both succumb to what is happening as the kiss becomes rougher. Our tongues slide together in perfect sync, like we were made for each other.

Dawson grips my waist, spins us again, and takes the few steps to my bed. My knees hit the mattress and before I know it I'm lying back with Dawson on top of me. Our heated and passionate kiss continues as I get wetter and wetter like he wanted, until I start to feel my stomach turning. *Oh no! No, not now! Fuck my life!*

I push against Dawson's hard chest, not even moving him a fraction, but he breaks from the kiss to look down at me. "Dawson, get off of me now!" His expression turns from desire to frustration, anger, and a little bit of hurt. That all changes to understanding when the first gag comes. *Way to kill the mood, Emery.*

Dawson quickly jumps off the bed, then helps me up. I take off, throwing the bedroom door open, one hand covering my mouth as the gagging continues. Getting to the bathroom door, I can't get it open fast enough before the vomiting starts. At least my hand catches it, but this is fucking disgusting, not to mention embarrassing. *This is just my luck!*

I make it to the porcelain god as the rest of the tequila dispels from my mouth. Dawson comes into the bathroom and stands behind me while pulling all of my hair back. "Dawson, get out of here!" I tell him between my hurling fit.

"Not a chance, babydoll," he says, running his hand over my head while I vomit some more.

"For the love of God, this is embarrassing. I warned you I had bad luck." When I have nothing else to come up, the dry heaving starts.

Dawson chuckles. "I think this is more my fault than bad luck. I shouldn't have let you drink so many shots."

"I'm a grown woman." That's all I can get out before exhaustion starts taking over. I lay my cheek against the cold seat of the toilet. I guess I have no shame right now either, because any other day my face would not be here right now. *Just filthy!*

"That you are," Dawson states as he walks out of the

bathroom, returning a few minutes later with a washcloth, my toothbrush and toothpaste. He soaks the washcloth in cold water then places it against my forehead. The coolness feels amazing. "Have you ever drank tequila before?" All I can do is barely shake my head *no* with my eyes closed. "This is why they refer to it as *tekillya*. You're gonna feel like shit tomorrow. Come on, let's get you in bed."

Dawson helps me stand by holding my waist and leads me over to the sink, where I wash my hands and brush my teeth. He holds my waist all the way to my room where he folds back the covers, helps me in bed, and crawls in behind me, fully clothed. Pulling me closer so my back is pressed against his front, with his arm around my waist, he takes my hand in his, threading our fingers together.

"What are you doing, sweet cheeks?" I ask. Glad my speech is back to normal. I realize I'm asking that same question a lot tonight. "Thanks for helping me in there."

"Staying to make sure you are alright. Now close those beautiful eyes." I do as I'm told, taking in the comfort of Dawson and the feel of his thumb rubbing along my hand. It doesn't take long before I am warm, safe, and fast asleep. I swear before the darkness took over I heard Dawson whisper in my ear, "Fall with me."

nine

DAWSON

Waking up in Emery's tiny ass bed is not the most comfortable place I've slept. I can't even remember the last time I slept in a twin size bed, but I wouldn't want to be anywhere else. It just lets me know that what happened last night was in fact real. Yelling resumes outside the door, I jump off the bed just as I hear Emery. "Get these money grubbing harpies off of this bus now!"

"Ow. You bitch!" An unfamiliar female voice screams.

"I said get off this bus and I didn't mean tomorrow. Now get to moving, all of you. And you, you hussy, put some fucking clothes on!"

"Ahhh! Okay!" Another unknown female voice screams. No doubt the guys found some girls to bring back to the bus. Laughter sounds out from Elijah.

"Don't you fucking laugh, Eli! This shit is not funny. When I said I didn't want to see it, I fucking meant it. Now get them gone before I beat the shit out of these skanky twats." You can hear the frustration in Emery's tone, but there is a hint of humor there.

"Alright girls, time to go," Elijah tells them and a few minutes later the bus is quiet.

"Sit down, Em. I wanna talk to you about something." I slowly and quietly open the bedroom door. I stay in the hall so

I can hear what Elijah has to say.

"What is it?" Emery's tone sounds nervous. It makes me want to go out there and stop Elijah, but my curiosity wins, wanting to know what he has to say.

"I want to talk about Dawson. We all know he didn't go to the party last night and we also know he didn't sleep in his bed. That only leaves one place for him to sleep. It might not be my business, but he isn't just our bandmate, he's our brother, Em. You need to be careful."

"Nothing happened." Emery's voice quiets like she is telling a secret.

"Doesn't matter if it did or didn't. It's going to, yo. We all know it, we all see it, and a shift happened with you two. You're a fucking awesome manager, but if you are going to let something happen with him, you be sure it's what you really want and what you are willing to risk for him."

"Eli." I wish I could peek around the hallway to see her right now, but I can't. Emery will see me and then the conversation will be over. I need to know her answers.

"No, let me say what I have to say, Em. Dawson was hurt really bad from a girl that was supposed to be our manager. She was also like a sister to the three of us and Dawson hasn't dealt with it well. If you hurt him, he won't survive it. Dawson isn't like the rest of us, he doesn't go looking to get fucked or have one night stands. He wears his heart on his sleeve and when he gives it to you, he doesn't want it back. He's loyal to a fault, he's passionate, and trusts too easily, but when he falls in love with you, and he will, he loves you with everything and he loves hard. So I am telling you to be careful not for yourself, but to be careful with what you give him."

"We're just hanging out and having some fun."

"Not to Dawson. We all love you, but I'm telling you right

now, do not start this with him if that's all it is to you."

"I won't hurt him." And that's my cue to step in. I walk back to shut the bedroom door louder and walk out of the hallway, stretching my arms like I just woke up.

"What's going on?" I look between the two. Elijah is wearing a knowing smirk while Emery is looking like somebody killed her cat.

"Nothing. I'm going to take a shower and then I'll go find us some breakfast," Emery says as she stands from the table, walks by me, not once making eye contact. For a moment I think about following her, but I think what Elijah told her needs to set in.

Taking her seat, I put my elbows on the table and run my hands over my face before looking at Elijah. "You heard that didn't you?" he asks while tearing up a piece of napkin on the table.

"Yeah. You didn't have to do that," I tell him when I lift my head to meet his stare.

"Yeah, I did. But it goes for you too, yo. Don't screw her around if you aren't ready for what she has to offer." Elijah shakes his head then continues, "Don't even start it. Fuck man, I hope for the sake of everyone this shit doesn't end badly."

"What if it's already been started?"

"Then I hope you are both ready for it. You have to let go of the past and so does she. Someone hurt her, but you didn't see her face, Dawson. She said it was just fun, but that's not how she feels. She's gonna give you every part of her and you need to be careful with that. Don't hurt her." Elijah's blue eyes bore into my grays, letting me know how serious he is.

"I kissed her." I lean back in the booth while tapping my fingers on the table.

"Figured something happened." Elijah looks out the bus

window then adds, "Rico, Colt, and I have talked about it and we know you are going to do what you want, but we don't want to lose her." Elijah runs his hands over his face and pulls at the longer hair on the top of his head while looking down at the table.

"We will be careful I don't want to screw shit up with the band." Taking a deep breath I continue, "I've never had a kiss like that, Eli, not even with Grace. It was like an explosion within me." It's my turn to shake my head. I remember the feel of her luscious lips on mine, the touch of her wet tongue, and her vanilla scent surrounding me.

"The kind of explosion Mama S tells us about?" Elijah questions while looking out the bus window and tearing up that damn napkin again.

"Yep." I sit back in my seat, folding my arms across my chest.

"Maybe she'll be your "one" then. Maybe you will finally be able to let go of Grace and all that happened. What's with you and managers?" He laughs and turns his head back to me.

I chuckle. "In my defense, Grace was my girlfriend before being the manager."

"So true." Elijah nods his head in agreement.

"Would you guys really be okay with it though? I mean, if we decided to give it a shot. I know you said you would, but be honest." Trying to keep myself busy while waiting for his answer, I start picking up the mess on the table. I walk over to the sink and throw away the napkin and cut up lime from last night.

"Yo, we've seen this coming since the day she walked in the studio. It was just a matter of time, and I don't think it's our decision. You're our brother before bandmate, we want you to be happy again so if Em is gonna do that, then go for it." Elijah

Saving Dawson

leans against the wall and kicks his legs out onto the seat.

"So what the hell was that before you got all deep with her?" I turn around, leaning against the counter, my hands gripping the sides, crossing my ankles.

"Your girl can kick some ass." He laughs before continuing, "We brought back some chicks from the party. I guess we all passed out and they were naked. I learned my lesson: make them leave before Em comes out." We both laugh some more.

"How the hell could Rico and Colt sleep through all the yelling?" I look towards the beds.

"We got pretty fucked up last night. I think it would take a fucking miracle to wake their asses up." He laughs before getting up and going to his own bed.

—

After Emery's shower she walked with Thomas to go grab some breakfast. I can tell that what Elijah told her is bothering her because Emery wouldn't speak before she left, let alone look at me. Maybe a part of Emery is still trying to wrap her head around what happened with us last night. Maybe she isn't ready to face it yet, I guess I'll give her some time.

When Colton and Rico woke up, the four of us decided we would clean up the bus before she got back. It helped ease the tension I'm feeling inside. I'm really hoping that she doesn't regret the kiss because I want to do it more, and I'm hoping Emery doesn't try to play it off as she was just drunk.

After the whole bus has been cleaned, and me constantly thinking about what happen, I have decided I'm going to have a talk with her and I will use the power of persuasion if need be. I know I said I would give her time, but I can't risk Emery pushing away from me. I know the kiss was more than just a drunken moment and she knows it too.

Emery calls a meeting after everyone has finished the

breakfast her and Thomas brought back. "New rule! I don't give a shit if you guys bring skanky hoes back here, but please, for my sanity, make sure they are gone before I step out of that bedroom door." She lifts her arm, pointing towards the hallway. "I have my own set of tits and an ass to look at, I don't need to see them from the little hoodrat groupies. Thank you guys for cleaning, and I hope you used disinfectant while cleaning the table you just ate off of, with bleach. You nasty fuckers better be wrapping it up." Emery's lip turns up in utter disgust while laughter breaks out from all the guys except me.

"Aww don't worry about us, Em. If we run out of condoms, there's always saran wrap," Elijah jokingly tells her, but I know the guys are always prepared and never run out of condoms. Emery shakes her head then smiles as the guys are still laughing. My lips twitch with the smile I hold back. She's so fucking cute, and even when she tries to get onto them, she makes it funny. I see her smile fall when she makes eye contact with me. Fucking finally I get a glance before she quickly looks down at the notepad in front of her.

Emery clears her throat as she continues, "So anyway, the itinerary for Virginia is as follows: your set starts at eight P.M. and ends at nine, the road crew will have you guys set up about ten minutes before, so this leg of the tour you won't have time to do a practice run before you go on stage. There are a ton of other bands, mostly local, but it's going to be huge. We will stay there for the night and then head to North Carolina."

"We got it, Em. Be sure to kick the bitches out, get our practice in now, and clean to keep you happy," Colton tells her with a smile on his face.

"Exactly! Okay, so you guys practice and I'm going to make some phone calls. I'll be in my room if you need anything." Emery doesn't look at me again when she starts to walk away.

Saving Dawson

I watch her until I can't see her anymore while I wait for the guys to get ready. We run through the whole set, until we feel that it's good. Rico and Elijah start playing video games, Colton goes to his bed, and I take this chance to go back and talk to Emery.

I don't hear her on the phone so I knock a couple of times. "Come in," her musical voice invites through the door.

Opening it, I stick my head through. "Can we talk?"

Emery lifts her eyes from the Kindle she's holding to meet my gaze. "Yeah sure, sweet cheeks." She gives me that perfect smile that eases some of my tension and doubt. When I sit on the edge of her bed, Emery asks, "Are you mad at me?"

"No, I'm not really mad. Just wondering where your head is at." I look down at my hands and feel the bed dip. Out of the corner of my eye I watch Emery get on her knees, crawl over to me and wrap her arms around my waist. The breath I didn't know I was holding releases from my lungs and every doubt I had evaporates.

"Dawson, I..."

Placing my finger over Emery's lips, I cut her off. "Shh. I need you to understand that everything Elijah told you is true. This isn't just a game for me and it's not just for fun. We don't need to put a label on it right now, but I want this with you. Whatever this is I want it." Wrapping my arms around her waist, I pull her onto my lap and ask the question I need the answer to. "Do you regret the kiss?" Emery's eyes stare into mine as she shakes her head *no*. "Good, because I don't either. In fact, I want to kiss you again, Emery. I wanna kiss you a lot. Like right now, I want to kiss you real bad, babydoll. I need to feel that mouth against mine, feel those perfect lips mold to me, feel that tongue dance to a rhythm made just for us." I cup her face in my palms, bringing her closer to me.

Her mouth parts in that adorable "o" shape and when I am just an inch shy of taking what I want, she pushes against my chest. "I need to tell you something."

"Tell me later. Right now is just me and you." Emery moves in, closing that inch that separated us. There it is, that explosion, the same one I felt last night. "Do you feel it?" I ask against her lips.

Emery pulls back. "Yeah. I feel it." Thank fuck I'm not the only one. I smash my lips against hers, Emery's mouth opens for me as I slide my tongue along hers. My hand moves into Emery's hair that she has been wearing down since last night after the concert. Gripping a handful at the back of her head, I keep her in place while our tongues dance together in perfect sync.

I don't know what it is about Emery, but it's never been this way with another girl, not even Grace. I can't get enough of her and I don't know if I ever will. After a few minutes, I break from the intimate kiss and gaze into her eyes. "You are so beautiful, so fucking perfect."

Chuckling, she says, "I'm far from perfect, sweet cheeks. There's still a whole lot you don't know about me." Her head dips down.

Using my finger and thumb, I press against her chin, tipping her head back up to look at me."You are perfect to me, Dorothy, and that's all that matters. There's nothing you could tell me that would change my mind. You got that?"

"Yeah. But..." I cover her lips once again, stopping her from continuing.

"No. No buts." I tell her as I shake my head. "So what where you doing in here?"

"I called Jacey, then home. When you knocked on the door, I was reading. I stocked up on ebooks because I figured it would be pretty boring being on this bus. Boy was I wrong." Emery flashes me that beautiful smile.

"Elijah and Colton can keep you entertained that's for sure." The smile I was holding back earlier appears now. "So what were you reading?"

Emery's face blushes, "Just some romance book."

"What's it about?" Oh this should be good by how red her face is right now. Filthy books for my filthy mouthed girl.

"You really want to know about my books?" Her head tilts a little to the side while she is looking at me curiously.

"I wanna know about you, and if that involves you reading book porn then yeah, I wanna know." I run my thumb over her cheek and her eyes close at my touch. My heart beats at the beauty of this woman on my lap.

She tells me all the dirty details of the bdsm and I think I even blushed a few times from some of that shit. When I asked if she was into that kind of stuff, she said not all of it, but she wouldn't mind trying some things, and I about came in my pants right then and there. Just the thought of tying Emery up and being at my mercy is getting me rock hard. If I turned Emery's cream colored skin to a beautiful pink, it would be out of trust and love. That's different than what happened to Grace. Having Emery look at me the way she described those women looking at their men has me so hard and turned on, it's outta this world. Even if that shit is fictional I'm kinda jealous, because I want to be her everything.

The lights on the stage go down. The crowd is wild tonight as we take our places in front of thousands of people. The darkness surrounds us when Colton starts our first song. I look to the side, getting one more glance at Emery as I start to sing the lyrics.

For the next hour I work the crowd, jumping around on stage and letting the music transform me into the rock star thousands are hollering for. With each passing song, the audience falls in love with us more, the screams get louder, the bras and panties pile up, and we are loving every motherfucking second of it.

When our set is over, I'm hot, sweaty, and my voice is raw as I run off the stage. I find Emery not too far away, talking with someone, going behind her, I lift her up then kiss her neck. Laughing, she says, "Put me down, Dawson."

"At least you knew who it was." I laugh as well, while setting her back on her feet. "Who are you?" I look to the man she was talking to.

"I am Ben Stevenson, manager of the band Outside Temptation. I was just telling Emery here how I thought she was doing an excellent job with your band. I remember seeing you years ago on tour you were good then, but now I'm impressed. If you need anything, give me a call." He pulls a business card from his jacket.

"Thank you, but we won't be needing that." I take Emery's hand and lead her away. "That guy's a douche bag, Dorothy."

"Yeah I know. I thought about nut punching him a few times before you walked up." I shake my head and laugh as we make our way to the bus.

After the guys shower and get ready, they decide to go party again while Emery and I stay on the bus. Thomas has already left for his hotel, so once again we are left alone. The half empty bottle of tequila is still on her bedroom floor, and what better time to play that other game than right now?

Emery just got out of the shower and I love it when I get to see her without all the makeup, in just a tank and shorts. It's like seeing the mask come off and getting to see the real

Saving Dawson

Emery. She is gorgeous made up don't get me wrong, but like this, she's pure stunning, it takes my breath away. She almost looks like just your ordinary girl next door, not the pinup-style woman everyone sees. I feel like the real her is just for me.

"Hey, babydoll. You wanna play that other game now?" I give her a devilish smile from where I'm standing against the counter.

"What did you have in mind? I don't want to drink that much again tonight." She gives me the stank eye from her seat at the table. "My head was killing me today."

"Follow me." I head into the hallway with her hot on my heels. "Lay on the bed." I command as I shut the door behind us.

"I'm serious, I don't want to drink very much." Emery bites on her bottom lip while crawling onto the bed then lying on her back.

"Trust me. You won't be getting drunk." Giving her a serious look she nods at me, I grab the tequila bottle from the floor. Opening the lid, I take a swig but don't swallow it. I straddle Emery's lap, lean down, and press my lips against hers. I push the hot liquid from my mouth into hers and she takes it, swallowing what I gave her. Some spills out the side of her mouth and I use my tongue to trace the line of escaping liquor.

Lifting back up, I place my hands at her sides, pushing up the tank to where it sits right under her breasts. Lightly running my fingers over her skin, I watch as the goosebumps coat her flesh. I take the bottle of tequila, tipping it to where the liquid falls onto her creamy colored abdomen. A shiver runs through her body, making some of it run down her sides. "Sit still or you'll make a mess." Scooting back some, I straddle her thighs and bend down, using my tongue and lips to soak up the tequila. A moan leaves her mouth and I lift my head to look at her.

Emery's head is pushed into her pillow, eyes closed tightly, fists clenched, and mouth formed in that perfect "o" shape. "Dawson, this doesn't seem like a game," she tells me, with heavy breaths.

"Then let's call it rehearsal," I say as I pepper kisses on her stomach.

"What does that mean?" she asks, bringing her head up so she can see me.

"It means I'm going to make music with your body." I run my tongue around her belly button then up to where the tank is.

"What? How are you going to do that?" She almost looks scared now and that causes me to laugh.

I lift my head to hers, kiss the shell of her ear and whisper, "Relax and trust me." A shiver goes through her body and a light moan slips out.

"I've only been with one guy, Dawson." Emery's voice is quiet and unsure.

"And I've only been with three girls, Emery. Trust me to make you feel good. We can stop anytime you want." I'm practically begging her, because if she can't trust me then a relationship would never work. I need her to trust that I will take care of her just as I have to give her my trust to not destroy me. She gives me a nod and relaxes back into the bed.

"To answer your question, you see, I'm gonna have your heart and pussy throbbing like the beat of drums. I'll strum your little clit like the strings of a guitar. I'll have those luscious, wet lips screaming my name like the lyrics of a beautiful song. Do you trust me?"

"Oh, how you have a way with words. I trust you." That's

Saving Dawson

all I needed to hear and I believe her. No hesitation in her voice, no tension in her body, and her fists unclench, then Emery's hands move up to the pillow, gripping it tightly.

Using my hands to hold my weight, I lean down, taking her mouth once again. I keep the kiss slow with all of my passion and desire showing her how much I want her. Only Emery. Moving my lips to her neck, I place open-mouthed kisses along her burning flesh and back up to her mouth.

One of my hands trails up her side, under her shirt and bra, to find her full breast with a hard perky nipple. While cupping her breast in my hand, I knead and massage her perfect C cup, then I use my finger and thumb to roll and lightly pinch her hard bud. After showing the same attention to the other, I start moving down her body, where my mouth lands on her stomach. The sound of the moans and mewls coming out of her mouth are turning me on so fucking much. Her hands have moved from the pillow to my hair, her hold is tight and for the first time, I miss my long hair. I don't want to push her too far, but with my mouth on her, Emery's cries of pleasure and pulling my hair, I might just bust a nut in my pants. *You're not a teenager anymore,* I tell myself, but with this woman I don't think my age gives a shit at how fast I could blow.

Licking, kissing, and sucking the soft skin on her stomach, I use my hands to feel her body. I move them over her legs, sides, tits, up her neck, and back down.

Her phone starts to ring. Emery jumps up so fast you would have thought the bus was on fire. She picks up the phone, looks at the number, then tells me she has to take it and for me to leave her room.

I do as she asked, all the while thinking what just happened, what is she hiding, and is she really as serious about this between us as I am? My anger is back and this time Emery will have to come to me.

ten

EMERY

Another week has come and gone being on this tour. I'm frustrated with Dawson and concerned about Colton, Rico, and Elijah. I miss home and I especially miss my daughter. Do you know what the worst thing is for a mother? It's being away from your child, then having them call you crying because they miss you and want to see you. That is what happened the night we were in Virginia and I made Dawson leave my room.

My mom said she was having a hard day and wouldn't go to bed, so I had to sit and listen to my baby cry herself to sleep. I wanted so badly to jump on a plane, go back home just to wrap my arms around Sicily and comfort her. But I have to be strong and I have to keep telling myself that I'm doing this to better our lives. After I got off the phone with Sicily that night, I silently let the tears fall until I had no more to shed then I fell into a restless sleep.

I knew that Dawson was pissed as soon as he walked out, and while I wanted to make sure he was okay, I couldn't do it. I don't have time for the mood swings and if he's going to be with me, he needs to learn a little patience. Besides, there is still a whole lot that Dawson doesn't know about me and I don't even know how he would handle my situation.

I know I need to tell Dawson about Sicily, but I'm just not ready. I don't bring men in and out of her life. In fact, I have never introduced her to a man before. There hasn't even been a guy in my life since her father, other than my dad. I don't know what this is between Dawson and I, and I don't know if it is just having fun while on tour or if it'll be more and continue afterwards. I hope it will, but I don't know where he stands now and I really never wanted to introduce her to someone until I knew it was serious. I know he said before that he wanted more, but I've learned men will tell you a lot of shit to get what they want. They aren't always truthful about it either.

Dawson's still being mad at me from that night in Virginia doesn't sit well with me, and while I don't want to deal with his mood swings, I regret not going in and at least trying to talk to him. I should have let him know that it was my mom that called, who knows what was going through his head. I told him I didn't have a boyfriend, but the expression on his face that night said it all. He thinks I'm hiding something, which I am, but not what he thinks. Would he even want to take on the baggage that comes with being with me? At twenty-two he's just starting his career, and we wouldn't be the normal couple starting a relationship if that is what he actually wanted. Gah, why does it have to be so confusing?

We're now in Georgia and he barely speaks to me. After the North Carolina show, he didn't come hug me like usual. He just went straight to the bus and stayed in his bed the whole night. In South Carolina we got to stay in a hotel for a couple days, and not once did he come to my room, even though he was right next door. I didn't go to him either, but truth be told, I don't want to go back to how it was. I'm scared that he will tell me that all this was a mistake between us. I'm worried that he'll go back to the angry man he was when we first met. I miss hearing him call me babydoll and Dorothy, I miss calling him

Saving Dawson

sweet cheeks and seeing his beautiful smile. I miss his perfect lips on mine, I miss his touch, and I miss someone taking care of me for once. I just miss it all.

Rico, Elijah, and Colton are living the rock star lifestyle with all the partying they're doing. They only stay on the bus long enough to shower before they're gone. They come back late into the night or early in the morning, then sleep half the day away. The longer we're on tour, the less and less I see of them. I see changes in Colton, and not for the better. It makes me wonder if something isn't going on with him.

My phone rings, bringing me out of my thoughts. Jacey's name appears on the screen, which is weird because she doesn't ever call. I always call her. "Hello."

"Hey, Emery. Listen, I need to tell you something, but try not to freak out on me." Who says that? Now I am going to freak out.

"That's not something you start a conversation with, Jacey. What's going on?"

"Well at first I thought it was no big deal, but now I'm not so sure. I have a couple of guys from Bear's club coming to you for security until I can get a team together." I stand up from the bed in my hotel room and start pacing.

"Jacey, what the fuck is going on? Why do we need security?"

"You are starting to freak out. I said don't freak out stay calm. Some of the fan mail has become…stalker-ish."

"What does it say?" My pacing picks up, short legs moving faster with adrenaline.

"At first it just talked about watching the band, wondering why the girl in the video wasn't blonde like Dawson's ex."

I stop in my tracks. "Jacey, the video hasn't even been released yet. It won't release until later this week. How would someone know that?"

"I don't know. I think maybe someone has been watching them for a while. Maybe someone they went to school with. You did post pictures and shit from when they were doing the video."

"Yeah, I posted pictures of the band, not the couple in the video." I throw my free hand up into the air and then place it on my hip.

"Well it's gotten worse. There's a letter saying how you will never be good enough for the band, especially Dawson. You aren't what they need." I can hear the hesitation in her voice.

"You aren't telling me something. Spit it out, Jacey. I'm starting to get really freaked the fuck out." I knew they would have stalkers, but I didn't think it would be this soon.

"The last letter I read was dated yesterday. It says that you have one week to quit your job or your family will be in danger. It also says, 'I always win, bitch.' All of the letters are typed, so we can't tell if it's a man or woman." Jacey sounds just as scared as I am, but she's trying to hide it.

"I'm coming home!" I yell into the phone.

"Calm down. I have guys on your parents' house, just stay in Georgia until the guys get there. I'm sure this is just some crazy stalker fan, so stay where you are until we know more. It'll be safer for you there than coming home."

"Fine. Bye." I hang up without waiting for a response.

Guess it's time to tell Dawson after all. Jacey has lost her goddamned mind if she thinks I'm sitting here a thousand miles away while my family is being threatened. *Not a fucking chance!*

I walk over to the hotel room next door and knock. Dawson opens the door without a shirt and I gulp hard at the sight of his toned chest. I feel my insides heating up for a moment until I remember why I came over here. "What do you want, Emery?" Ugh, my real name! I remember when I used to want to hear my real name from him, but now I long to hear one of those two nicknames he gave me.

"We need to talk, Dawson." He opens the door further, letting me in, and I walk to the bed, sitting on the side while he grabs his shirt. *Oh, how it should be illegal to cover up all that hotness.*

"What do you want to talk about? You ready to explain yet?" Dawson stands in front of me with his arms crossed and that angry expression he has mastered.

"I'm going home." I look down at my hands in my lap.

"What do you mean you're going home? You're just going to give up? I thought you were stronger than that, guess I was wrong about you after all." Dawson leans against the wall, his jaw grinds and his fists clench.

My eyes meet his, my expression matching his angry one. My hands go to my hips as I stand ready to match his mood. "What the fuck are you talking about? I'm not giving up on anything." I throw my hands in the air and continue, "Is there even anything to give up? You haven't spoken to me in a week, Dawson." I take a few steps so we are chest to chest and I poke him repeatedly in one of his defined pecs. "I have to go home to make sure my family is safe because you guys have some crazy stalker that's threatening my family."

Dawson grips my wrist with his hand. "What are you talking about?"

"Jacey just called me and told me about some letters that came in your fan mail. They said I have one week to quit my job or the person is going after my family. I have a daughter, Dawson. I can't be here with Sicily there and someone threatening her and my parents." I look down at my wrist he's holding, it's safer than seeing the hurt in his eyes. "I'm sorry this is how I'm telling you about her, but I don't have a choice. It was my mom on the phone that night in Virginia, my daughter was having a bad night and needed me, not another guy."

Dawson lets go of my wrist and takes a few steps back. "You have a daughter? Why the fuck wouldn't you tell me that?" I feel his eyes burning through my skin as he waits for my response.

Meeting his gaze, I give a half grin trying to ease the tension. "You never asked," I respond with a shrug. I know it's a bullshit answer, but the truth is we played that drinking game and that's the only shit we know about each other.

It's Dawson's turn to throw his hands up. "You are twenty-one and agreed to a three month tour, why would I ask if you have a kid? And this is what you were hiding?" The anger Dawson was holding onto evaporates.

"Yeah, the truth is that I don't know what this is between us and I don't want to bring someone into Sicily's life unless it is serious. Like I told you, I've only been with one guy and that was her father."

"So your daughter is the reason you were crying the day we left for tour? She's who you were talking to on the phone that night in Virginia, and there isn't someone else?" Dawson looks relieved as he starts putting everything together.

I plop back down on the bed. "No there isn't anyone else, Dawson."

He walks to stand in front of me, bends down, and places his hands on my thighs. "Thank fuck for that. Don't hold back from me, Em. I want to know everything about you, I want to know about your daughter, and I want this whatever it is between us. I want it and I have no intention of stopping anytime soon. I don't care that you have a daughter I just want you to be honest with me." His hands come up to cup my cheeks. "I want you, babydoll." He leans in, lips softly touching mine in a chaste kiss. "Don't leave. Please don't leave. Have Sicily come to you, get her here and we'll go from there," he says against my mouth.

I pull back a fraction so I can meet his eyes. "Dawson, a tour bus isn't a place for a three year old."

"I'll talk to the guys. We will make it a place for her. I don't want to do this tour without you," he tells me while still cupping my cheeks.

Giving Dawson a nod, I answer, "Okay I'll make some calls, sweet cheeks." I smile brightly and he chuckles.

"Fuck, I missed that. I missed you, Dorothy." He leans in for another kiss before standing.

I spend the next hour on the phone with Daphne, my parents, and Jacey, getting everything set up, and telling Dawson all about Sicily. I told him everything that Jacey had told me, from exactly what the letters said to how they have guys coming here for security and that they have men watching my parents' house.

Daphne and Sicily will be here a couple of hours before the show, and my parents are going on a trip somewhere else. Jacey was fine with all of that and was happy I wasn't coming home. She believes it'll be safer if I stay here and I'm fine with that as long as my daughter is with me and my parents are safe as well.

eleven

DAWSON

Emery has a kid! To say I'm shocked would be an understatement, and out of all the shit that was running through my head in the last week, that wasn't one of them. After everything was said and done, Emery went back to her room to get ready so we could go to the airport. I sat on my bed, going over every detail of what she said to me, and I came to one conclusion, I needed Sarah.

I pick up my phone off the nightstand and call home. "Hello." Sarah's warm voice comes through the line, immediately soothing the tension I've been feeling.

"Hey, Sarah. I need some advice." I sit on the bed, elbows on my knees with one hand holding the phone to my ear while the other rests on my forehead.

"Is everything okay, Dawson?" You can hear the worry in her tone.

"Yeah, everything is fine, everyone's good. This is about Emery."

"Are you still being mean? What happened?" Sarah's tone turns stern and it makes me laugh.

"No, I'm not being mean, Sarah. We moved past that a long time ago. I think I'm falling in love with her." I bite my bottom lip in anticipation for what she will say.

"Oh, Dawson. I thought you agreed to keep it professional."

"I did, until I kissed her. Every time I touch her or kiss her, I feel it. I feel that explosion you always tell us about."

"But..." Sarah knows me too well. She knows if I'm asking advice from her that it's more complicated.

"But... Emery has a daughter." I blow out a breath after I say the words.

"Oh! Ok. So are you concerned about her daughter, or are you thinking it's too much to handle?" Understanding coats Sarah's tone. One of the reasons I love her so much, she never judges.

"I don't know. I'm not concerned with her having a daughter. I feel like if I'm going to love her then I need to love that little girl also because they're a package." I pace the room as my words start coming faster. "I don't know if it's too much. I didn't think I would have to think about taking care of a child at twenty-two."

"Whoa. Whoa. Dawson, calm down." Sarah laughs into the phone before continuing, "Did Emery ask you to take care of her daughter?"

"Well no, but..."

"But nothing, Dawson. Yes, she has a daughter, but she isn't asking you to be the little girl's father. Talk to Emery about your fears and all of your concerns. Love has no boundaries, and if you love Emery, you're going to love that little girl like she was your own. Just like Grady and I did with you four boys." Sarah is a wise woman and I can feel her smile through the phone. She is right, they loved all four of us when they didn't have to.

"Thanks, Sarah. I love you," I tell her, thankful she has made me feel so much better about the situation.

"I love you too, and tell the others I love them and to call me. I want to meet Emery soon, Dawson." We hang up and I think about what Sarah had to say. I guess I'll have to talk to

Saving Dawson

Emery tonight after the show.

I walk over to each of the guys' rooms and tell them to meet me in my room. When they all come in and take a seat, I start talking. "We need to have a meeting," I tell them as I take my position against the wall, folding my arms across my chest and looking at each one of them. "We have a stalker fan that is threatening Emery's family. They want her to give up her job as our manager. They know things that no one should know, so Jacey thinks that someone has been watching us for a while. They know about Grace, and Jacey is sending some guys here to be security until we get a team."

"Fuck, is she okay?" Rico asks from the chair at the desk he's sitting in.

"She wanted to go home, but I talked her out of it. She has a three year old daughter that will be here in a few hours. I know you guys probably don't want to tour with a kid on the bus, but we have to do this, especially after everything Emery has done for us. We need to help her now." I plead my case, hoping that they will be ok with all of this. I know keeping Emery here is for my own selfishness, but maybe they will ease up on some of the partying they're doing.

"A daughter!" Elijah's shocked voice matches all of their expressions - eyes wide, mouths hanging open.

"We love Em, so we'll agree to whatever," Colton recovers quickly.

"Alright, that means no partying on the bus, no chicks around Sicily, and watch the language." My voice turns stern so they know I'm serious.

"We got it. Cute name, Sicily," Rico answers as he nods his head.

"Thanks guys. I'm going with Emery to the airport to pick Sicily up."

"She's not on a plane by herself, is she? What's she like? Where's her father?"

"Eli, calm down, papa bear." I laugh at the defensive tone he already has for the little girl. "No, she isn't by herself. I think you'll be surprised to see who she's with. I don't know what she is like, I just found out about her a couple of hours ago, and I don't know about the father, but I'll find out."

"Hey, we know that Eli already gave you his opinion on you and Em, but Rico and I wanted to let you know that if you wanna start something with her, then we are good with it. Be sure it's really what you want though, especially now that there's a kid involved. We don't want to lose Em, so take it seriously, Dawson." Colton's bloodshot eyes bore into mine. I worry about him the most with the partying, and I hope he can keep his shit under control.

"It's already started, Colt. There's no going back." I look him right in the eyes, letting him know just how serious I am. My mind is made up. I want Emery.

—

We stand at the terminal, waiting for the passengers to come through the gate. Emery is bouncing from foot to foot, moving her head side to side, trying to see around the people that are coming through. I grab her hand, entwining our fingers, trying to give some calm to her anxiety.

I see Daphne first, with all of her colorful ink on display. My eyes roam down her tattooed arm and hand that is holding a much smaller one. Sicily is a beautiful little girl, the spitting image of her mother with those same big green eyes and that long wavy hair except it's a shiny chestnut color. I can only assume that's what Emery's would look like if hers wasn't dyed. When she spots her mother, the cutest set of dimples show in her chubby little cheeks, accompanied by a huge smile. I

Saving Dawson

wonder if Emery had those same dimples before she pierced her cheeks.

Sicily pulls her hand free from Daphne and breaks out in a full run. "Momma! Momma!"

Emery bends down, holding her arms out for the little girl. "Come here, baby!"

Sicily flies into her mother's arms and Emery stands up while they hug. "I missed you so much, Princess."

"I missed you too," Sicily says with a wobbly little voice, still holding tightly to Emery. Emery makes eye contact with me and there are tears threatening to fall, but she's happy. This reunion shows me how much they love each other, and my chest aches to one day be a part of both of their lives. I place my hand on her back, rubbing up and down, giving her comfort and letting her know I got her.

"Hey, Daphne," I greet my tattoo artist, who happens to be Emery's best friend. "You brought the equipment, right?"

"Hey, Dawson. You know it. I gotta keep myself entertained around a bunch of rock stars somehow." She gives me a smile that I return. "He does smile!" She fakes being surprised by covering her mouth with her hand before laughing. I can't help but to laugh also.

Emery hugs Daphne while still holding Sicily and it's like one big happy reunion. "Thank you so much for this, Daphne."

"No problem, Emery. I'll stay until you find someone who can watch Sis. Zane is with my parents, you know how much he loves them." Daphne rolls her eyes as she pulls away from the hug.

Emery laughs. "Yeah, because they let him do whatever he wants so he can come home and annoy you. How was she on the plane?"

"Perfect," Daphne replies while running a hand down

Sicily's long hair.

"Sicily, you have to walk now so we can go get your bags." Emery puts her back on her feet and Sicily hides behind her mother's legs, but peeks around to look at me.

I bend down to her level and hold my hand out for her to shake. "Hi Sicily. I'm Dawson, it's really nice to meet you. I've heard a lot about you."

She takes my hand and shakes it. "Hi," she says in her quiet, shy voice. "Are you da one my momma says is Mr. Hot Pants? Your pants don't look hot." Sicily looks like she is really trying to figure it out. Daphne and I bust out laughing while Emery's face has turned the same shade of red as her hair.

"Come on, Sicily. I don't know where she hears these things." Emery takes her hand and begins walking towards the luggage. Daphne and I follow behind until we come to a stop. Walking up behind Emery, I move the hair that is covering the side of her neck.

I kiss the soft skin and when I let out a breath, goosebumps cover her creamy flesh. I whisper in her ear, "I better be the one she is talking about." I pull back, chuckling.

Emery turns, giving me the stank eye look. "It wouldn't be anyone else, sweet cheeks."

We grab all the luggage, head outside, and wait for a taxi, all the while Sicily keeps sneaking looks at me. Then when I look at her, she turns away real fast. It makes me smile and warms my heart, and I have suddenly formed a very protective feeling over this little girl and her mother.

"Atlanta! How the hell are you tonight?" The crowd goes crazy as I scream into the mic. "Are you ready to fucking rock?" I growl louder and elongate the words as I bend backwards.

We go through a couple of songs before I walk off stage,

Saving Dawson

taking a drink of water that Emery has for me. I kiss her neck before running back out. "So Atlanta, let me tell you a little about us. We are four brothers that made a band eight years ago in a garage. We waited a long time for our dream to come true and now here we are, getting to share it with you! Thank you Georgia for having us! We are The Betrayed!"

Halfway through our set, I introduce all of us and let the guys do their solos. I end the night singing *You Don't See,* like usual, and the crowd loves us. I tell the screaming fans that Caged Animals will be coming out to tear this motherfucking place down, then I replace the mic on the stand.

I run off stage, going straight to Emery. I pick her up and kiss the side of her neck. God, I missed this - finding her right after the show, picking her up, and giving the soft skin on the side of her neck a kiss. Yeah, we're going to need to talk soon because my feelings are growing strong for this stunning redhead.

When I sit Emery back on her feet, the guys are standing there, all in the same position. Theirs arms are folded across their chests and they aren't looking too happy. "Uh, awesome show tonight," Emery says, trying to figure out why they are looking like that. I smile behind her and see Elijah trying to contain his laughter.

"So, Emery Ashland, I thought we were all closer than that. We don't even know you at all. Maybe this won't work out after all," Colton tells her in his most serious, stern voice.

"What are you talking about?" Emery looks worried as she clutches onto me.

"Do you or do you not have a daughter?" Rico questions.

"Well, yeah," she answers, tilting her head to the side. Emery is trying to figure out where this is going.

"When do we get to meet her? Why didn't you tell us?

Who did she fly here with?" Elijah goes on one of his question fits again.

"Eli, calm down." I laugh as I spin Emery to look at me. "They're just fucking with you. I told them about her earlier and about what was going on." Her shoulders relax as she turns back to them.

"You guys are assholes! You can meet her tomorrow, because it's late and she should be sleeping. Daphne is with Sicily back at the hotel."

"Daphne as in the tattoo artist, Daphne?" Elijah questions.

Everyone laughs and all the guys hug Emery. "The one and only. Now I'm going to get a cab ready, I'll be out back." I let Emery go as I focus on the guys.

"We had a hell of a show tonight," I tell my brothers with a smile on my face.

"Yeah we did," they all respond, then Rico says, "So Daphne, the tattoo artist, is the one that brought Sicily. Man she's fucking sexy as hell." Before I have a chance to say anything two members of Caged Animals walk up.

"Man, way to bring in a show, guys," Traxton, the lead singer says while fist bumping all of us.

"For real, four years did y'all fucking good. You get better with each show on this tour," Jag, the drummer gives his input while tapping out a beat on his leg.

"Thanks for giving us the opportunity to do this with you," I tell them.

Colton and Rico walk over to where the other three members of Caged Animals are standing. It makes me wonder what exactly they are talking about. Savage has already left and went back to their bus I'm sure to get ready for the party tonight.

"We're happy it was you guys. We haven't had the best luck

with bands in the last four years." Traxton brings me back from looking around the room. I remember hearing about problems they've had with getting into fights with other bands. Drugs and alcohol played a big part in it. Over the years, Traxton has stayed in contact with us and he's about the same age as Elijah and I, so we became close on tour. He became like a brother to us, but we haven't seen them since that tour because they live in California and we stay in Kansas.

"Alright, have a great show tonight, we gotta go. Our taxi is ready." They give nods as they head on stage.

We walk out the back doors, meet up with Emery, and head to the hotel.

twelve

EMERY

The taxi drops us off in front of the hotel and as we all walk in, we go our separate ways. I walk into my room to see Sicily asleep on one of the queen sized beds with Daphne lying next to her watching TV.

"Hey, how was the show?" Daphne asks in a quiet voice so she doesn't wake Sicily.

"It was good," I reply while grabbing shorts and a tank to change into. "Are you okay here for a little while?" I use the same quiet voice as I walk over and kiss Sicily on top of her head. "I need to go talk to Dawson," I say over my shoulder as I walk to the bathroom.

"I'll be just fine. Take all the time you need," Daphne says outside the bathroom door, with humor in her voice.

Opening the door, I come face to face with her evil little smile. "Get your head out of the gutter, nothing is going to happen."

"If you say so." She chuckles then stretches and yawns. "I saw the way he was with you, the way he was looking at you. It's goin' down eventually, or should I say Dawson's goin' down, because he looks at you like you're a buffet he wants to devour and get all he can eat." Daphne ends her statement laughing so hard she snorts.

I fake gasp because he totally does look at me like that. "He does not." I hit her on the arm as I walk out of the bathroom, free of my makeup and my hair hanging down my back.

I walk next door, knock, and wait for Dawson to answer the door. He opens a few seconds later, freshly showered, wearing a pair of loosely hanging sweats and a beater. With one hand on the door and the other on the frame, I take a minute to appreciate all the sexiness of Dawson. All the tattoos, muscles, tapered waist, those lips, and those gray stormy eyes that are darkening by the second.

"Hey, Dorothy. Come on in." His tongue runs across his bottom lip as he opens the door further. "Sicily sleeping?"

"Yeah." I clear my throat and try to ignore the tingles in my belly as I turn towards him. "So where do we start?"

"Why don't you start from the beginning," Dawson says as he closes the door and I sit on the edge of the bed.

"I had just turned seventeen and it was the middle of my junior year in high school. Trey and I were pretty good friends, but then he told me one day how much he liked me. He asked me to be his girlfriend that day, and of course I said yes because I had always liked him too, but was too scared to say anything." Dawson pulls me up the bed so I am lying next to him, my head on his chest and his arms wrapped around me.

I continue with my story. "We became inseparable the last four months of school. He would take me out on dates or we would go to the weekend parties our classmates threw, and we became the 'it' couple at school. For the first two months of summer, it was amazing. We were together all day, every day, and we were in love. So in love. We even talked about our future, like where we would go to college, when we would get married, and when we wanted to have children." Dawson holds me tighter in his arms as I start the last part of my past.

"We were going swimming that day and there was a party later that night. I sat on the front porch waiting for him, but he never showed. I waited for hours until my parents made me go inside. I tried calling him, but his phone had been disconnected, his parents wouldn't tell me anything, and he deactivated his

Saving Dawson

Facebook account. There was no way for me to get ahold of him and I cried myself to sleep for many nights after that. I never heard from him again, but I tried for months to find him. Especially when a few weeks after he left I started feeling sick and missed my period. When I found out I was pregnant with Sicily, I was scared and embarrassed, but my parents stuck by me. I decided I didn't want to stay in Arizona, so my dad found a job in Kansas and we moved." I run my hand from his chest to the hem of the beater. Pushing it up a little, I use my fingernails to trace along the skin of his abdomen. Feeling a bit braver, I go underneath the beater, feeling his six pack and up his defined chest. His flesh is soft and smooth, and as my nails rake over his body, goosebumps coat his skin. *It makes me happy that I can affect him as well.* "So that's my story. What's yours?" I ask, continuing my exploration.

Dawson's fingers find the bottom of my tank and he pushes up the material. His fingertips are delicate as they run along my spine. "I told you my parents were killed in a car accident when I was fourteen. I moved in with Sarah, Grady, and the guys the night that it happened, but I took some time to grieve, I guess is what they called it. I wasn't grieving though, I was adjusting and moving on. I had my parents taken away, I was thrown into a new home with people I didn't know, and had to start at a school where I was the new kid." Dawson adds pressure behind his rubbing so it's more like a massage on my back. Which feels really good, and I continue running my nails over his bare skin.

"On the first day, I bumped into this girl that was so quiet, she went unnoticed. Grace was shy and a little nerdy to be honest, but I didn't care about any of that and she became my best friend. Over time, I fell in love with her and eventually she became my girlfriend. Grace was a loner so we didn't hang out with friends, we just stayed at my house with the guys, working on music to become the band we are today.

"Grace never talked about herself, and I was never allowed at her house, which I found odd. I questioned it a lot, but she would get mad and eventually she confessed to being abused at home. With Grady being a cop, he got her out of the situation quickly and moved her in with us. Her foster parents actually just got out of prison after four years." Placing my lips against his stomach, I lightly kiss where his happy trail begins. Dawson stills for a second before continuing with his own past.

"When we finally got the band formed and started playing out of the garage at home for the kids we went to school with, naturally Grace became our manager. Everything was great and awesome and perfect for a while, but then Eli, Grace, and I moved out after graduation. Grace and I moved in together and shit started changing pretty fast. She started changing. We were fighting all the time, she would go out a lot and I would be with the guys. She stopped going to see Sarah and didn't really want much to do with the band. Grace got us that tour with Caged Animals, then Jag's wife went into labor so the tour was cut short. I was excited to go home because I missed her so much, and while I was gone, she wouldn't answer my calls or text me back, so I kind of figured something was going on. What I didn't expect was to walk into a filthy, disgusting house and her in our bed with someone else. She acted like it was my fault the shit happened and she didn't really take responsibility for her actions. I ended it, she called Sarah and told her a bunch of lies, the guys and I moved. I haven't seen her since." Dawson squeezes me tighter and I lay my chin on his stomach so I can look at him.

"I'm sorry you had to go through all of that," I tell him as I stare into those stormy grays.

Saving Dawson

"Yeah, I'm sorry for you too," Dawson responds as he continues to rub my back. "It's in the past, so it's time to move forward, right? Do you still love him?"

I think about his question. "I thought I did for a long time after he left, but no, not anymore. It's the past, I'm ready for the future. Do you still love Grace?"

Dawson shakes his head *no*. "Not anymore. I used to argue with people when they would tell me it was just puppy love or not real. I'm starting to know they were right."

Still looking into Dawson's eyes, I ask, "What are we doing?" My voice sounds wobbly with my nervousness.

He sits up and I follow. Dawson pulls me onto his lap so I'm straddling his legs. He cups my face with his hands and tells me, "I want you, Emery. I want you to be mine and I hope you want the same."

I nod my head *yes*. "I do. I want everything." Dawson pulls my face to his then crashes his mouth against mine. Our mouths move and our tongues touch; the kiss is primal, demanding, and possessing. Dawson's hands move from my face to my back, down to my ass, and he grips my cheeks tightly, pressing me against him more. I feel his bulge and the wetness forming between my legs.

Involuntarily, my hips start moving, rubbing against his hard erection that I know is pushing to be released. My shorts are a thin fabric so there isn't much that I'm not feeling. Little moans fall from my mouth, but Dawson catches them as the kiss deepens. His hands move me faster and my clit pulses as I keep the grinding rhythm going.

I pull away from the kiss to catch my breath, but it's not working. The cries of pleasure that come from deep inside of me intensify, as do the growls and grunts coming from Dawson. One hand leaves my ass so he can grab a handful of my hair, pulling my head back so he can suck on the side of my neck.

"Dawson, I'm gonna come." His other hand lets go and moves under my tank and bra. He roughly massages and kneads my full breast before pulling and rolling at my hard nipple.

"Let go, babydoll. Come for me," Dawson says as he sucks on the flesh of my neck harder. No doubt I will have a hickey tomorrow, but right now I could care less.

"Oh God." My hands grip his beater tightly as the orgasm gets closer and closer.

"That's it. Fuck, I can't wait to be inside of you, feel your tightness around me. The next time you come, I'm going to have my mouth right here." The hand that was on my breast skims down my body under my shorts and panties to my very needy clit. "Come for me, babydoll. I wanna feel how wet I can make you. Just know next time my tongue and mouth are going to be soaking up all of your juices like that tequila, only I bet you taste so much better."

The feel of his hand cupping my bare pussy, mixed with the flicks of his finger against my throbbing clit and the dirty words coming out of his mouth, sends me over the edge. I scream out his name as the orgasm takes over my body. My eyes close and I convulse, trying to keep the steady rhythm I had going.

Dawson's hands move back to my ass, helping to keep the pace going. Opening my eyes, I watch as Dawson's head falls back against the headboard, his mouth parts and his teeth bite into his bottom lip. "Are you going to come for me? I want you to come for me Dawson," I tell him as I start to recover from that brilliant orgasm he gave me. Now it's his turn. "Imagine my mouth wrapped around your hard dick, sucking you so good as I swallow every bit of your cum." He moves me faster, matching his heavy breathing while the sounds grow louder from him. "I wish you were inside of me right now, filling me so full. I wanna feel you on top of me, surrounding me, and pushing inside of me. I want you to control me, Dawson." I lean closer so my chest is against his. Keeping the fast grinding motion, I bite the side of his neck and suck softly on the skin. "But right now, I want you to come for me."

Dawson grips my ass harder, hard enough I will probably bruise. "Fuck, Emery!" Dawson yells out in a rough and raw tone as his own orgasm releases from his body. Watching Dawson come is the sexiest sight I have ever witnessed. He keeps me against his chest by wrapping his arms around my waist. I realize in this moment I am falling for this man. I am falling so in love with him and that scares the shit out of me. What if he doesn't feel the same way?

"I've never came in my pants, not even as a teenager." Dawson laughs as he reveals that little bit of information.

I laugh too. "Me either, but it was pretty fucking awesome."

"Yeah, it was," he says as he kisses my forehead. "Will you stay with me tonight?"

"I can't. I told Daphne I was just going to come talk to you. I need to be there in the morning when Sicily wakes up." I feel bad because I really do want to stay, but I need time with my daughter.

"I understand." Dawson gives me one last kiss before I get off the bed and he slaps my ass. I go back to my room, shower, and fall asleep next to my daughter with Daphne in the next bed.

———

I'm losing my fucking mind! It's been one week since Daphne and Sicily joined us on tour. It's also been one week since two guys from Bear's club came also. Pretty Boy and

Chayser have joined us to be security until we get a team. Where they come up with these names, I have no idea. The threatening letters are still coming, but they aren't any closer to finding out who it is.

It was so not a good idea uprooting Sicily because my sweet daughter has turned into a little hellion. She is a complete diva with an attitude and doesn't like to listen. That might have something to do with the four rock stars she has wrapped around her finger that give her anything her little heart desires. Especially Dawson. She has fallen in love with all of them as much as they have fallen in love with her.

Dawson and I are now together and have been since that night in the hotel room. He isn't afraid to let everyone know it either, always touching or kissing me every chance he gets. We have heavy makeout sessions after the shows, but nothing like that night. We always end up going our separate ways before something can happen. Which I am okay with because we haven't been in a hotel since and I'm not having sex on the bus. That doesn't mean he doesn't leave me wanting more and almost begging for it until I come to my senses.

Coming out of my wandering thoughts, I look at my daughter. With my hands on my hips, I tell her, "Sicily, come on. You have to get ready so we can go."

"I don't want to." Sicily throws herself on the bed, using her whiny voice, and kicking her legs.

"One." I start doing the countdown before she has time out, but I really don't have time for this.

"Two."

"Otay!" she yells and I blow out a breath.

After I have her dressed, we meet the guys and Daphne in the living area of the bus. The taxis are outside waiting for us so we all jump into them and head to the restaurant.

Saving Dawson

Once we are seated in the private area, our waitress comes to take our order. Her southern accent is heavy when she speaks. "Hey y'all, my name is Marina and I'll be your server today. What can I get y'all to drink?" Everyone tells her what they want and Sicily orders chocolate milk. Marina bends down in front of her. "Aren't you just the sweetest little thing." Sicily gives her that cute dimpled smile. "I'll be right back with those," Marina says as she stands then walks off.

As the afternoon progresses, I watch Marina with Sicily. I asked several times for her to sit with us, but she declined, and I think it had something to do with the fact her boss was yelling at her every time she left the room. An idea forms in my head. "Hey, Marina do you have any family?" She shakes her head *no* and I smile then nod. "Do you have anything keeping you here?" Again with the head shake. "How would you like to go on tour with The Betrayed?" I look at the guys to see the smiles and shaking of their heads, but they don't say anything.

"Are you kidding? I would love to!" Her pretty smile forms on her very beautiful face. She starts to hand me the check, but I give her the credit card first. When Marina returns, I tell her she's leaving with us. She doesn't object, just goes and clocks out, then quits her job. We take Marina to her apartment so she can grab some clothes and then head back to the bus. I needed to find someone because I can't keep Daphne for long. She has her own life to get back to and a child of her own to take care of.

"Okay, so basically you will be watching Sicily while I manage the band." I let Marina know the deal once we are back on the bus. "Are you good with that?" I guess I should ask.

"Yeah, that's no problem. Thank you for the opportunity, I really hated that job." We smile at each other.

"Daphne, I'll get you a plane ticket home." I'm going to

miss my best friend. In the week she has been here it's been fun with our late night talks and her tattooing the guys.

"It's been fun, but it's time for me to get back to real life. I'm going to miss you," Daphne says as she hugs me tightly.

Later that night, we all go to the airport and wait until Daphne boards the plane. When we get back to the bus, Colton gives his bed up to Marina, so he sits at the table while the rest of us go to bed.

thirteen

DAWSON

Alabama, the seventh leg of this tour and an awesome fucking crowd as usual. Since we are gaining more fans, Emery had us stand outside after the show signing autographs. That's something we haven't done before and it was a lot of fun, made this all seem more real that people want us to sign our names on their shit. I can't lie, it was pretty fucking cool meeting our fans and listening to them tell us how much they love our music.

You Don't See has hit number fucking one on the billboard charts. The video and our album have both released and are doing amazing. It's all so surreal that everything we worked so hard for is happening. We couldn't have done any of this without Emery, and honestly, she is the best thing to ever happen to the band. Do I regret giving her such a hard time to begin with? Sometimes and I have apologized numerous times for how much of a dick I was to her, but Emery just smiles and says everything happens for a reason.

Emery and Sicily Ashland have consumed my beating heart. I feel like they have restored that part of me and everything I do is for them now. I fall in love a little more every day with Emery, but Sicily has me wrapped around her tiny finger and I wouldn't have it any other way.

I walk with Emery onto the bus and Sicily is still wide awake with Marina beside her in the living area. Marina is amazing with Sicily and I'm glad that Emery chose her. They are sitting on the couch watching *The Wizard of Oz* and it hits me like a ton of bricks. The panic I haven't felt in so long starts to take over. I fall against the wall trying to get my breathing under control. My forehead is coated with sweat and I'm shaking uncontrollably. Emery comes to stand beside me placing her hand on my shoulder. "Breathe, Dawson. Are you okay?" The feel of Emery and her musical voice start to soothe me. I wrap my arms around her holding her to my chest.

Emery looks over at Sicily and tells her, "It's time to go to bed now."

"I want Dawson." Sicily sticks her lip out to pout.

"Dawson's not feeling very good right now, baby."

"Pwease?"

"It's okay, I got her. I'm okay now," I assure Emery as I take a few more deep breaths then kiss her forehead. I walk over to Sicily, pick her up, and carry her into the bedroom. "Alright Munchkin, get laid down." I throw her onto the bed and her sweet laugh fills the room. I put the cover over Sicily, tucking her in the bed and hand her Pinky the pig, then I lay next to her. Emery told me the story of the princess she likes to hear so I sing it to Sicily like a lullaby until her eyes start to get heavy and she's yawning. Kissing her forehead, I wait for Sicily to fall asleep, but right before she asks me a question that I wasn't expecting to hear from her.

"Dawson, do you wuv my momma?" Her green eyes stare at me as I try to think of what to say.

"I'm getting there more every day. Why?" I furrow my brows wondering why she would ask that.

"Betus if you wuv my momma, den will you be my daddy? I want a daddy like da pwincess." My eyes fill with tears and I

Saving Dawson

have no idea how to answer that.

"We'll see, but for now you have to go to sleep. Do you like The Wizard of Oz?"

"It's my favite. Goodnight, Dawson." She leans up to kiss my cheek.

"Goodnight, Munchkin." I lay there staring at the ceiling until Sicily is fast asleep. I think about her question and what it means. Do I love Emery? Absolutely. Do I love Sicily? Yes. Can I picture my life without them? No.

I quietly stand from the bed and walk to the bedroom door, shutting it behind me. Emery is standing in the hall right outside the door when I turn to walk down the hallway. "Did you mean what you said?" she asks as she leans against the wall with her arms crossed and tears threatening to fall.

"Come to a hotel with me tonight. We can be back in the morning, but we need to talk and it can't happen here." I grip her hips, pulling her against my chest and softly place my lips against hers. Feather light, I whisper, "I don't beg ever, but I'm willing to now." I kiss her more in depth before pulling back slightly. "Please."

"Okay, let me call a taxi and tell Marina." I release Emery from my hold and let her take care of what she needs to.

"So did you hear what Sicily asked me?" I ask after Emery gets out of the shower in the hotel room.

"Yeah I heard. Did you mean what you said? And just because we are together doesn't mean that you need to be Sicily's dad or take care of her or anything like that. I've been doing it on my own aside from my parents all this time. I don't want you to feel like you have to..."

"Hey." I stop Emery before she can say anymore shit. I pull her down so she is straddling my lap. I rub my palms up and down her bare, smooth thighs. "I love you, Emery. I have for a while and I love that little girl. You know why I call you Dorothy?"

There's that cute little "o" shape I love to see on her mouth while shaking her head no. "When I was younger, my mom made me sit with her and watch *The Wizard of Oz* every year. I haven't watched or even seen a part that movie since my mom died. My first crush was Judy Garland." I laugh at the thought before continuing, "That's why I started panicking earlier, it brought back memories. I never really dealt with my parents' death, I just kind of moved forward without them. I wouldn't do or look at anything that reminded me of them. Anyway, the first time I saw you when you walked into the interview, you reminded me of a pinup style Dorothy and I felt like a teenager with a crush again. I felt my heart start beating at the sight of you and that's something I have never felt with anyone. Not even Grace. I was like the tin-man, ya know? Getting his heart and all. The guys thought I was crazy, but I went and had Daphne start a piece on my back that's from the movie. Kind of to bring my past into my future. I told her to leave off Dorothy because at the time I wasn't sure, but when she was on tour with us for a week I had her tattoo not only Dorothy, but also a munchkin."

"Oh Dawson," Emery says as she covers her mouth with her hand. "It's Sicily's favorite movie. I've watched it enough with her, I should have put two and two together, but I just thought you were being an asshole." That makes us both laugh remembering how we used to act towards each other with no doubt me instigating it.

I gaze into her eyes. "You don't have to say it back, but I want you to know I love you. I love you, Emery Ashland, and I love Sicily. If you are okay with it, I want to be her dad. I want to take care of you two as long as you'll have me."

The tears start falling from her eyes, but her smile is so bright. "I'm okay with that." Using my thumbs, I swipe away the tears on her cheeks. "I love you too, Dawson. So much."

I look into her eyes. "Say it again."

She laughs, but replies, "I. Love. You."

"Thank fuck." I grip her face in my hands and crash my mouth to hers in a desire filled kiss. Emery's arms wrap around my neck loosely, and fingers lace in my hair, lightly tugging, keeping me connected to her. Releasing the top of the towel Emery has covering her body, I pull at the place she has it tucked. The towel falls, landing on my knees, but I push it to the floor. Staring at her bare thighs, I rub up and down the soft skin of her sides, over the curve of her ample breasts, and keep going until I cup the side of her neck as my tongue continues to explore her mouth.

Emery pulls back slightly, but keeps her arms wrapped around me. "Can I see the tattoo?"

Flipping her over so she is lying on her back, Emery's arms release me as I stand up. Keeping eye contact with her, I pull the shirt over my head then slowly turn around. I hear the quick intake of Emery's breath before her fingertips trace along my flesh. My head rolls to the side as the touch of her hands apply more pressure going up and down my back. A low growl comes from deep within my chest as her touch causes a shiver to run through me before I turn around, facing her once again.

"Dawson, that's me on your back wearing the dress I had on when we first met. And that…that's Sicily." Big green eyes bore into my stormy grays as she falls back down onto the bed. Sitting at the edge, looking as if she is in shock.

The tattoo is of a yellow brick road with the tin-man, Dorothy, and a munchkin holding hands staring towards the emerald city. As the road goes on, the lion stands to the side as well as the scarecrow. The evil witch sits back in the bushes, you wouldn't be able to see her if you weren't paying attention, and half the sky is dark with monkeys flying around. The other half is clear with the good witch guiding us along the path.

I drop to my knees before her. "Yeah, that's you and Sicily." Cupping her face with my hands, I tilt my head to the side. "That's how serious I am about this between us. I don't want a day without you, both of you. I don't want a night without you lying in bed, falling asleep in my arms. And for the rest of my yellow brick road, I want you next to me, walking hand in hand with me." I inch closer and closer, so close our lips are only a centimeter from touching. "I love you, babydoll."

"I love you too, Dawson and I want all that, everything you want, I want it too. I don't want to be without you." Emery's lips come down on mine softly at first, growing more intense by the second until I break free.

Emery watches my every move as I stand and remove the rest of my clothes. Her mouth forms that perfect "o" shape as she takes in all of me for the first time and I do same to her. As we stare at each other I suddenly feel nervous. "Scoot up the bed and lie back. I want to see all of you."

Emery bites on her bottom lip, but does as asked. When she gets to the top of the bed, her knees fall to the sides, nothing hidden from view and it's a beautiful sight. Emery bares it all for me to see, confident with herself and no shyness in this moment, which turns me on so fucking much. I didn't think it was possible to get any harder than I already was, but I was so wrong. I need this woman so much, that is lying before me naked, waiting, and perfection. "You are so fucking perfect, Emery. So fucking stunning. So beautiful." Her hands grip the sheets tightly as her chest moves up and down rapidly. "I

Saving Dawson

need you now, babydoll. Do you need me?" I question, but I already know the answer, and her pussy glistens with more of her arousal. I get no answer, just a head nod.

"I need words, Emery. Don't get quiet on me now, babydoll. I wanna hear those explicit words coming outta that filthy mouth of yours. Tell me what you want, what you need that only I can give you." I crawl up her body until I am lying over her and my face is only inches from hers.

Emery's cheeks turn rosy pink from embarrassment before murmuring, "What I want no one has ever done." My brow arches at her confession because I'm not exactly sure what she is referring to.

"Tell me." I whisper against her ear.

"I want your tongue down there." Emery tries to turn her head but I place one hand on her cheek, making her stay focused on me.

"You want my tongue where?"

"On my pussy, Dawson. I want you to make me feel good, I want you to make the ache go away." The smirk pulls at my lips and Emery bites down on her plump bottom lip.

"You telling me that he never put his mouth on your gorgeous pussy? You telling me that I'll be the first to give you that kinda pleasure?" My cock is about to explode with just the thought of giving this to her.

"Yes, that's exactly what I'm saying." I nod with an evil grin. I'm not finished listening to her dirty mouth.

"Then what do you want?"

"God, Dawson." Emery blows out a breath then gives me that filthy mouth I love. "I want you hard, I want you deep, and I want you so fucking rough. Ruin me for all other men, Dawson, and make it so fucking good that you break me." She takes a deep breath then exhales before continuing, "But if you do this, you make damn sure this is what you want because there is no going back. Everything you give to me, I will give right back and I'm going to love you just as hard, rough, and deep."

Dipping my head into the crook of her neck, I kiss the soft skin and then meet her lust filled gaze. "We are already passed the point of going back, babydoll. You are all I want." My lips smash down on hers in a kiss full of want, need, and hunger. Emery's nails scrape up my back then are on my head, gripping handfuls of hair and keeping me right where she wants me. My hands explore her body moving over every inch of her hot, bare flesh until I get to her heated, wet pussy.

With our mouths still connected in a heated, passion filled kiss, my fingers run over her slit. Emery purrs into my mouth while her hips buck, wanting more. Breaking from the kiss, I move down her body with my tongue grazing over her neck, nipples, stomach, and the top of her mound. Running my tongue on her pussy like my finger just did, I taste her sweetness for the first time. "Fuck! You taste so godammed sweet. Are you ready for me?"

"Please, Dawson. Help me, make me come. God, I've dreamed about this so many fucking times. I need it now." Emery's head burrows into the pillow and one hand finds the top of my head, grabbing a handful of hair.

My arms go under and around Emery's thighs so I can keep her positioned on the bed. Her pretty clit begs for my tongue to touch it. So I do. With every lick Emery's cries become louder, with every flick against the sensitive spot she tries bucking against my face, but I have her pinned to the bed. Running my tongue down her slit and into her opening, the sweet flavor coats my taste buds. Pushing in and out of her a few times, I swirl my tongue back around her little clit. The sensations have

Emery's top half thrashing on the bed as her cries of pleasure fill the room.

"I'm close, Dawson. Please don't stop!" No way in hell would I stop now. I focus on Emery's face, her eyes are closed, rosy pink fills her cheeks, and her mouth is open. Panting breaths come quickly as her impending orgasm draws near.

"Open your eyes, babydoll," I command as I sit up on my heels, taking her lower half with me. This causes her to spread open more for me, her feet rest on my shoulders with her toes curling. She does as told and when I see those beautiful greens, I devour her more until she is screaming out my name along with God and a whole vocabulary of creative words. Emery's orgasm releases from her body and the taste explodes onto my tongue as I watch her come apart. Her body convulses as she grips the sheets tightly in her fists and she tries hard to keep her eyes open, but loses the battle.

I lay Emery flat on the bed before crawling up her body, peppering kisses on her flesh as I go. "How was that?"

"That was..." She shakes her head back and forth. "That was the best feeling ever. Better than my dreams or fantasies."

"Good." I grab the condom off the nightstand, rip it open with my teeth, and sheath my cock with the latex barrier.

Gripping my dick in one hand, I run it up and down Emery's pussy, my eyes roll into the back of my head. I push inside of her and the feel of Emery so tightly wrapped around me already has me wanting to come. I take a minute to get control and for her to adjust, bringing my hand up to her face, I stare into her eyes. "You are beautiful. The most beautiful woman I have ever seen. I can't believe you are mine and I promise never to take that for granted, Emery. I love you so fucking much." Running my fingers lightly over her cheek, I bring my lips to hers, kissing with an intimacy I never knew existed.

Emery kisses me back with just as much love as I'm giving her and her hands move from my back to my ass. She pushes me inside of her more and I can't hold back any longer, I have to move. I rock in a steady motion of pushing deep inside and pulling out until only the head of my cock is filling her. My rhythm is controlled and deliberate as I make love to my Dorothy.

"Don't hold back, sweet cheeks. I need it harder. Give me what you promised," Emery whispers against my lips. Rolling my hips harder, pushing in deeper, and thrusting rougher, I do as she has asked.

The sounds of our moaning fill the room as we move in perfect sync, like we were made for each other. Emery's nails dig into my back and ass cheeks while I bite the sides of her neck and pull her nipples into my mouth. Sucking on the tight, hard, perky buds causes Emery's back to arch as I change my angle.

Pushing up onto my hands I stare down at Emery's closed eyes. "Give me those eyes, babydoll." Slowly they open and she watches me through her hazy emeralds. "You gonna come for me?"

Emery nods her head as she digs her nails deeper no doubt drawing blood. Pushing harder, faster, and rougher, I rub against her g-spot and the feeling has her screaming out. "Right there!"

"Where, here?" I question with a sly smile as I hit it again.

"Oh God! Yes!" Emery bucks her hips, matching my thrusts. Our bodies slam together from the force and it is fucking amazing. Emery is amazing. Making sure to hit her g-spot with every push, I send her into her second orgasm. Her pussy walls clench around my cock so fucking tight and it feels so fucking good. Our moans, her screams, and my grunts fill the quiet dark room as we both come, holding each other tightly. Her name falls from my lips over and over into the crook of her neck as she shamelessly screams mine.

After disposing of the condom and cleaning both of us up, I climb back in the bed, pulling Emery into my arms. I think I wore her out because not long after her head hit my chest, she was out. For the last hour I have laid here staring at the ceiling while running my fingertips up and down her bare skin. My mind drifts to Grace and I know this isn't the best time, but I can't help it. Something has been bothering me and I have a bad feeling about the stalker.

I slide out from underneath Emery, grab my phone out of my jeans, and head into the bathroom, shutting the door behind me.

After the third ring, Jacey answers. "Dawson, this better be fucking good. Do you know what time it is?"

"Yeah, I'm sorry it's so late, but I've been thinking about some shit."

"That's great Dawson, but still it's two in the morning. You need to get to the point." Jacey huffs out a deep breath.

"How many interviews did you set up for us?" Biting my bottom lip, I wait for her answer.

"Four. Why?" Anger dissipates from her voice and worry takes over.

"Because we interviewed five people, Jacey."

"What!? I set up Emery, Gary, Lily, she was the bossy bitch, and Katie the bimbo."

"We also had Jamie, and she was just like my ex. I freaked the fuck out and had to leave the room. I think it's her, Jacey. Can you get us a flight back to Kansas? I need to find out where she is." I try keeping my voice calm and quiet so I don't wait

Emery.

I hear Jacey yelling at Bear to wake up, but he just grunts in response. "Kellen fucking Rhodes, you get your ass up right now or I'm throwing a bucket of ice water on you! Your name might be Bear, but your ass isn't in hibernation so get the fuck up!"

"I'm up! Now let go of my fucking nipple, and if you ever throw fucking ice water on me, I'll spank that ass until you can't sit for a week. Got me?" What the fuck? I think I actually heard her moan.

"Jacey!" I raise my voice trying to get her back on track. Opening the bathroom door slightly, I peek out to make sure that Emery is still sound asleep.

"Right, sorry Dawson. Okay what's your ex's name? I'll call Caged Animals manager and get you a couple extra days."

"Grace Sullivan. I'll get the plane tickets."

"Bear, get Hacker on the name Grace Sullivan. I want to know any and everything there is to know about this girl."

"Thanks, Jacey."

"No problem. You guys stay safe."

We hang up the phone, and I call to get our tickets, then crawl back in bed. Pulling Emery into my arms once again, I kiss her forehead and take comfort in having my girl in my arms with her vanilla scent surrounding me. I don't sleep a wink the entire night. Kansas, here we come.

fourteen

EMERY

The next morning Dawson brought me up to speed on the conversation he had with Jacey while I was sleeping. I can't say I like it too much that he was thinking about his ex after the incredible night we had, but if it brings us closer to the stalker then I guess I'll deal with it. I also can't say that I'm not freaked the fuck out that his ex is a crazy bitch. We rushed back to the hotel at dawn to pack up our things and to get Sicily before we headed to the airport.

The plane ride was quiet between Dawson and I, although I don't think either of us really know what to say about what happened last night. Dawson's mind seems to be somewhere else, probably on what's going to happen and if he will get any answers. No matter how nervous I am my mind keeps reflecting back to last night. The way his hands and lips caressed my body, the way he made love to me, hard and rough, giving me just what I needed. The way he was so gentle after with cleaning us both and pulling me into his arms. I was so comfortable and felt so safe tucked in next to Dawson, I instantly fell asleep. Waking up in his arms just confirmed that I am so madly in love with him. Both of us have had shit luck when it comes to love so all I can do is hope that we make it through this obstacle together.

After our flight landed at KCI airport in Kansas City, it

was a long taxi ride back to Wichita with a cranky Sicily, but we made it. Dawson had the driver drop us off at his parents' house, from there Sicily fell asleep so Sarah offered to watch her. Normally I wouldn't let a stranger watch my daughter, but her and Sicily got along great. It helps that Sarah is a nurse and Grady is a police officer, I got good vibes from the couple that took in four teenage boys. I don't think I will have too much to worry about while I go with Dawson.

Dawson parks alongside the curb in front of the single story pastel yellow house. I have mixed feelings about being here. I'm a little nervous, a little scared, and a lot anxious. I don't know what to expect being here, are they even going to talk to us? Dawson squeezes my hand in comfort and when my eyes meet his, he gives me a nod. Nodding back, I relax knowing we are in this together.

After opening our doors, we meet on the passenger side of his truck, I take a deep breath while looking up at the house. His fingers lace through mine as we start to walk up the sidewalk. I hope we have some answers by the time we're finished.

Dawson knocks on the door and after a few minutes an older man answers with a scowl on his face. The man is tall with a lanky build, his short buzz cut shows a bit of greying hair and his glasses slide down his nose, almost swallowing up his face. The overalls he's wearing look to be a few sizes too big. "Whatever you're sellin' we ain't buyin." He goes to shut the door, but Dawson stops it from closing by grabbing ahold of it and using his strength to keep it open.

"We aren't here to sell anything, we need to speak with you and your wife about Grace." The man freezes for a few seconds before turning back around. He takes a good look at Dawson.

Saving Dawson

"You were in the courtroom that day, a little older now but I remember you. Was wondering how long it would take for you to show up. Come in." The man holds the door open for us and I swear my heart is going to explode with the anxiety I'm feeling. The man yells into the house, "Jeanette!" I assume that's his wife's name. The man leads us into a small living room. "Have a seat." He points to the brown love seat while waiting for his wife.

The little frail woman walks into the room, standing only about five feet tall, thin as a rail. Her greying hair is pulled into a bun, and wrinkles show heavily, making the woman look older than what she should be. Jeanette hasn't had an easy life by the looks of it. She wipes her wet, boney hands on the front of her long, flower print, homemade dress. Jeanette walks right into the arms of the man then asks, "What's going on, Ronnie?"

"They're here to talk about Grace. Let's sit." Jeanette tilts her head a little, looking between Dawson and me.

"You're Dawson?" she asks, but it's more knowing than a question.

"Yes ma'am," Dawson answers with a tight nod. "And this is Emery." He takes my hand in his once again, letting me know we are in this together.

"Knew you would come eventually," Jeanette says while sitting next to her husband on the opposite matching brown couch as us. She starts telling us the story of a very disturbed Grace. "When Grace came to live with us, she was just eight years old. She had already been in and out of several foster homes for such a young age. They all said the same, she was too much trouble. We felt bad for her, it was like no one wanted this poor baby, she was just a little girl, ya' know, and we were younger then. We thought we could give her all the love her heart desired. We never could have children of our own and we wanted to be parents so bad. After a few visits at the group home, we got to bring our little girl home with us. Everything was fine at first, but then we noticed she was very antisocial. Grace never was like the rest of the kids her age. We just thought maybe it was because of never having a family, or not having her biological parents in her life and being in and out of so many homes. So we went ahead with the adoption and then everything started changing. Grace became very violent, she would throw uncontrollable fits, and then there was the lying. She would try playing us against each other and it worked for awhile, almost so much that we started talking about divorce and Grace was loving every minute of it. Ronnie and I would be arguing about something that had to do with Grace and we would catch her peeking around the corner with a smile, or she would be laughing at us." Jeanette blinks away the tears shining in her eyes. She stares at the wall like she is lost in time.

"Why would Grace do that after everything you guys did for her?" I ask more confused than before.

"When she was ten, we started taking her to therapists, but they were no help. Grace has a way of making you believe she's normal, but she isn't," Ronnie answers with hurt in his tone, he holds his wife just a little bit tighter.

"What do you mean she isn't normal?" Dawson questions, sounding as confused as I am.

Jeanette turns her attention back to us. "It took some time, about two years, when Grace was twelve, we had started recording her at home without her knowing. We had cameras installed all over the house to catch anything. We just wanted answers. The final therapist watched the videos and Grace was diagnosed with being a sociopath. Everything is a game to her and she can never actually love anyone. She will make you

Saving Dawson

think she does and she will tell you whatever she needs to to get what she wants. You were her first friend, Dawson. I don't know what made her come after you, but I'm sorry she did." Jeanette gives Dawson a sympathetic look while Dawson puts his hands on his head.

"She never told me she was adopted. Why wasn't I ever allowed here?" Dawson question as his gaze travels between the three of us.

"I'm sure she made her story sound a lot like yours with her parents dying and she was in a foster home too. Her parents didn't want her, Dawson, they left her at the hospital after she was born. They were young, had no help, and didn't want the responsibility of having a child. We never said you couldn't come here, Grace didn't want you to get too close to her real life. We lost all control over her when she was in middle school."

"What about all the bruises and scars? I saw them." Dawson's eyes narrow as he takes on an accusatory tone.

"I'm sure you did, but those were self-inflicted, Dawson. We never laid a hand on her. She was our daughter, and no matter what, we loved her. We never would have abused her. Especially when all we ever wanted was to have a child we could care for and love, whether it was our blood child or not. When Grace would get angry, she would take a belt or knife and whip herself or cut her legs and arms. She would always claim that she would turn us in for child abuse and that everyone would believe her. We didn't know what to do anymore so we let her do what she wanted. I know that wasn't good parenting on us, but we had no other choice. We didn't want Grace taken from us, or to be taken from each other, even though that's what happened in the end."

"So you two ended up in prison for no reason?" Dawson

looks skeptical.

"Yes. A few months before everything happened, Grace started talking about wanting to live with you. She would say things like 'Dawson lives with a cop, do you know how easy it would be for me to ruin your lives?' Or 'don't you forget I always get what I want no matter what.' It was like she was taunting us, and for no reason. In the end she got what she wanted, all those police officers never once believed us. Grace had the proof. She had all the marks, she had the story, and her game ended because she ruined our lives and got to live with you. She ruined us just like she always promised she would."

"She didn't play games with me though. I was with her for four years before I saw a change in her." Dawson shakes his head in disbelief then runs his hand through his hair.

"She was playing a game with you the entire time, I can assure you of that. You may not have known it, but she was," Ronnie answers with a hint of anger in his voice.

"How long has it been since you saw her last?" My voice is shakier than I would like. I'm trying to be strong for Dawson, but inside I'm hurting for all of these people she destroyed. I sit back on the couch, hoping that we can get her before she gets to us.

"It's been about six months. She came by, letting us know how good her life is now, and she said she hoped we had a good time in prison. We asked her to leave and not come back. We can't let her destroy us anymore than we already have. She'll always be our daughter, but we can't have her around to do any more damage," Ronnie explains, sounding almost guilty for feeling the way that they do, but I don't think anyone could blame them. I look at Jeanette, seeing her wipe away tears that have fallen, and my heart hurts for these two people.

We stay for a while longer, telling them about our situation

Saving Dawson

and trying to figure out where she could be. By the time we left I was mentally, emotionally, and physically drained. I'm scared that something really bad is going to happen, but Dawson keeps reassuring me that everything will be fine. He says we have security so she won't be able to get to any of us. With her though, I'm not so sure about that.

We spent two days catching Sarah and Grady up on the stalker and us believing it's Grace. Dawson told them everything we learned from Ronnie and Jeanette, and they were in disbelief just like Dawson was. Grady made some calls to his friends at the station, but by the time we left Kansas, there was still no word on Grace. Grady made a trip over to the Sullivan's to formally apologize for taking part in their arrest. Ronnie and Jeanette accepted the apology and said they understand that they didn't have a leg to stand on with all the proof Grace had.

The time we spent at Sarah and Grady's was nice. They welcomed Sicily and I in with open arms and treated us just like part of their family. I really got to know them and the amazing people they are for taking in four teenage boys. Sarah told me all about how they were as kids and how the band started. They reminded me of my parents in a lot of ways, like how much they love those four guys, how supportive they always have been of them following their dreams, and the love that Sarah and Grady have for each other.

We also met up with Jacey and Bear at the studio. They informed us that just like the police, Hacker couldn't find one damn thing on anyone named Grace Sullivan. It's like she up and disappeared after the split with Dawson. So now we made it back to the tour with some good information, but no answers on Grace's whereabouts. Jacey let me know that my parents are safe and sound on their "vacation", but she still says it's safer that no one knows where they are. She has men watching over them still so that helps to reassure me, even though I would like to know where exactly they are.

Now that we're back on tour, it's time to get back to work and hope that everyone can stay safe.

fifteen
DAWSON

We walk off the stage, just finishing up the show in Tennessee, and although we put on a great performance as always, we knew our hearts weren't in it. After coming back from Kansas, I let the guys know what was up with Grace and the situation at hand. We're all a little paranoid and watching over our shoulders because we don't know what her next move will be. Our security teams do their jobs, but Grace is a sneaky bitch so I don't think she would have a problem getting past them. We are all losing sleep and exhausted from worrying about what will happen. I think we would all rest easier if we just knew where the fuck she was at. I can't wrap my head around how someone could just up and disappear like she did. It's like we're playing a game of chess - all of us are Grace's pawns and it's her move. All we can do is sit by, wait, and hope that we all stay safe. She'll make her move eventually, everyone does.

Emery wanted to stay behind to finish up some business she had so I agreed to go check on Sicily. I'm okay with her staying back because she has security, plus the guys also stayed for the rest of the show. Walking onto the bus, Marina and Sicily are sitting on the couch, and when Sicily sees me she jumps up.

"Da...Dawson!" Sicily runs into my arms and I catch her,

holding tightly for a big hug.

"Hey, munchkin. You ready to go lay down?" I ask as I kiss her forehead. She has gotten into a routine of staying awake until we finish up so I can put her to sleep. I'm telling you, this little girl has stolen my heart right along with her mom.

"Yeah. Sing to me."

"You got it." I look to Marina. "You doing okay? Was she good tonight?"

Marina smiles brightly. "She was perfect as always, and yeah I'm good. How was the show?"

"It was good. Everyone should be coming back soon."

"Okay, I think I'm going to head to bed." Marina stands, walks over to us and runs her hand down Sicily's back. "I'll see you tomorrow. Sweet dreams."

"Night Mawina." I smile and tell Marina goodnight also before heading back to the bedroom.

I lay Sicily down on the bed after pulling back the covers and I tuck her in tightly. I lay down next to her on top of the comforter and start to sing quietly. After a few songs she is still awake so I decide to tell her. "Hey, Sicily, it's okay with me if you want to call me dad."

"Weally!?" She sits straight up and I can see the smile on her face.

"Yeah really." I smile back. "Alright you gotta lay back down."

She does as she's told and I start singing some more. After a while longer she's still awake, which is unlike her. "What's wrong?"

"Where Mama at?" Come to think of it, Emery should have been back by now. Instantly getting worried, I stand up and get Sicily out of bed.

"I'm not sure. Let's go find her." Keeping my voice calm

Saving Dawson

so I don't scare her, I pick Sicily up and we head to the venue.

Walking back stage, I don't know what I expected, but it wasn't to have my world turned upside down.

sixteen

EMERY

Dawson walks off the stage after their set in Tennessee, with the guys right behind him. As routine goes, he walks up, grabs me around the waist, lifts me and spins me around before kissing the crook of my neck. "Good show tonight."

"Thanks, Em," they all tell me, but we all know the atmosphere isn't as light as usual.

"Dawson, I need to stay back and finish up some work. Can you go check on Sicily?"

"Yeah, but I don't like the idea of leaving you." He looks unsure and a bit worried.

"It's cool man, we got her," Colton tells Dawson, reassuring him that I'll be fine with them, plus I'll have one of the security guys with me.

With a long kiss goodbye, Dawson finally agrees to go back to the bus without me.

—

After speaking with the sound and lighting techs about some changes to be made, I stand backstage looking at my clipboard. Caged Animals just closed out the show, but I don't pay that any mind. I'm ready to get back to the bus and spend the rest of the evening with Dawson and Sicily.

"Emmy." I hear from behind and I freeze. Stunned, I

haven't heard that name in four years.

His hand touches my shoulder and I spin around lightning fast. "Don't you dare fucking touch me."

"Come on Emmy. Its been four years, don't be like that." He tries to give me that smile that once melted my heart.

"Yeah, four years with no word from you. I waited on my porch for hours that day and you never showed. You couldn't even say goodbye. What are you doing here anyway, Trey?" I cross my arms over my chest, waiting to hear his sorry excuse.

"I've seen you around on the tour, I was just waiting for the right time to say something. I thought maybe we could go talk."

"The right time!? The right time would have been calling me four years ago, or at least telling me you were leaving." Trey takes my hands in his. I try pulling away, but his grip is strong.

"I have money now, Emmy. I could make a good life for us."

"Mama!" I hear my daughter's voice, I turn my head and sure enough, there stands Sicily in a very angry Dawson's arms. Oh my God, this cannot be happening right now.

Dawson looks down at our hands that are still connected. Trey's hands have loosened on mine so I pull away. "Dawson, it's not what it looks like." Dawson's angry eyes look between Trey and me. Out of the corner of my vision Trey is staring at Dawson and Sicily.

"What is it then, Emery? Or maybe you would like to tell me what the fuck is going on, Traxton." Dawson's face is deep red, the veins in his neck are protruding. I have no doubt if he wasn't holding my daughter right now there would be a fight.

"Traxton? Wait a minute, as in Traxton, lead singer of Caged Animals, Traxton?" My eyes narrow on Trey as I wait for answers.

"Is she mine, Emmy?" At least he has the decency to whisper, or maybe it's shock. Either way, I'm glad only I could

Saving Dawson

hear.

"Meet me tomorrow at the café down the street at noon. Don't be late." I walk away and head for Dawson and Sicily. I take her in my arms, hugging tightly. "Dawson, we need to talk."

When we got back on the bus, I woke Marina up so she could put Sicily to sleep on the couch while Dawson and I talk. As I head towards the bedroom, I keep thinking *how the hell am I going to explain this to Dawson?* I don't even know what the fuck just happened. Slowly opening the door and closing it, I lean against the doorframe. "I didn't know."

"You didn't know what exactly?" Dawson's gaze meets mine. He sits on the edge of the bed, hunched over with his elbows on his knees, looking defeated.

"That Trey and Traxton were the same person. When I set you guys up on this tour, I didn't do enough research. I didn't even look into Caged Animals, I just knew that you guys had went on tour with them so I thought it would be fine." I take the few steps and sit on the edge of the bed next to him.

"So you are telling me that Traxton is Sicily's father."

"Yes." Dropping my head, I don't know what to say or do. I never thought I would be put in this situation. I never thought I would see Trey again. *Fucking small world!*

"Seeing him again, did it bring back your feelings?"

I whip my head around to face Dawson so fast I could've given myself whiplash. I place both of my hands on his cheeks, turning him to face me. "No. Not at all. I love you, Dawson. You, not anyone else, and nothing will change that. Trey is my past, but you are my right now and hopefully my future. I have to meet with him tomorrow so I can tell him about Sicily, but that's it."

"I can't stop you from telling him because he has a right to know, but I can make sure he knows you are mine." Dawson leans in, bringing his lips to mine. The kiss is raw, primal, and possessive, and he pulls away all too soon.

"I'll be back." And before I know it, he's gone.

Laying back on the bed, I cover my eyes with my forearm as I think about what tomorrow is going to bring. I have to tell Trey, or Traxton, whatever the hell he is calling himself now, about Sicily. I have to protect my daughter so if he chooses to be in her life, he better not fuck it up like he did with me. I have to protect myself and not get caught in his web, and I need to protect Dawson. What the hell have I gotten myself into now? *Wanna talk about my bad luck again?*

seventeen

DAWSON

Walking onto the Caged Animals bus, the first thing I notice is the smell and smoke of weed lingering in the air. I've smoked with my brothers a lot, don't get me wrong, but this shit it hits me like a freight train.

Next I notice Rico and Eli sitting on the couch, high as hell with some groupie whores on their laps. "Where the fuck did y'all go?"

"Dawson, hey what's up? Did you come to party for once?" Elijah asks with a stupid grin on his face.

"No, I didn't come to party. I came to talk to Traxton. And answer the question, when I came back to find Emery, none of you were there. Where the fuck did you go?" Crossing my arms over my chest, I wait for the excuse.

"Shit, the guard said he would be there, is she okay? Did something happen?" Rico answers while he's about to get up.

"She's fine, but I trusted you guys. I think this shit is getting out of control, but we'll talk about that later. Where's Traxton?"

"He's in the bedroom." Eli tells me, pointing in the direction I need to go.

Knocking on the bedroom door, I wait for Traxton to answer and when he does, I push my way past him then take a look around. I don't see any drugs or alcohol lying around so I guess he decided to stay sober tonight.

Turning in his direction, I start talking. "We've never had a problem before and I don't want to have one now. I know who you are to Emery and I know she is meeting with you tomorrow, but you need to understand that she's mine now. I'll be there when you meet with her and y'all can talk about what you need to, but if you so much as look wrong at her and I don't like it, then we will have problems. Respect me and what's mine and we will be good, understand?"

"Do you love her, Dawson? Is she happy?" Traxton sits on the edge of the bed.

"Yeah, I love her. I didn't want to at first, but she has a way to her, ya know?" I smile at just the thought of my Dorothy. "I can't speak for her, but I'd like to think I'm making her happy. She'd made me happier than I've been in a long time." I lean against the closed door. This situation is so fucked.

"Yeah, I know all about how Emery is." Traxton shakes his head and chuckles. "It didn't take me long to fall in love with her either. I know I fucked up the day I left, but I couldn't say goodbye to her. Listen, I won't step in your way as long as she's happy. I can admit when I fucked up and it's my own fault someone else stepped up. Hell, it's been four years and she's an amazing girl. Treat her right, Dawson, because if you don't, I'll be there to pick her up."

"I won't fuck up. Don't worry about that." I hold my hand out for him to shake and after he does I head back the way I came.

Quietly closing the bedroom door, I crawl in bed next to Emery. She stirs when I put my arm around her and pull her close to me. "Is everything okay?" she asks, half asleep.

"Yeah, everything's fine, babydoll. Go back to sleep." I kiss the back of her head and before long, exhaustion from the day

Saving Dawson

takes over and I fall into a deep sleep.

"So she's my daughter?" Traxton asks in the booth seat across from Emery and me.

"Yes. I found out I was pregnant not long after you took off and I tried to get in touch with you, but there was no way, and I think you know that," Emery tells him with her attitude coming to the surface.

"I'm sorry, Emmy." Traxton hangs his head while stirring the cup of coffee in front of him.

"Don't call me that."

"Fuck, Okay. I'm just, I'm so fucking sorry. If I would have known…" Traxton shakes his head and when he looks up I see tears shining in his eyes. "Are you gonna let me meet her? Are you going to let me be in her life?"

Emery opens her mouth then closes it." Why don't you start with telling me what happened, why did you leave?"

"I never wanted college like you did. You had our whole lives planned out and yeah, I went along with everything you said because I loved you so much and it was what you wanted, but it wasn't what I wanted. I wanted to make music and when I found out that Caged Animals were coming to Arizona for tryouts for a new lead singer, I went and got it right on the spot. I couldn't say goodbye to you and I knew I was fucking up by leaving like I did, but you're strong. I knew you would be okay eventually."

Emery's mouth hangs open in shock, "You knew I would be okay eventually? Jesus, when did you become such a dick? Do you even realize what I had to go through?" Emery's voice rises as she starts to get angry. "I had to move, I had to give up college, I had to change my whole fucking life because you knocked me up. Yeah, I was okay eventually because I had to fucking be for our daughter, you jackass."

"I'm sorry! I'm sorry! I'm fucking sorry, how many times do you want me to say it? I'll never be able to make it up to you, but I'm that little girl's father and I won't mess that up." I see the seriousness in his expression and I hear it in his voice. I know Emery does too.

"Her name is Sicily," I tell him, then look to Emery. "Don't deny her this chance. I would give anything to have my dad back, but he gets one chance. If he fucks it up then he's out of her life." I look back to Traxton. "You understand that? Don't fuck it up. She's the best thing that will ever happen to you."

"I won't. Thanks Dawson." I nod my head then get out of the booth before helping Emery up.

"Are you sure about this?" Emery's worried eyes bore into mine.

I caress her cheek with my thumb. "Yeah, babydoll. You two can set up a date later for him to meet her. If he does fuck up, I'll still be here. I won't let Sicily get hurt. I promise. I love you."

"I love you too." Emery moves in, giving me a chaste kiss before we head out of the café.

eighteen
EMERY

It's the last leg of the tour before we're home. It's been an interesting three months, that's for sure. A lot of good has happened, and some bad, but it's all worked out in the end. Not long after meeting with Traxton at the café, I let him meet Sicily, but I didn't introduce him as her dad. That's a little fast for me, although he's been great with her so far. He spends a lot of his time with her even though we still have Marina. We'll see what happens after this tour and then maybe I'll tell her who he is. Right now though, she's happy with Dawson being her dad and I won't take that away from her.

There still hasn't been any word on Grace or her whereabouts, but I think we're all just trying to move forward. We still have the security and that might be why she hasn't tried anything yet.

"You're Emery Ashland, correct?" A female voice asks beside me, breaking through my thoughts.

"Yes. And you are?" My brows furrow when I look at the woman standing next to me. I don't recognize her.

"Oh sorry. I'm Sherry Knox, manager for Caged Animals." She gives me a kind smile and holds her hand out.

Shaking it, I say, "Oh hi it's nice to finally meet you."

Laughing, she lets my hand go. "It's nice to meet you too. I wanted to talk to you about another tour for next year."

"Okay. You can send all the info to Jacey and we will look it over."

"Actually, I have all of the paperwork with me on the bus. We need an answer now if you want in. Come with me and we'll just go over it now. If we go now, it'll be quiet before all the guys get back."

I'm not sure what the rush is, but since she's the manager for Caged Animals, there wouldn't be any harm in me going. "Okay, let me just tell Traxton so he can let Dawson know when he gets off stage."

"Great. I'll wait right here." She smiles again.

—

The bus door shuts behind us. "I didn't think I was ever going to get you alone," Sherry says from behind me.

I spin on my heels. "What are you talking about?"

She huffs out a big breath. "Oh come on! With all that security guarding you or the guys always around. I had to come up with something to get you alone." She starts to pull at the collar of her button up blouse. "Ugh. This latex gets so hot."

She pulls off the latex mask, making her look like a totally different person. Next she takes off the dark haired wig she was wearing to reveal long blonde hair. *Oh my God! Please tell me this isn't who I think it is.* "Who are you?"

"You know exactly who I am. Now sit down!" She yells the last part making me jump back. "I'm the stalker everybody has been looking for. I'm the one that sent you all those letters, I'm Dawson's ex-girlfriend, Grace Sullivan."

I stay standing and start to head towards her. I gotta get off this bus. "Let me go." I try pushing past her, but it doesn't work, she's strong.

"I said sit down!" The punch comes fast to the side of my head. My vision blurs a bit, but I shake it off and go for her again.

I throw my own punch, connecting to Grace's jaw, but that's the only shot I get in before she tackles me to the floor of the bus and starts hitting me over and over until all I see is black.

DAWSON

Saying goodnight to the Oklahoma crowd, I walk off stage and immediately look for Emery just like I do after every show. I don't see her though and instantly get concerned. As I'm walking around in every direction, looking, Traxton finds me. "Hey Dawson, Emery wanted me to let you know that she went to our bus with our manager."

"And you let her go?!" I yell, worry growing deep inside of me. "Go to our bus and make sure Sicily and Marina are safe. Something's not right."

"What'd you mean?" Now I'm not the only one looking worried.

"Emery wouldn't have just left, she always stays until our set is over. Just go now, I'm going to your bus."

Running for the back door, I throw it open and break out in a full run for Caged Animals bus. I try to pry the door open, but it doesn't work. I run back towards the venue and find a security guard. "I need on the Caged Animals bus now! Get me on there, then call the cops." I start back towards the bus and he is hot on my heels.

The shot rings loudly, but I'm able to open the door now and when I climb in, the sight before me almost makes me sick. An unconscious Emery is sitting at the table, head slouched over where it lays on a smiling Grace's shoulder. Emery is beat the fuck up, her face is already swelling, blood coats her creamy skin, and the bruising is horrible. "What did you do, Grace?"

"Well I asked her to sit down and she didn't want to listen." An evil laugh comes from the girl I once loved. "All of you thought you could beat me at my own game. Shame on you, I always win."

"Why are you doing this?" I take a step towards them.

"Stay where you are, Dawson or I'll hurt your precious Emery even worse." Grace puts one elbow on the table and rests her chin on her bloody fist. "You should've hired me. That sweet Jamie would have been the perfect manager. She was so much like what you thought I was in high school, she would have been good for you. But you didn't do what you were supposed to so I had to come up with a new plan. I became the Caged Animals manager and it wasn't hard to do either. Because I had the experience from you guys, they just hired me right then and there, the stupid fools."

"What do you want?" I question. "Don't hurt her anymore, please."

"Aww. Look at you. Are you scared?" Grace throws her head back laughing.

"Just tell me what you want."

"I want you to hurt."

"You did hurt me, Grace. When I walked in our house and you were with someone else, that hurt me." I tempt to take another step.

"Not good enough. I want you to hurt more."

"Did you ever even care about me at all? I met your parents and they said you didn't." Grace gets up from the table, letting Emery fall over onto the seat.

"Well, they are my parents so they know me pretty well. Although they were stupid fools for ever thinking I'd care about them too. Just like you and your family. You all act so

Saving Dawson

happy, ugh! It makes me sick. It was all just for fun, Dawson. Just like it is now." Grace steps up to me, slapping my cheek twice. I turn my head away and step back so she can't touch me. "Now you are going to fire her and leave her."

"I can't do that, Grace. I won't do that." I shake my head *no*.

"You will if you don't want her hurt." She starts to head back to the table.

Someone grabs my shoulder, pulls me back off the bus, and then I see officers swarming the area. I hear yelling, but can't make out what's being said and then, what feels like forever, I see them bring out a handcuffed Grace. Next, an officer carries out Emery, who's still unconscious, and takes her over to an ambulance.

—

Emery spent the next two days in the hospital with me right beside her. She ended up with a concussion, but other than that, nothing serious was wrong, thank God. Between Traxton, Marina, and the guys, Sicily was taken care of. Everyone took turns coming to visit and the day she was released, we went back to Kansas. Jacey, Bear, Sarah, Grady, and Emery's parents were all waiting for us.

Sicily had a lot of questions about what happened to her mom, and to keep her from being scared, we all told her it was an accident. She was so happy to see her grandparents, and they decided to keep her until Emery is well enough. Emery will be staying with me so I can take care of her and I'll be on the hunt for a house of our own.

I'm glad it's all over and Grace will be out of our lives now. It's also really good to be home. Although, Jacey says we will be back in the studio soon working on new music. While on tour, our album hit number one, which is fucking awesome. What's next for The Betrayed? A new album, a new tour, and let's see what kinda trouble we can cause.

epilogue
EMERY

SIX MONTHS LATER

"Mama, is Daddy T coming?" Sicily asks from the doorway of our new home with Dawson.

"Yes. He should be here soon," I respond for the tenth time in half an hour. Sicily gives me a big, blinding smile before running off.

We finally told her a couple months ago that Traxton is her father and she was so happy. She said, *now I'm better than the princess*. I asked, *how is that?* Her response was because *the princess has one daddy and I have two*. I laugh but had tears in my eyes because when I started this journey, all Sicily wanted was a dad and now she has two. That is how Daddy T and Daddy D came about.

After everything with Grace, and Caged Animals getting tricked by her, they decided to relocate. So they moved to Kansas, had Jacey sign them, and I became their manager. It works well for everyone and I'm glad that no relationships were ruined because of who Traxton is. Out of it all, I think him and Dawson became even closer and have a mutual understanding and respect for each other.

Tonight everyone is heading to Insanity for a special performance that Dawson put together for The Betrayed.

He said that's where it all started with Jacey and their lives changing forever.

I walk into the club, quickly realizing that the only people in here are all of our friends and family. Jacey directs me to a seat right up front and takes the seat next to me. Soon after, Traxton brings Sicily in to join us at the table. The guys take their places on stage, but they don't start playing.

Dawson sits on a stool in front of the mic then picks up a guitar. "Thank you everyone for coming out tonight. Let me tell you a little something, almost nine years ago I became the lead singer of this band. We were four boys that had a dream and in this club, that dream started coming true. I haven't picked up this guitar in eight years, but tonight, as I am on this stage, I will for her." I immediately recognize the song and it's my favorite. *She's My Kind of Crazy* by Brantley Gilbert, and Dawson sings it perfectly. I didn't even know he could play the guitar, but he is amazing.

When the song ends, he sits the guitar down and...OMG! "Emery Ashland, we had a rough start, no doubt my fault, but we got past that. And for some reason you fell in love with me." The crowd laughs and I'm doing a combination of laughing and crying while Dawson is on one knee. "Part of my dream has been filled with this band, but I need the rest to be filled. I always dreamed I would find a girl to love like my dad loved my mom, like Grady loves Sarah, and like your dad loves your mom. You are that girl for me, you are my one, babydoll. So will you do me the honor and help me fill this dream of mine and become my wife?"

The tears freely fall down my face as I jump out of my chair, make my way on stage and practically tackle Dawson. "Yes! I will marry you!" Dawson puts the princess cut diamond

Saving Dawson

ring on my finger then stands, picks me up, spins me around, and gives me a kiss that should be considered illegal in public. When he pulls away, we face our smiling and clapping families.

In nine months, my life did a one-eighty. Some good, some bad, but I made it through strong as ever. New friends and family have come into my life, past people have returned, now all we can do is move forward from here and see what tomorrow brings.

about the author

I live in a small town in Kansas where I work at a nursing home. Before I started writing I was an avid reader and still love to sit and read a good book in my free time.

I published my first book a little over a year ago so if you haven't heard of me check out my MC series. I am so thankful that I am able to live my dream and as long as you all keep reading I'll keep putting out my stories.

Until next time...I love you all!

XOXO

Connect With Colbie Kay
Facebook, Twitter and Goodreads

excerpt

CITY LIGHTS
(Book 1 of Satan's Sinners MC Series)

CHAPTER ONE

ZOEY

It's spring almost summer, I used to really love this time of year. The trees are full of leaves, the grass is green, it's not too hot or cold, and it's just perfect outside. You can feel the wind blowing on your face and through your hair. I would always get so excited, school was almost over for the year, you get three months of freedom. You can go swim or just hang out with your friends all day, every day. But like I said, I used to love it. That was until I turned sixteen and started dating my very first boyfriend. Now six years later, here we are, it's our anniversary; and he's supposed to be taking me out to dinner. I'm pretty shocked because we never do anything together anymore. He would rather keep me locked in the house while he goes out and does whatever he wants. I think to myself a lot, why don't I just leave and let him kill me? It would be so much easier, but then I think about my family. I'm twenty two years old and I have my whole life ahead of me. I guess it's just easier if I stay. I hope one day something will happen and I'll be able to get out.

I met him when Ever, my twin sister, and I started our sophomore year in high school. I was taking an art class. That first day I was sitting at my desk, when I looked up he was standing in the doorway. I thought he was the cutest boy I had ever seen. Some would consider him to be preppy. He was tall with short blonde hair, blue eyes, smooth skin, he was just handsome, then I saw his clothes; he was wearing khaki shorts, a light blue polo shirt, and light brown loafers. This ended up being the way he dressed every day, the only thing that ever changed was the color of his shirt. When it got cold outside he switched out the shorts for slacks. Looking back on it now I think to myself, who would want to dress the same way every day? He walked over to the seat next to me and sat down. He held out his hand and I took it as we introduced ourselves. His voice was deeper than most of the boys in my grade, but come to find out he was a grade higher than me, he said his name was Andrew Conners.

 A few weeks later we had to pick a partner for a project. I was so excited when Andrew picked me, I couldn't have been happier about it. That first few weeks before the project I would steal glances at him, then sometimes I would catch him looking at me. Any chance we got to talk to each other we would take it. We became close friends while doing that project together, and as the weeks went by the more we would flirt. We liked each other but I wasn't allowed to date until I turned sixteen. The day our birthday came I was at home sitting outside at the patio table looking at a magazine. My mom called for me and said I had some company. When I looked up from my magazine to the sliding glass door, he was standing there. He stood there for a minute fidgeting with his hands, until he took a deep breath, walked over to me, and asked me out on a date. Of course I jumped at the chance to go out with him, I had been infatuated with him for weeks. My parents agreed that I could go. We were happy at first, but over time my family started to see changes happening with me. They tried everything they could to get me away from him, but I wouldn't listen, if they yelled, I'd yell back, if they grounded me I would just sneak out. I was so stubborn and thought I was in love. My twin sister was another person that didn't like him, she wanted me away from him. But if I wasn't going to listen to her, I wasn't listening to anybody. God, how I wish I would have now. I just always wanted that kind of love, the love that songs and books are wrote about. What I've got with Andrew is nothing at all like that.

I sent a text to my sister to ask if she wanted to have a girl's day with me, so I could be ready for tonight. Thirty minutes later she was ringing my doorbell. Ever is finishing up with school, she is going to be a fashion designer. I became a nurse, so I was finished with school before her. She always looks so fashionable and put together. I open my door, and there she is wearing a white form fitting top with black capris and white matching heels. Her hair is pulled up in a ponytail and she has little makeup on. I wave her inside, she looks me up and down, *"You are not going out with me looking like that."* She then points her hands at me, cocks her eyebrow then crosses her arms over her chest staring at me. I look down at myself. I guess sweats, a holey T-shirt, with a messy bun on top of my head wouldn't be good to wear to the mall.

"Let me go change."

I walk off to my room, I'm gonna take the advantage of Andrew being at work. I put on a nice fitting hole less t-shirt, shorts, I slip on some flip flops, and pull my hair into a ponytail. I know we are identical, but when I see my sister I see someone who is beautiful, confident, and so sure of herself. I used to be like that, but not so much anymore. Even though we are identical, I don't see me in her at all. I walk out and she has a smile on her face.

"That's much better, now let's go."

She drives us to the mall, which I think is her favorite place to go of all time. It takes us a couple of hours, and about ten stores later before she finds my dress. It is black, tight, and ends right above my knees, it has spaghetti straps and it goes straight across my chest. I feel sexy when I put it on, that's something I haven't felt in a long time. Next is shoes. We go into a couple of different stores until she finds the right ones. They are black open toed stilettos with a six inch heel. We then have to find accessories, she finds me silver hoop earrings and a silver chain necklace and a black clutch purse. Then we go to one of the nail salons that's in the mall. We both get mani, pedis done. I go with French for both. While she chooses a bold red. We leave the mall and go to a hair salon, she must come to a lot because they get me right in without having an appointment. I had them put some pink streaks in my blonde hair, I love it. By the time they are done I'm starving. So we decide to go to lunch. We chose a Chinese restaurant, we both order our favorites Pepsi and Cashew Chicken. I've had more fun today then I've had in a really long time. Let me tell you why that is.

Andrew has alienated me from all my friends and family. I miss them all so much, especially my sister. Ever and I used to be inseparable. Even though we look exactly alike, there are so many differences between us. She was born deaf, the doctors never could figure out why I could hear and she couldn't. My parents took classes and learned how to sign, they taught us as we were growing up. Ever was always more shy because not very many people know sign language. I was more outgoing, always had a lot of friends. She clung to me, and I was okay with that. Growing up we were in our own little bubble. We were best friends until Andrew came along and took me from her, through it all nobody could replace her. She will always be my best friend, even if I don't get to spend a lot of time with her. I look over at her and I can see that she is worried about something so I sign, *"Are you okay, sis?"*

"I have a really weird feeling, like something bad is going to happen to you. I only get that feeling with you. Are you sure you want to go out with him tonight?"

"It'll be okay, we're just going out to dinner. I do want you to know that I love you though and I'm glad you worry about me."

"You are my twin, of course I'm gonna worry and I hate that douche bag your with."

"I know you do and I don't like him either, but I'm stuck right now. Maybe someday something will change, until then I just have to deal with it. Let's go so you can make me beautiful."

By the time we get back to my house it's time for me to start getting ready. I'm already exhausted from all the shopping. It's a job in itself to go anywhere with Ever when there is clothes involved. But I wouldn't have changed a thing about it today with her. I jump in the shower and when I'm done getting dressed I let Ever work her magic. When she's done with my hair and makeup I look at myself in the mirror. I let out a gasp and cover my mouth with my hand. I look like a totally different person. I look beautiful, I never expected it to turn out like this. Right now I see my sister in me. My hair is pulled up in a tight ponytail, my makeup is done more dramatic, and it looks so good, with a smoky eye and sassy red lips. I hope he likes it.

I give her a hug and tell her goodbye. Now I just have to wait for him to show up. I start thinking back to our first date, man how things have changed.

"Zoey, you look beautiful. Are you ready to go?"

"You look nice too. Yeah I'm ready."

"Oh, here these flowers are for you." He pulls assorted flowers from behind his back and hands them to me.

"Andrew, they are so pretty, thank you. I'll put them in some water real quick." When I come back from putting the flowers in water, he leads me outside to his beat up Buick. He opens the door for me. He takes me to a quiet little Mexican restaurant. The conversation is so easy because we've been friends for a while now. I'm having such a good time.

"What are we doing after we eat?"

"Well, I know you love those girly movies, so I thought we could go see the one that just came out, 10 Things I Hate About You."

"Really? I've been wanting to see that movie so bad." We smile at each other.

We get to the movie theater, he opens my door to let me out. He holds my hand all the way into the theater, buys our tickets, and we make our way over to the concession stand.

"Do you want some popcorn and candy?"

"Sure, I like the Crunch Candy." He gets my candy and grabs Twizzlers for himself, a large popcorn and two big Pepsis. When the movie is over he takes me home. While holding my hand, and he walks me to my door. *"I had such a good time Andrew, the movie was so good."*

"I did too Zoey. I'll call you tomorrow." He leans in and gives me the softest kiss on my lips and then walks away. About half an hour later, I get a text, *"Just wanted to say goodnight beautiful."* With a big smile on my face I text back *"goodnight."*

Pulling myself from the memory I look at the clock. I've been waiting for over an hour and I'm starting to get angry. Finally at eight o'clock, he's just pulling up and starts honking. I can't keep him waiting, he gets so mad if I make him wait. I walk outside to his silver Toyota Tundra. There's no opening doors, or helping me get in anymore. So I do it myself, quite the gentleman, huh, when I'm seated I ask, "Why are you late?" I look over at him and he doesn't look happy.

"One of us has to make some god damn money in this

fucking relationship and it sure as fuck isn't you, working in that shithole you call a clinic. What the fuck did you do to your hair? It looks like shit. Why the fuck do you have a dress on? You know you are not supposed to wear anything other than pants and long sleeves. You think I want to take you out looking like that? You're such a fucking embarrassment, this is why I never want to take you anywhere." He's so pissed off. Maybe Ever was right to have a bad feeling about tonight. I put on my best face and look over at him. "God, Andrew it's just a little pink in my hair... let's just go out to dinner, and have a nice night."

"You're really trying my patience tonight. I think you need to shut your fucking mouth, before I make you shut it."

I try to turn on the radio but he slaps my hand away, with more force than necessary. I turn my body towards the door and stare out the window. No more words are spoken the rest of the way. It takes about twenty minutes to get to the restaurant because we live outside of Wichita and have to take the highway. We pull up to a nice looking Italian restaurant called *Gremaldi's*, when we get inside I notice it's quiet and not very busy. I can't help but wonder if that's why he chose this place. He doesn't like to have me around people. The hostess seats us in a booth and tells us our server will be right with us. While we are waiting I look around the place. It's like I've stepped into Italy, it's very nice with pictures hanging on the walls. The atmosphere is very calming, the lighting is low, and I can see they have a room where you can do wine tastings. When the waiter comes over I notice that he is very good looking, I'd say about six feet, black hair, with a short black beard, his eyes are a crazy light brown color almost the color of whiskey, and his complexion is darker than a regular tanned skin tone, maybe he's mixed. He is wearing a white long sleeved button up shirt and black slacks with black dress shoes. The way his shirt fits, I can tell there is a whole lot of muscle under that shirt. He introduces himself as Jason and says that he will be our server for the evening. Andrew orders for us both of course, "We would like a bottle of Gavi, she will have the Pristine Caesar salad, and I'll have the Chicken Parmesan."

"I'll be right back with your wine, Sir." Jason gives a slight nod and turns and walks away.

"Andrew, I didn't want a salad."

"Well, guess what that's just too fucking bad. You don't need all those carbs anyway. You need to watch your weight."

I think to myself, fuck this is going to be a bad night. He's always terrible when he drinks. Jason comes back bringing the bottle of wine, uncorks it and pours a glass for Andrew lets him taste it then pours a glass for me, and then says he will be back with our food as soon as it is ready.

When the food comes I give Jason a polite smile, but when he walks away I guess I have made Andrew mad.

"What the fuck do you think you're doing? Sitting over there being a whore, and flirting with the waiter. Is that why you wore that dress? To draw attention to yourself." His face is starting to turn red from his anger.

I look at him shocked "I wasn't doing anything. I was just being polite, and no I wore it for you, to look good for you."

He stands up and grabs ahold of my arm, "Zoey, let's go now! I'm not sitting here with you anymore." I try to pull my arm free but it's no use, he tightens his hold, he's too strong. I tell him quietly that he is hurting me but he doesn't care. I look back to see Jason standing there glaring at Andrew, then he looks at me and I see the concern in his eyes. Andrew drops money on the table and basically drags me out of there. When we get in the truck he starts yelling at me about the waiter, me questioning him, and my hair. Andrew doesn't like change, this is why he has had the same look to him since I met him. He pulls onto the highway and I keep trying to tell him I didn't do anything wrong. He pulls over on the side of the road and turns to me. I can see the rage in his eyes. I know what's about to happen. "Please, don't do this Andrew. I'm sorry I won't do it again. Please." I whisper to him, but it's no use. There's no way around what's about to happen.

  I see him make a fist and draw back his arm, I flinch, then try to shield my face, but it doesn't help. He hits me in the side of my head, it's hard and hurts. He doesn't stop there, he just keeps hitting me over, and over again. I try fighting back, I throw my fist and open hand slaps, and I claw at him with my fingernails, anywhere and everywhere I could reach. I fight with everything I have in me, but nothing helps. He's just too strong and so much bigger than me. I start crying, I don't like to show weakness but I can't help it. I start begging, "Andrew, Please, Stop! You're hurting me! Please, just stop!" But he doesn't, the punches just keep coming. I feel them everywhere, my face, head, arms, legs, and stomach anywhere he can hit he does. I can feel the blood running over my face. I'm pretty sure he busted my head open. My eyes feel wet, they sting a little, and I have a coppery in my mouth. I'm sure my lips are busted too. Fuck, it's never been this bad. I don't know how long he's been hitting me. It feels like it's been hours, but it's probably only been minutes. Suddenly, I don't feel anything, and I think it's over. Nope, I was wrong. I feel his body lean over me, he reaches out his arm, I hear the door open, and then he's pushing me out of his truck. I grab onto his arms but he pry's my hands free then I'm falling. I feel my body hit the cold hard asphalt. I can feel little pieces of gravel dig into my legs and the palms of my hands, then the back of my head hits the road. I hear the squealing of tires and I know he just sped away. Leaving me, laying on the side of the road to die. I can't move, my whole body hurts from all the punches I took and the fall from the truck, and my eyes are swollen shut. How did my life turn into this? I just have to lay here and wait. Hoping somebody will help me but then the blackness takes over.

HANGER

I'm sitting at the bar in the clubhouse about to take my shot of Jack Daniels Single Barrel when my best friend/ VP Gunner comes and sits next to me. "We ride out in five, Hanger. I hope this shit gets settled tonight." We have been best friends our whole lives and he can pull in as much pussy as me. He's not as tall as I am but he's a good six foot, his hair is long on top and shaved off on the sides' and is a blondish brown with a beard about the same color. The chicks dig his blue eyes. One look at 'em and he's got 'em crawling at his feet. He's solid muscle that comes with one helluva punch and he's my right hand man.

"Me too, Brother. I wanna find out what the fuck is going on and who is doin' it." I take my shot of Single Barrel and head outside, to get on my one and only love. She is beautiful. She's a 2010 FLSTN Softail Deluxe, with chrome ape hanger bars, she's Candy Apple Red, with metallic black flames going up the sides of her gas tank. All my brothers are here ready to go, but the prospects will be staying behind to watch over the clubhouse. I get on start her up and head out. We jump on the highway heading into the city, we gotta meet up with the Cobras and see if they have any information for us.

We get there in thirty, Snake the President meets us at the gate of their compound, he looks up and has one of his prospects open it for us to head inside. We've never had problems with the Cobras before, but if shit doesn't get figured out we might start. When we park our bikes he leads the way into the clubhouse. I follow him to his office, leaving my guys in the bar; when we get there he shuts the door behind us and takes his seat behind the desk. I take a seat across from him and we get right down to business. I don't have time to beat around the bush I got shit to do.

"Snake, you know my pushers aren't bringing in the money they should be. Someone is taking from me and I wanna know who the fuck it is."

"I haven't heard anything about it yet, but I have it narrowed down to either a new club in town, trying to take over, or it's the Italian mob. You still got Romeo working at *Gremaldi's?*"

"Yeah, I still got him in there and he'll stay there until he finds somethin'."

"Hanger, I figure whoever is messing with your shit is the same as the ones running guns on mine. They're taking from me as well. We gotta work together to figure out who the fuck it is, but we gotta be smart about it and take them down."

"Alright, Snake. Let's just keep each other informed, but I'm telling you now, you don't wanna fuck with me. If I find out that it's your guys, I'm coming after you and there won't be a Cobras M.C. left when I get done. I will destroy you. Yeah?"

"Yeah." I hope for his sake it's not his club doing this.

We shake, sit and talk about some other business. When everything is settled it's time for us to leave. We're on the highway headed back and we're not too far from our exit when I spot something on the side of the road. It doesn't look right to me. I give the signal for the guys to slow down and we all pull over onto the side of the road. I get off my bike, grab my flashlight out of my saddlebag, and walk slowly up to see what it is. Fuck, if it's not the worst thing I've ever seen. Growing up in the most notorious M.C. in Kansas I've seen a lot of fucked up shit. Kneeling down keeping the light on her.

I check her pulse to make sure she's still alive. I look around, she doesn't have a purse or anything, so I can't find out who she is. I look back and yell, "Gunner, get over here right fuckin' now."

"What's up, Prez?" I turn and look at him, that's when he sees her.

"Prez, what the fuck is that?" I look at him like he's a fuckin' idiot.

"Gunner, you're not that fuckin' stupid. You see what the fuck it is." He looks at me. "What are we gonna do with her?"

"You need to go get my truck. Don't forget the ramp, and ratchet straps so we can load up my bike. We are takin' her with us and gonna have Doc check her out."

"Do you think that's a good idea, we don't even know who she is?"

"Don't question me, Gunner, just go get my fuckin' truck. Have the boys follow you, I'll wait here with her." They all leave and I just sit here and stare at this poor girl. She's so fucked up. I can't tell what she looks like. Her hair is covered, and matted with blood, but I can see some blonde.

I don't know how long I've been sitting here, but I look up and see my truck. So I stand up, with the girl in my arms and walk over to my truck. I lay her gently in the back seat. Then help Gunner load my bike. I have Gunner drive so I can sit in the back with her. We get back to the clubhouse and Gunner lets me know he made all the club whores leave. I thank him, then I get out, take her in my arms, and go inside.

I head straight for my room and shut my door with my foot, and I lay her on the bed. There's a soft knock on the door. "Who is it?" The door opens just wide enough for Doc to stick his head in, I tell him to come in. He is our clean cut brother, came from the Army. Clean shaved face, buzz cut, no tats you can see. He is just as tall as the rest of us and packed with muscle, his jaw is set hard and firm. When you look into his dark green eyes you can see something is haunting him rather it's from his days in the army or something else, I don't know. I won't ask. It's not our way, if he wants to talk he can come to me, until then I'll let it be.

"Gunner, said you need me."

"Yeah, I'm gonna need you to look at her." I point to the girl lying in my bed and he says. "God damn, Hanger. What the hell happened to her?"

"I don't know, Doc. We were on the highway and I spotted her on the side of the road. You think she's gonna be alright?"

"Let me check her out real quick." He checks her over. "Her vitals look good. Most of the cuts aren't very deep, except the two on her head. They are gonna need some stitching but other than that she should be alright. She needs to be cleaned up, and get some different clothes put on. She'll be in a lot of pain when she wakes up. I can give her some pain meds and a sedative, when she needs it." He pulls out the thread and needle from his little doctor bag I didn't notice before, then starts stitching up her head.

"Thanks Doc. When you are done will you send Chatty in? She's the only one I'll trust cleaning her up." He leaves, then there's another knock on the door. Chatty walks in. She looks at the bed, then looks at me. She has a shocked look on her face but I can see the pain in her eyes. "Hanger, what happened to her? This poor girl. What do you need from me?"

"Chatty, I don't know what happened. I found her like this on the side of the road. I need you to clean her up and put some different clothes on her. I don't trust anybody else to do it. You gotta be gentle with her." She doesn't say anything as she walks into my bathroom and comes back with a large bowl of warm water, and a few washcloths. "I will use one of your shirts to put on her, and I'll be as gentle as I can."

"I'll be back when you're done." I say as I'm walking out of my door.

I make my way to the bar and get a Stone Arrogant Bastard Ale from Bam Bam, when I hear the front door open and in walks Romeo. He comes over and sits next to me. I get him a Dogfish Head, and grab my baggie outta my pocket. I line two rails, roll up a bill. I do one and pass the bill to Romeo. He does his then I ask. "How was your shift at *Gremaldi's*? Did you find anything?"

"No, I didn't find shit, but I think they are starting to trust me. I've got someone there that I'm getting close to."

"Oh yeah? Who's that?"

"Her name is Giovanna, her uncle is Antonio, the owner of *Gremaldi's*. She's starting to notice things about her family that she doesn't like."

"Don't let pussy cloud your judgment, Romeo. Be careful when it comes to that girl."

"The pussy is good, but I know what my job is. I'll get it done, Hanger."

"Okay." We continue to sit there when he starts talking about the rest of his night.

"Most of the night was pretty slow, boring, until a couple came in the girl was really pretty, she had on a black dress, her boyfriend was a douche. He got aggressive with her. Fuck, Hanger. I wanted to destroy him. I can't stop wondering what happened after they left. I hope she was okay, he didn't even let her eat. I never understand why girls wanna be with dickheads like that." I turn and look at him.

"What the fuck did you just say?" He starts to repeat it,

but I jump up out of my seat.

"I heard you. What did she look like?" He's giving me a curious look. I must seem like a fuckin' crazy person right now.

"She had a black dress and shoes on, had blonde hair with pink streaks, she had it pulled into a ponytail, the girl was fucking beautiful, Hanger." For some reason his comment about her being beautiful pisses me off. I grab his arm and drag him to my room.

"Chatty, were coming in." I don't even wait for a reply. I bust in and look at Romeo "Is this her?" He looks at her and studies her clothes then looks at me and says "Fuck. Yeah that's her, Hanger. What the fuck did that asshole do to her? How the hell did you end up with her?"

"Apparently, he beat the fuck out of her, then left her on the side of the highway to die. Motherfucker. Did you get a name or anything so we can find this guy?"

"No. He paid with cash, no reservation. As soon as they got outside, I went to the window watched him put her in a silver Toyota Tundra."

"Chatty, come get me when you're done." She just nods and keeps washing the girls face and hair. We head back to the bar where we take our seats. The front door opens again and in walks one of the whores.

"Shug, you know you ain't supposed to be here tonight. Tell me why the fuck you are here."

"I'm sorry, Hanger. I know, it's just Romeo called told me to be ready for him. So I thought it was okay for me to come back."

"Yeah, man. I'm sorry. I had no idea what was goin' on. I can send her on her way."

"No, its fine. Just stay the fuck away from my room."

They head to his room while I continue sitting on the stool, drinking my beer, tryin' to figure out what the fuck happened to that girl, but I can't. It makes no god damn since to me.

About thirty minutes later Chatty walks back into the bar.

"I tried to get as much of the blood off of her as I could, but it's gonna take a long, hot shower to get the rest. That poor girl, it's gonna take some time for her to heal from whatever happened with her. I hope you find whoever did this and make them suffer."

"Oh, I will Chatty. Don't worry about that. Chatty, have you ever had anybody do something like that to you? I'm tryin' to figure out why it would of happened."

"Good. No, I haven't and I don't know. I think some guys are just assholes. They try and show who is boss by beatin' on woman. Try and have a goodnight, Hanger."

"I will. You too, Chatty."

I go back in my room and pull a chair next to the bed. I won't be leaving her alone. I grab my guitar, sit in the chair, and start singing while I play, Angel of Small Death & the Codeine Scene by Hozier.

Made in the USA
San Bernardino, CA
21 February 2017